Praise for Colin Bateman's novels:

'An Ulster Carl Hiaasen' *Mail on Sunday*

'Such are Bateman's skills with narrative and characterisation that one is gripped to the last page' *Literary Review*

'If Roddy Doyle was as good as people say, he would probably write novels like this' *Arena*

'Bateman has barged into the previously unsuspected middle ground between Carl Hiaasen and Irvine Welsh and claimed it for his own' *GQ*

'When you require a novel to help you unwind while raising a subtle smile, Bateman has once again come up trumps' *Big Issue In The North*

The Horse With My Name

Colin Bateman

headline

First published in 2002
by HEADLINE BOOK PUBLISHING

First published in paperback in 2003
by HEADLINE BOOK PUBLISHING

A HEADLINE paperback

10 9 8 7 6 5 4 3 2 1

ISBN 0 7553 0240 0

Typeset in Meridien by
Palimpsest Book Production Limited, Polmont, Stirlingshire
Printed and bound in Great Britain by
Mackays of Chatham PLC, Chatham, Kent

HEADLINE BOOK PUBLISHING
A division of Hodder Headline
338 Euston Road
London NW1 3BH

www.headline.co.uk
www.hodderheadline.com

For Andrea and Matthew

1

I was shaking hands with the vicar in the rain when the phone rang. I dried off on that week's towel and crossed the bedroom. A voice at the other end said, 'Dubliners are skin-gathering showers of shite.'

I said, 'Excuse me, you might have a wrong number,' and put the phone down. I flipped the answer machine on so that I wouldn't be disturbed again, but by the time I got back to the shower the water had run cold, the vicar had gone and my headache had returned.

I believe you actually have to have the shower in a small, separate room to be able to describe it as en suite; this one sat in the corner beside my bed, the plastic curtain hanging off the railing. You never know quite when the urge to shake hands with the vicar will come on you, so to speak, and this time it had come halfway through shaving in the shower, so I was left with a five-day growth on one side of my face and the other side cut and bleeding from a six-week-old razor which had, according to the packaging on the floor, been cut from the hull of the *Ark Royal*. There remained three inches of water at the base of the shower which was draining away a drop at a time; only with the power off could I hear the weird sucking sound it made as it battled to escape. It had been a while since I'd experienced a weird sucking sound so I decided to investigate. I had two fingers down the drain when the phone rang again, and the machine clicked in. The voice said, 'I'm serious, Dan, they *are*. But give me a call anyway, I might have some work for you.' He left me his number, no code, so I presumed it was Belfast. I recognised the voice, but couldn't quite place it; I was still running possible names through my head when I came up with the remains of a leg of chicken from the drain, the sucking sound ceased and the water started to gurgle appreciatively away. I took a nibble at the leg. It tasted vaguely spicy. I gave some thought to the possibility that I might have stumbled on the Colonel's secret recipe, but not a lot.

I sat on the bed and warmed myself before the three-bar electric fire with the glowing coal-effect façade. In the absence of a television in my little bedsit palace I had taken to watching the façade and been pleasantly surprised at the standard of programming. You couldn't always pick up the Liverpool game but you got a great view of the mountains at sunset. However, I'd managed to put my foot through it a couple of nights before while trying to locate the equally unsweet toilet in the blackness of a heavy session and now it sat dark and cracked like a fellated Krakatoa; from Technicolor to black-and-white movies with one drunken footstep. It wasn't my only entertainment, of course. There was a pub round the corner and my laptop, though I used one more than the other. Somehow, the words wouldn't flow, but the beer always would. It had something to do with a little white coffin and the fact that my life was a disaster. I had tried to commit suicide by putting my head in the fridge, which was just about the standard of everything I attempted in life. There was a biography of a fat boxer which had cost me thousands in libel payments, there was a thin novel about a teenage messiah which had been remaindered within six weeks, there was a *making of* book about a hit Hollywood movie which was not, and there were a thousand and one columns taking the pish out of the fighting Northern Irish, except they were now the ones taking the pish out of me. Jobless, hopeless, loveless; generally *less* everything.

I listened to the message again, but still couldn't fit the voice to a name. I finished a can and sat thinking about things for a while, and then remembered why I'd gone to the expense and trouble of showering. I groaned and stood up. I still had my one suit hanging behind the door, but the knees were green from playing football in the park; I couldn't turn up to marriage guidance like that; I would look like a loser. That and the big sign on my head which flashed a neon *LOSER* every time I breathed in. There were tracksuit bottoms and some scuffed trainers under the bed; there was a greyish-white T-shirt with *Harp* written in the corner I'd won in the pub movie quiz; there was my bomber jacket with the lining hanging loose, although you could only tell that if it was unzipped. I'd get there and Patricia would be wearing her wedding dress, just to rub in the fact that she had a date for the divorce hearing.

Fuck it. What was the point? She'd got some big promotion in work and seemed to be rolling in it, but I loved her too much to sue her for alimony. I had a bill in my bottom drawer for a little white coffin, but I wasn't going to bother her with that. What were they going to do, repossess? Over my dead body.

I walked into the centre. It was only about twenty minutes. For once in my life the rain stayed off. There is a Buddy Holly song about *raining in my* . . . but the last word wouldn't come to me. It seemed like it should be *soul*, but I wasn't convinced. Something with *s*: suit, soap, soup. *It's raining in my soup*. I liked that. It wasn't right. But I liked it.

Belfast was buzzing.

That was the slogan they used after the ceasefire. In Stormont they were doing the familiar two steps forward, three steps back, but there was a kind of peace, the kind that involved shootings, kneecappings and riots, about which a lot of reformed terrorists did a lot of tutting and shaking of heads. There was a similar kind of peace about to settle over the headquarters of the Presbyterian Church where the counselling was scheduled to take place. Patricia, in her despair, had found solace in the church, despite our experiences on Wrathlin. Some might argue that I had found solace in a bottle, but I couldn't afford a bottle; solace in a can. The ring-pull mountain sat in one corner of the room; there was no longer any benefit in keeping them; the standard of my beer had dropped with my circumstances and I could no longer delude myself that I was drinking only to attain those air miles, that World Cup football or that outside chance of a Mini Metro. If the men at the ring-pull factory went on strike or some lager version of Auric Goldfinger cornered the market in world ring-pull supplies then I might be in a position to cash in, but in the meantime my ring-pull mountain wasn't enough to convince the bank manager that I was a safe bet on a mortgage, an ATM card or even an account.

I walked through the doomy doors of Church House and told them I was looking for sanctuary. They told me sanctuary was only available on Tuesdays and Thursdays between six and eight p.m., and could I come back. I wasn't sure if they were joking. There were two of them, sisters from the looks of them (although, of course, not *sisters* in the habit and revolver sense), and they wore identical hats and looks of disdain and told me that I'd gotten the wrong day for the AA meeting. I set my can down on the counter and said I was here for marriage guidance, but I could come back for the other one. I suggested to them that they should form a larger organisation called the AAAA, for drinking drivers, but they didn't know what I was talking about.

They pointed me in the right direction, which was any direction which took me away from them, and I heard them fussing and whittering to each other as I headed for the stairs.

There are no elevators in church buildings. It's a fact. Not even for the disabled. I suppose it's something to do with ascending to heaven, or hell in the case of the marriage guidance office three flights up. It wasn't called marriage guidance any more, of course, that was too old-fashioned; there was a proper organisation called Relate, somewhere, but that would have been too straightforward for Patricia. This was my third visit and they should have called it Relate To This You Misanthropic Bastard. Instead they called it Providence. I'm sure there was a reason. It was run by a woman called Mary Bowland. When I first met her I told her one of my favourite books in primary school was *The Forest of Bowland Light Railway* and she told me to sit down and be quiet or I'd be kept behind. She gave us a lot of guff about love and God and problems and God, all the time Patricia nodding and me staring at Patricia. That was the first time. The second time Patricia slapped me and I pulled her hair and Mrs Bowland had to call in a passing curate to separate us. This third time I slouched in and took my seat and smiled at Mary Bowland and apologised for last time. She nodded and made a note. Patricia had not yet arrived.

I asked if I could smoke and she said no.

'Drink?'

'No.'

'Drugs?'

'No. Mr Starkey?'

'Call me Clive.'

She looked at her notes. 'Clive?'

'I'm thinking of changing my name. Although I'm more Clive Dunn than Clive of India.'

She blinked and said, 'Dan, Patricia called. She won't be coming.'

'What?'

'She thinks it's pointless. She's decided on the divorce.'

I nodded. 'You could have called me. Let me know.'

'It was only half an hour ago. I tried to leave a message.'

'You have to give at least twenty-four hours for the dentist.'

'I'm not a dentist, Dan.'

'Aren't you?'

I sighed.

She sighed. 'Dan, I know this is all very painful for you . . .'

'Not half as painful as . . .'

'Don't say it, Dan. That was one of her big complaints, that you never take anything seriously.'

'*Au contraire*. Or on the contrary. I take everything

7

seriously. If I happen to be hilariously funny in my responses it's just my way of covering up the hidden pain. It's more of a cry for help than anything. Tears of a clown, as Smokey said.'

We looked at each other for several long moments. Actually she wasn't a bad sort, she was trying to help, she just happened to be blinkered by religion. She had short dark hair and a thin aquiline nose. She wore pale lipstick and a shirt buttoned right up. She closed her file of notes. 'I very rarely say this, Dan; in fact, I'm not meant to. But you know I've been having one-to-one sessions with Patricia, so I happen to know that she loves you. The problem is that you won't talk to her about what happened . . .'

'About dead kid.'

'Dan . . . all you really need to do is go round and talk to her about it. I think you'll find that once you take that first step, things will change. You do have to talk to her, Dan, you know that, don't you?'

I nodded. 'I don't know where she lives any more. The court . . . the police . . . well, you know . . .'

She took a deep breath. 'This could get me sacked.' She opened the file again. She turned it round so that I could see and pointed at Patricia's name and her address on Windsor Avenue. 'On the condition that you won't go round there and throw stones through her windows again.'

I shook my head. 'Nor potatoes.' Her brow crinkled. I shrugged. 'Deal,' I said. She smiled. I stood up. I reached across to shake her hand; she hesitated, suspecting, I suspect, that I would suddenly withdraw it and stick my tongue out like a child, but then she grasped it.

We shook. I held on to her hand.

'I understand your pain, Dan. I had a nephew who—'

I stopped her. 'You don't understand the meaning of the word pain until you've had your pubic hair caught in the rotorblades of the Action Man canoe.' I nodded and let go of her hand. I walked out of the office and down the stairs and out into the street. It was raining.

Raining in my *heart* . . .

I smiled. Buddy. My wife had thrown in the towel, although unlike me she undoubtedly had more than one. Windsor Avenue. It was only a hop, skip and a jump away. People forget how small Belfast is. You can walk almost anywhere worth walking to. I set off. I felt suddenly hungry and stopped off at a sandwich shop but everything they had left seemed to involve avocados or peaches so I made do with a packet of Tayto Cheese and Onion from the newsagent next door. It wasn't raining so badly that I was in danger of getting soaked. It was vaguely pleasant walking up through the shoppers, the office workers and the tourist.

Fifteen minutes took me to the foot of Windsor Avenue, and then I was standing opposite her house. It was a three-storey terrace on a pleasant leafy street. There was no sign of her car, although she might well have changed it. The likelihood was that she was at work. I contemplated breaking in and shitting in her shoes like a burglar, or just making do with the toilet and forgetting to flush it so that she'd know I'd been there, but I couldn't decide which was more appropriate; not for the first time I was falling between two stools. So I decided what would be would be and rang the doorbell. There was nothing for quite a while. I was just turning away when there came the sound of bolts being drawn back and the door finally opened. I turned back to a tall man with a short beard and fashionably rectangular glasses. He had pale skin and a copy of the *Daily Mail* in his hands, held open with one finger to the page he was reading. He looked me up and down with the blind indifference of a mortician in retirement week.

'Oh, hello,' I said. 'She doesn't take long.'

'Pardon me?'

'I said, would you be interested in a copy of *The Watchtower*?'

'Excuse me?'

'Or double glazing? I find it much more practical to double up. You can look into the window of your soul and be nice and snuggly at the same time.'

'I'm sorry . . . I . . . not today, thank you.'

He closed the door. I rang the bell. 'Only raking,' I said when he opened it a fraction. 'Is Trish in?'

'Patricia?'

'That's the one.'

'No. I'm sorry. She's at work. You . . . ?'

'Oh. Just a friend. Passing by, y'know?'

He nodded. 'Can I give her a message?'

I nodded. 'Tell her that I still love her. That I will always love her. That I have done terrible things to her and we have suffered a terrible loss but that if we just give it a real chance we can work it out, we can go back to what we had, what was beautiful and fun and sexy and just the greatest thing since sliced bread. Tell her she can go ahead and divorce me, that doesn't make any difference, it's only a piece of paper, if she needs time, sure, she can have more time, if she needs me to promise things, I will promise them and this time I will mean it, but just please God don't throw us away. Tell her I want to talk, I really want to talk, I've seen the light and I want to get it all out in the open. I want to talk. Talk is what I want to do. Talk, and everything will be okay.'

He had closed the door halfway through, but I continued just in case he was still listening.

I turned away. Normally I harbour feelings of violence when Patricia takes a new lover, but there was nothing. I was above it, or beyond it, or beneath it. I started to walk. I was about a hundred yards from home when it finally came back to me whose voice it was on the phone; I knew immediately that I shouldn't call, that it would mean nothing but trouble. And I knew just as immediately that I would.

For Trouble is my middle name.

2

Actually it's *James*.

We were standing in the first-floor lounge bar
of the Europa Hotel. Me and Mark Corkery. Or
Mark Corkery and I. He was drinking shorts and I
was on pints. He had recovered sufficiently from his
opening, 'Jesus, you look rough,' to concentrate on
the catalogue of physical disasters that had befallen
him in the past year. There was a car crash, a skiing
accident, a train derailment and then in Decem-
ber a decrepit Shorts Skyvan on the way to an
air show outside Dublin had deposited part of its
landing gear on Corkery's house, demolishing the
top floor and inflicting on him what he described as a
severe concussion, and what someone less charitable
might have described as brain damage. 'They think
my personality's changed. They say I'm moody and
bad-tempered and I've lost interest in sex. You'd be
fucking moody and bad-tempered if you'd broken
your leg, your arm, three ribs and your skull in the

past twelve months, and you wouldn't be particularly into sex if the landing gear of a Boeing 747 had landed on your arse while you were giving your girlfriend a fucking good seeing-to, would you?'

'Fair point,' I said. 'I thought it was a puddle-jumper.'

He grinned. 'Aye, well, it felt like a fucking 747.' He drained his glass and said, 'Anyway, so how's Trish, how's the kid?'

'Divorcing and dead, respectively.'

'Fuckin' wise up.'

'I'm serious.'

'You're fuckin' not.'

'I fuckin' am.'

'Jesus Christ.'

'And he was no help.'

We stared at our drinks for a while. There was barely another soul in the lounge. In the good old bad old days it would have been full of foreign journalists covering the Troubles and local reporters making a mint selling them stories so that they didn't have to leave the safety of their drinks. It was a vicious circle and I'd been part of it. That's where I'd met Mark Corkery. There are some journalists you describe as *old school*. Corkery was very definitely *reform school*. He knew every trick in the book, and it was frequently a stolen book or a banned book. He was known as the King of Crap. He was everyone's friend and had everyone's ear and he had complete freedom to write, spread or print lies about anyone or everyone without fear of being sued or kneecapped because the lies he wrote, spread or printed invariably weren't half as bad or dangerous as the truth. He made a fortune over the course of twenty-five years, and lost it over a different kind of course. He was a fiend for the geegees. He bet every penny he ever had and nobody had ever seen him celebrate a win. The cessation of the Troubles (ish) had seen the work dry up for all of us, but it had hit Corkery the hardest. The bad guys had gone legit, the good guys had moved on or passed on, now it was all about grey men in grey suits talking talks about talks, and the only thing they agreed on was that they didn't want to talk to the likes of Corkery any more. As far as anyone knew he'd retired, or been retired. He still had a kind of a swagger about him, but it was quite sad standing with him in that empty lounge, like having a drink with the oldest swinger in town, knowing that he too would go home lonely and unloved at the end of the night. I told him about Trish and Little Stevie. Gave him more detail than I'd probably given to my wife. I wouldn't have opened my mouth in the old days because it would have ended up on every front page in the land. But times had changed and I'd already jokingly searched him for a tape recorder. He finished his drink and ordered us another and said, 'That's awful.'

I said, 'I thought you'd know. It's been in all the papers.'

'I don't read that crap.'

I raised an eyebrow. He didn't notice.

'Anyhow,' he said, 'I've been out of the country.'

'Let me guess. Dublin.'

He smiled. 'Skin-gatherers, the lot of them.'

'Meaning . . . ?'

'If they could sell the flakes of skin that fell off your arse in the street they would.'

'Ahm, one might describe that as a sweeping generalisation.'

'It's a fucking fact, lad,' he snapped. His whiskey arrived and my pint. I was handling them better these days. There'd been a few years where I'd gotten out of practice and could be legless by six, but now I could easily hit double figures without making a complete fool of myself. It wasn't much of an achievement, in the grand scheme of things, but it was something.

'So,' I began, starting what I'd been putting off for an hour, 'you were thinking of offering me some work.'

'Oh. Aye. I was. The thing is, Dan, I'm having trouble with the IAR.'

I took a sip of my drink. I ran my eyes over him. He was in his early to mid fifties and despite what I knew there was no obvious crack in his head. He wore a faded black trenchcoat and had dirty silver hair. He had stubble to match mine, although on both sides of his face. He did not appear to be any more inebriated than I was.

'That'll be the IRA,' I said.

'What?'

'The IRA are after you.'

He glanced behind him. 'Are they? Why for?'

I glanced behind him. Clearly they weren't. They'd all retired anyway and taken up gardening, although they were careful not to dig where the bodies were buried. I took another drink. 'Perhaps we could start at the beginning again. You're having trouble with . . .'

'The IAR.'

'I think that is the source of our problem. The I . . . A . . . R . . . ?'

He nodded, then smiled abruptly. 'Dan, for Jesus' sake, you of all people should know. Dan the Man.'

'Why thank you.'

'Dan . . . Dan the Man.'

'Why thank you again.'

'For fuck sake, *Dan the Man*.'

'Can we get back to the subject of this concussion, Mark? Did you think of asking for a second opinion?'

He looked at me, shook his head, then took another drink. 'Dan. For fuck sake. Do I have to spell it out to you?'

'Thus far your spelling hasn't—'

'Shut up, would you? Listen. What do you know about horses?'

'*Horses?*'

'Horses.'

I thought for a moment. I shrugged. 'Brown. Four legs. Eat grass. Sleep standing up. Lester Piggott. Champion. Trigger. Dick Francis. Princess Anne.'

'And gambling on horses?'

I shrugged again. 'Nothing. When I was eight my dad put a couple of shillings on Fearless Fred for me in the National and he fell at the first. I was inconsolable for days. I haven't had a bet since.'

'You lucky bastard. What about Geordie McClean?'

'What is this, twenty questions?' He raised an eyebrow. 'What about Geordie McClean? You know what I know. You gave me most of my info when I was doing my book on Fat Boy.'

'I mean, what about him these days?'

'Nothing. Still runs some boxers, but his big chance has come and gone. Strictly small potatoes. Or croquette potatoes. Or should that be *crooked* po— Sorry, this could go on all day. What *should* I know?'

'That he got out of boxing because there were too many fucking meaningless titles to make it worth his while. Because half his boxers are either thick as shite or have had the sense knocked out of them.'

'And?'

'So he got into a sport where once you have a winner you not only make a fucking fortune off him, you can also bottle his sperm and make ten times as much selling it on.'

'He's into football?'

'Dan.'

'Okay. He's into horses. What's the big—'

'He's making millions. He's the man behind Irish American Racing—'

'IAR. At last.'

'You *have* heard of Irish—'

I shrugged. 'I've been lying low.'

'He's been shaking up the system. He's been doing a Murdoch. He's been making enemies left, right and centre.'

'Okay, but what has this got to do with the price of fish?'

'Dan, you didn't happen to see the racing on Channel 4 on Saturday?'

'I was probably on the other channel. Nature documentaries, that kind of thing.'

'One of Geordie McClean's horses won. An eight-year-old called Dan the Man. He named it after you.'

We adjourned to the Crown Bar across the road. It was one of the oldest pubs in the city. The National Trust owned it. It was all snugs and big mirrors and liked to promote the fact that the James Mason IRA movie *Odd Man Out* had used it as a location way back in the fifties, whereas anyone who cared to check would find that the movie had actually been made in a London studio with a set mocked up to look like the Crown. Not that it mattered. Not that anyone cared. Not that you could tell the difference from the stills on the wall. It was just an *interesting fact*. There was no TV and no juke box, but there was a cigarette machine. The condom machine in the toilets gave out empty crisp packets and elastic bands. Or should have.

We were hiding in plain sight. Better to talk seriously in a crowded pub than whisper in an empty lounge. Corkery had moved on to the Guinness. 'Geordie McClean has three injunctions out against me. I'm on the run, but he won't get me.'

I've never been able to stomach Guinness. I switched to cider, mostly because I'd no wife any more to tell me to grow up. I said, 'Why is he after you?'

'Because I'm the Horse Whisperer.'

'Uhuh.'

'You must have heard of the Horse Whisperer.'

'Uhuh. Nicholas Evans. Book. Robert Redford. Film.'

'No! Not that cak. The *internet* site.'

I looked at him. I was surprised he'd even *heard* of the internet. I'd always thought of him as a man who'd find a ballpoint pen new and fangled. 'I'm sorry,' I said, 'you've lost me again.'

'Jesus Christ!' He fumed into his pint for several moments. 'Okay. All right,' he began again, 'sorry'n all. Sometimes you get immersed in a world and you start to presume everyone knows what you're talking about, you can't see the wood for the trees. And I forgot your knowledge of racing amounts to brown horses and Trigger. Okay. All right. It still might work. Okay. All right. Dan, I'm the Horse Whisperer. That's the name of my internet site. It's the inside track on the racing game. News, gossip, rumours, all sorts of shit. Everyone who's anyone reads it, everyone feeds me info; just like it was here with the fighting. The powers that be would like to present a nice PR job on the racing, y'know, all nice happy families and pretty horses, when the truth is it's the most vicious fucking thing I've ever been involved in, and that's including the 'Ra. Cut-throat, Dan, fucking cut-throat. Bribery. Corruption. Doping. Nobbling. Stable lads feed me, jockeys, train-ers, the man who sells the feed, the man who collects the shit, the man who pilots the helicopter, it all comes through the Horse Whisperer, and not a one of them knows who the fuck I am. That's the magic of it. It's completely anonymous. I mean, to look at me you'd think I was the type who'd consider a fountain pen new and fangled, not running a fucking internet site.'

'Nah, Mark, I always knew you had your finger on the pulse.'

'Anyway, they haven't a clue it's me.'

'Who's *they*?'

'The money men, Dan, who else? Up to now they've been taking it in the arse but haven't had the wherewithal to do anything about it. But now Geordie McClean's muscling in, bringing his Sandy Row wide-boy mentality with him. A few innocuous stories about him and he's slapped out a cartload of injunctions on the site; it's been thrown off half a dozen servers already, but if you know the internet you know there's more servers out there than you can fucking count, so he's not going to close me down that way. The only way he's going to do it is find out

21

who I am and then sue me for libel. And that's what he's trying to do now.'

'So that's why you're on the run.'

'Exactly.'

'And where do I come in?'

'I need to fight fire with fire. Because his is a new set-up, because he's brought in a lot of American expertise, because he runs the tightest fucking ship in the harbour, I've not been able to get a man on the inside. Nobody is feeding me info. I know he's up to something because you don't get to where he is in such a short space of time without tramping on toes. You know him, Dan, he's not Mister Nice Guy. I've got to find out what he's up to, but I can't do anything while he's chasing me from pillar to winning post. He has stables north of Dublin. I need you to go down there, ingratiate yourself and find out what the fuck he's up to.'

'Is that all?'

'Dan. I need you to do this for me.'

'I can't.'

'Why not? I'm paying. Better than you'd get here.'

'I haven't done any journalism for a long time.'

'Well you should. You're bloody brilliant.'

'I'll take that as a compliment, coming from the King of Crap.'

'You are. I always had time for you, Dan. And I did you more than a few favours.'

'I know that, but . . .'

'But what? Look at the state of you, lad, you look

like you've been dragged through a hedge backwards, your clothes are hanging off you, you're whiter than a ghost and you smell like a fucking dump.'

'Thanks. Can you put that in writing?'

We looked at each other for a while. I tried not to think about what he was telling me, though I knew already it was the truth. I'd known it for weeks.

'Dan. You're a journalist. It's in your blood. I'm sorry for your circumstances, but you need to do something about them. You need to get out of here, you need to get your teeth into something and it might as well be Geordie McClean. He named a horse after you and it's worth a fucking mint. I happen to know he loved the book about Fat Boy, tell him you want to do one on Dan the Man. He'll lap it up. He's a vain son of a bitch.'

'Geordie or the horse?'

'I can't vouch for the horse. Will you do this for me, son? It would mean an awful lot to me.'

I sighed. Everything had been going downhill for months. Like skiing down a mountain, it was rather good fun right up to the point where you came to the edge of a cliff, and the trouble was there was so much snow about you never quite knew where it was or when you'd reach it, there was just that absolute certainty that you would.

I looked at myself in the mirror behind the bar. I was not a pretty sight. The clothes . . . the hair . . . the beard . . . If Patricia had walked into the bar right then she would hardly have recognised me. How was

I ever going to win her back looking like this, living like this? Corkery was right. I should get out. Get out now. Do something positive. I knew bugger all about horses but I knew a lot about Geordie McClean. Why not fuck him up rather than myself? What had he ever done to hurt me? Not much, but since when did a journalist ever need a reason to fuck someone up? Besides, he'd named a *horse* after me.

I took a deep breath.

'Okay,' I said, 'I'll do it.'

It wasn't quite St Paul's conversion on the road to Damascus. If I'd been walking that road I'd have seen the light and then got flattened by a chariot. But it was a start.

3

You can upset your whole system by indulging in sudden, radical changes of lifestyle. People die from crash diets. They smack their cars into lampposts when they forsake nicotine. I had to edge myself into sobriety sideways. I woke that first morning of the new era with the dry bokes and a throbbing head, the predictable legacy of the cider I'd drunk long into the night, long after Mark Corkery had departed for what he described as his latest safe house.

The peculiar thing about a cider hangover is that you think you've escaped it completely right up to the point where you have to move your head off the pillow. It's at that point that your neck turns to concrete, your forehead into Spaghetti Junction and your stomach into that toxic waste lorry that has jackknifed in the fast lane, spilling its contents.

Oh shit, a knock at the door.

I rolled up into a sitting position. Then I rolled back into a lying-down one. If it was important they would come back, or break it down. It couldn't be the rent, the Government paid that direct. A survey. A charity collector. A boy scout. Another knock, another *thunderbolt*; I bent the pillow around my head like a horseshoe.

Horse.

Dan the Man.

The banging came again. 'What do you want?' I groaned. 'I have no money to give you. I haven't eaten for a week. If you have any food for me please slip it under the door.'

Then I *remembered* and dropped the pillow. My jacket was on the floor, the lining spilling out of it like a clot. The hangover was momentarily forgotten as I delved into the one pocket that remained stitched – nothing; I cursed and tried the other, bottomless one; my hand extended through the lining and up into the downy material along the back and . . . *aha!*

I pulled out an envelope. I'd unsealed it in the bar, of course, after he'd gone, but I'd not gone nuts with it, most of it was still there: £500, an advance, just to get me at least as far as the bus stop for Damascus.

'Dan? Are you in there?'

Shit!

'Stop playing silly buggers and open the door.'

'Trish,' I said.

There was a silence.

'Are you going to let me in, Dan?'

'I'd like to, but I can't. There's been an accident. What do you want?'

'To see you. What kind of an accident? Are you okay?'

'I . . . I think . . . I think it's *broken* . . .'

'*What* is?' she asked urgently.

'My heart.'

There was another silence. Then, 'Oh for fuck sake, Dan. Just open the door.'

I looked about me. My room looked like a hurricane had passed through it, and I looked like the one with the snooker cue had taken me drinking. 'No,' I said, 'not here. Somewhere neutral. Somewhere public.'

'Public house, you mean.'

'Are you trying to pick a fight already?'

'No, Dan, I . . .'

'There's a cafe at the end of the road. I'll see you there in twenty minutes. I need to finish this story, I need to phone it in. Okay?'

There was another silence, then an 'Okay.' Footsteps started to recede.

'Trish,' I called.

The footsteps stopped. There was a blunt 'What?'

'You suit that colour.'

I could *hear* her fuming.

My luck was in. As Patricia went out the front I went out the back. There was a row of shops immediately behind my palace and I went through them in minutes, pausing only to vomit. I've always been a one-stop shopper. In the old days I could do the

27

family shopping and be home with my feet up in the time it would take Trish to compose a list. It might not exactly reflect what she was after, but what it lacked in variety it made up for in ease of preparation and storage. Or to put it in Patricia's words, 'Just because they advertise Heinz 57 varieties, you don't have to buy them *all*.' This time I wasn't after food: a clean razor, a pair of black jeans, a fresh shirt; purchased, back home, showered, shaved, aftershaved, dressed and down that road in twenty minutes. Some kind of a record.

I would tell her about it, one day, when we were back together. We'd laugh about it. She'd say, 'You silly fool,' and tweak my cheek, then kiss me. Admittedly the look she gave me when I sauntered confidently through the door of La Belle Epoque owed more to dismemberment than tweaks or kisses. I slipped into the chair opposite and smiled at her. A waiter came by before we had a chance to fire the opening salvos and I ordered a hot chocolate to complement her own.

When he'd gone I said, 'There's no use begging me to come home, I have my own life now.'

She looked at me steadily. 'Wise up, Dan,' she said.

I shrugged. 'So who's the new guy? He looks like a psycho.'

'It's none of your business.'

'Oh you think not?'

'No.'

'You do think not or you don't think not?'

'I . . . oh shut up, Dan. You're so fucking annoying. I want to be angry with you but you just . . . oh *nothing.*' She sighed, then took a sip of her chocolate. There was a spot of fresh cream on the end of her nose when she looked up again, but I decided not to mention it. It was probably a fashion thing. She'd always followed the latest trends. Perhaps creamy noses were in. 'Are you okay?' she asked.

'Do I look okay?'

'You look okay. Are you eating?'

'Occasionally.'

'Dan . . .'

'I missed you at Weight Watchers the other d— I mean, marriage guidance. You might have called me.'

'I . . . look, I was going to . . . then . . . Why did you say Weight Watchers?'

'No reason, just a slip . . .'

'You think I've put on weight.'

'No I don't. Besides, you suit a little . . .'

'I have not put on weight. I'm on a diet. I go to the gym every—'

'Only joking, kiddo. Lighten up. You look great.' My own hot chocolate arrived and I took a sip, being careful to keep my nose out of it. We smiled pleasantly at each other for half a minute. It was too good to last. 'What's he like in bed, then? Does he take his glasses off? Or his beard?'

'Dan . . .'

'I think it's fascinating when you get a new man. Of course they never last long. No one measures up.'

'Dan, they all measure up.'

'So how come they don't stay?'

'Maybe *I* don't measure up.'

'Maybe you don't.'

She sat back. She stirred her chocolate with a spoon. 'If you're trying to undermine my self-confidence, you're doing a good job.'

'Good. Come home. Or let me come home.'

'Dan, I don't love you any more.'

'Yes you do.'

'I think I would know best.'

'It's the baby, isn't it?'

'It's everything.'

'But it's *mostly* the baby.'

She shrugged. 'Please don't come around to the house any more. I'm trying to make things work with Clive . . .'

'*Clive?*' She nodded. I burst out laughing.

'What's so funny?'

'Nothing.' I sucked in, quelled it. 'Sorry. Clive.'

'Dan, just don't take the piss any more, okay? I've met a new man, you're not going to like him, but that's tough shit. I *love* him. We're going to make it work. But it doesn't help having you hanging around like a sore head. Just leave us alone. We're over. We're finished. I don't want to end up despising you. I loved you once, it was good, then it went bad. There are too many bad things, Dan, things I can't forget. So let's leave it, okay? Get on with your life. You'll meet someone. You'll be fine if you give yourself a chance, but you need to get me out of your system.'

I looked at her. And unheralded, a tear sprang from my eye. I wiped it. I didn't look at her. When I spoke, I spoke quietly. 'But what am I supposed to do?'

'It's your life. You're a free agent. Do anything you want to do.'

'Eddie and the Hot Rods.'

'*What?*'

'Nothing.' I sighed again. She pushed her chair back and stood up. She looked at me for several moments, then extended her hand. I looked at it. 'Please don't do that to me,' I said.

She withdrew it quickly. 'Sorry,' she said. There was a hint of a nod, then she turned and headed for the door.

I shouted after her and she turned. I pointed to the end of my nose. Her brow furrowed. I pointed again, then the penny dropped and she glanced at herself in the mirror behind the cash desk. Then she turned and glared back at me. The word she mouthed might have been *bastard*, but it might not. She followed it with a slim little smile, and then she was gone. Out of the restaurant, out of my life.

I sat in that window seat for half an hour. The waiter looked at me once in a while, but every time he did I took a little sip of my cold chocolate. I was in the frame of mind to make it last for days. My favourite pub's side door was just visible a couple of hundred yards up to the right. I watched a pair of young girls, laughing between them, pull the door open and enter it. I could almost smell the alcohol.

But no.

Dan the Man.

Damascus.

Things were going to change.

I was going to turn my life around. I would win her back. She would see me on stage accepting a massive cheque for *Brown Beauty*, my literary novel on the life of a thoroughbred horse, and come running to me. She just needed to see that I could do it, that they weren't the usual hollow promises.

Things were going to change.

The waiter was at my elbow. 'Can I get you anything else, sir?' he said, whipping the empty cup out from under me.

I glanced longingly back down at the pub, then nodded up at him. 'Another hot chocolate,' I said. There was a hint of a curl to his lip as he wrote it down. As he turned I said, 'Oh, and do you have any liqueurs?'

I spent the next two or three days purging my system of alcohol. It involved copious amounts of health drink *Diet Pepsi* and a trunkload of chocolate digestives. I bought daily copies of the *Racing Post* and hung around in bookmakers' offices trying not to breathe in. They'd brightened up considerably since

I'd watched my dad back his losers all those years before; now there was satellite television on a bank of screens, a coffee bar, nice comfortable seats, friendly staff in crisp uniforms ready with a heartfelt good afternoon and good luck; but no matter what, they still stank of smoke and existed in a kind of timeless haze. Any one of them could have been a contender for the annual services to passive smoking award. But they weren't bad places, just hopeless. They should have suited me fine. I studied the form, I placed bets, I read the news and the profiles and the tipsters and I watched a hundred races from Down Royal to Listowel to Punchestown to Navan, and by the end of it I still didn't have a clue what it was really all about.

It was Greek.

It was half a dozen brown horses jumping over hedges.

It was munchkins in saddles with whips, and I could rent that from the video store without getting lung cancer.

I wouldn't know where to start a conversation about a bloody horse, let alone investigate Geordie McClean's shady dealings. Two or three times I tried the mobile number Corkery had given me, but it was always out of service. I was going to tell him to forget it. Thank him for the five hundred, tell him it had changed my life, but not my wife, and that I'd pay it back to him from my first pay cheque, because I was going to get a proper job, right away, first thing tomorrow, or maybe the day after. The last person I needed to get involved with was Geordie McClean. I was trying to sort my life out, not complicate it. A court reporter. I could do obituaries. Or the movies. Yeah, the movies. But God protect me from Geordie McClean and his infernal, eternal machinations.

On the fifth day after my final showdown with Patricia I was feeling fit and thinking positive. I'd given my palace a spring clean. I'd not touched more than a few drops. I dry-cleaned my suit and polished my shoes. I invested in a portable TV and visited a second-hand book shop. Patricia had thrown me out without my books and I'd gotten out of the habit; so I bought something heavy and something light to see me through the long, largely alcohol-free nights; the light for its entertainment value, the heavy in case someone tried to steal my portable TV while I slept. It was that kind of neighbourhood.

Despite having been out of the loop for some considerable time, I'd absolute confidence that I'd be able to land some work; maybe not staff, immediately, but there was plenty of freelance stuff out there if you didn't mind looking for it, and I'd never minded that. It wasn't like I was starting from scratch either; I'd taken a sabbatical from journalism to write my books, so my personal problems would not be common knowledge amongst my potential employers. Besides, most of the reporters I'd grown up with were now happily ensconced in senior positions as editors, publishers or television producers and therefore ideally

placed to give me a leg up. I had my contact book.
I started calling.

It wasn't the morning to phone.

The first was out of the office, the second at a
funeral, the third had the day off, the fourth was
also at a funeral. I thought maybe they were avoiding
me, so I stopped giving my name, but it was just the
same. Two more had called in sick, *six* others were
at a funeral. I began to doubt that *any* newspaper
or television programme would make an appearance
that day. I didn't want to phone Mouse. He was my
oldest friend, and arguably the best placed of all of
them to give me some work, but he'd been giving
me a wide berth for months; he'd pulled me out of
the deep end once too often. My problem was, every
time somebody threw me inflatable armbands I ended
up putting them on my feet and going straight back to
the bottom. I suppose eventually we all have to sink
or swim by our own efforts.

It could be avoided no longer. His name was the
only one I hadn't tried. If I was to get anywhere that
day, and it felt important that I did, there, then, before
something else knocked me back, then I had to call
him. I paced the room for a while, wondering what
to say, how to approach him, whether to apologise
or pretend that nothing had happened. I knew why
he'd dropped me and he'd every justification, but still.
He was Mouse. My friend. He knew what I was like.
You expect a little loyalty, or, indeed, a lot. Had I
not been there for him, every single time? Well, I

would have been if there'd ever been any need. But he was as solid and dependable and unadventurous as a rock. He should have been called Rock. My friend *Rock*. If only Hudson hadn't gone and spoilt the name for all time.

I punched in the numbers. He was now editor of the *Belfast Evening News*. 'I'm sorry,' his secretary said, 'he's at a—'

'Funeral.'

'At a funeral. Yes. He won't be back until—'

'Just answer me one thing. Who the hell is so important every friggin' journalist in the city is going to make sure he's dead?'

There was a little bit of a giggle at the other end. 'Do you know, I said *exactly* the same thing. I've been working here for five years and I've never *heard* of this fella Corkery.'

4

It's usually bad manners to read a book at a funeral, but I had my reasons.

I arrived late, of course, though not as late as Corkery. In keeping with most of the past year, and more specifically with the manner in which he had met his death, the hearse had managed to impale itself on the back of a trailer as it turned out of the funeral home and it had taken an hour and a half to first free it, then repair the damage. Nor was it simply a case of transferring the coffin to another vehicle. It was a small family firm and their only other car was on duty elsewhere. It would doubtless have tickled us all if Corkery's last ride had been in the back of a newspaper delivery van, as some had seriously suggested. I heard subsequently that enquiries were made but foundered on the lack of insurance cover, for the van, rather than Corkery, who was a bit beyond it.

It turned out to be one of the biggest funerals I'd

ever attended, the cars spilling out of the car park at Roselawn Crematorium to sit two abreast on the grass all the way back down the lane to the Saintfield Road. The taxi driver dropped me at the gates, said he had a thing about going through them. I had a thing about not giving tips to drivers who stop halfway there; he cursed me, I cursed him, and I hurried through the gates in the rain with a shouted threat not to visit a certain part of Belfast in the near future ringing in my ears. I charged down towards the crematorium, and managed to make it just as they lifted the coffin from the hearse and hurried it through the doors. I stood at the back, looking for a spare seat, but there was none, but I saw Mouse and knew he'd manage to make some space if he saw me coming. There was the usual doomy music playing as I hurried down and across, then backed into the slimmest of gaps. Mouse didn't bat an eyelid. Just his usual 'HIYA, DAN,' impervious to the half-dozen mourners who nearly jumped out of their seats as his voice boomed around the echo chamber that was the setting for Mark Corkery's final shift.

'Big turn-out,' I said.

'Give the public what they want . . .' he whispered. We grinned conspiratorially. 'So how're you doin'?'

'Fine.'

'I was speaking to Trish the other day.'

'All good, I trust?'

He rolled his eyes. We settled for a minute while a small, impoverished-looking minister appeared through a side door and took his place behind a lectern that was a little too high for him. There was a microphone which he had to bend down to his level, which resulted in a wave of feedback that had everyone wincing. He cleared his throat then and began to address us on the life and times of Mark Corkery. There were too many people in the place for me to see clearly who was sitting on the front row, if there were any obvious family members present. For some reason I had assumed that he didn't have any family, that he'd been an only orphan married to his job. Mouse wasn't aware of any either, and I had only Corkery's assertion that he'd been hit by the Shorts landing gear while making love to a girlfriend to suggest any kind of relationship with another human being, but any or all of that story could have been fabricated, he had the perfect track record for it.

The minister was whittering on. What he said bore little or no resemblance to the man we knew, the King of Crap, but that was pretty standard for funerals. I whispered, 'I hear he got hit by a car.'

Mouse shook his head. 'A car fell on him.'

'*Fell?* You mean he was walking down the street and a car fell outta the sky?'

'Don't be daft. He was fixing his car. Had it jacked up, working underneath, jack gave way. Result, one flat Corkery. The car was fixed, if that's any consolation.'

We grinned into the palms of our hands, then

sang 'The Lord Is My Shepherd'. Not just us, the whole congregation. I watched as the minister, still leading the singing, moved several yards across to his left, stopping by the large counter on which sat Corkery's coffin. With a dramatic flourish he lifted his index finger into the air, held it there for a moment, then plunged it down towards a red button set into the side of the counter. A moment later the plain wooden box juddered once, then began to descend, the minister with his hymn book in one hand and his finger still stuck on the button. There was something about the way he did it that reminded me of the National Lottery, and I suppose in a way it was.

As the service drew to a close I whispered to Mouse that I'd see him later, then edged along the row to accompanying tuts and hurried up the aisle. I went through the door, then looked about me for a few moments before I picked my place. There was a mock marble column just to the left of the exit which was ideal. I leant up against it, as lazy-looking as I could, then removed the lighter of the two books I'd bought in the second-hand shop and opened it at Chapter One. I started reading.

I probably wasn't doing my chances of employment much good, judging by the glares and stares of the mourners as they filed out, but I persevered. Mouse came past with an exaggerated tut; he knew I was up to something.

'We're having a few drinks, down in the King's Head,' he said.

'We?'

'The cream of Belfast journalism. But you can come as well. There'll be crisps.'

'Well if there's crisps . . .'

'Can I give you a lift?'

'I'm not finished here yet.'

He nodded. I winked back. He walked on. I smiled after him. Six months, and no hint of the fissure that had opened up in our friendship.

'*The Horse Whisperer*. Is that good?' I looked round. There was a silver-haired woman, red-eyed, black-dressed, medium heels, looking at the front of my book. Mid forties, possibly older, but knew how to look after herself. Her voice was South Belfast, cultivated without being plummy.

I shrugged. 'Only started.'

She nodded thoughtfully for several moments. She was looking me over. I wasn't sure I liked it much. She pursed her lips. 'You're either here to rub salt in, or you're Starkey.'

'What do you think?'

'You're Starkey.'

'Bingo. You'll be the girlfriend.'

She smiled. 'I'm hardly a girl.'

'You're *all* girls.'

'Does that charm get you far?'

'As far as the divorce court.' I put my hand out. She grasped it. 'I'm sorry for . . . y'know.'

'I know.'

'I heard a car fell on him, that right?'

She nodded.

'Accident?'

'What do you think?'

'I think he never worked under a car in his life. I'm thinking the only time he'd ever get under a car was if one of his betting slips blew under it. That's what I'm thinking.' She nodded. 'What'd the police say?'

'They'd rather believe suicide than murder, and they don't believe suicide.'

'Maybe we should have a cup of coffee.'

'I'm having some people back to the house, you're welcome to come along. But it may be a while before we can have a chat.'

'That's okay. I understand.' I was still holding her hand. I gave it another little squeeze and added, 'There will be food, won't there?'

She fixed me with a look as steady and unnerving as any I have ever experienced. Her voice, when it came, had shed any pretence of gentility; it was dragged all the way back from the darkest ghetto in West Belfast. 'Corky told me you were a smart cunt. Just don't try it with me, okay? I've enough shite to put up with.'

'Okay,' I said, meekly.

Just as abruptly, she softened again. 'There will be buns,' she said, 'but they're for the kids, okay?'

She'd said it was a house, but it was more like a mansion. Anything that has wings but doesn't fly qualifies as a mansion in my book. (Or, indeed, as a chicken.) There was a long driveway, tended lawns, a tennis court, an outdoor swimming pool, a garage bigger than most houses, ivy, sprinklers, white doves and a pair of spaniels. Out back, there were stables. There were mourners of course – some of the journos, but not many, the rest seemed to be relatives of hers, and when I spoke to them they knew little or nothing about Mark Corkery.

I went through the books in the library, largely antiquarian, and scoffed buns. There weren't that many kids to eat them and it would have been a shame to let them go to waste. They were little sponge efforts with soft white icing on top like my mother used to make. Patricia had fancied herself a dab hand in the kitchen, but her butterfly buns reminded me more of moths. Still, I was prepared to put up with them if she came back to me.

By mid afternoon I still hadn't set eyes on the girlfriend, even though the stragglers were leaving. It crossed my mind that I might have the wrong house, but eventually she struggled through a door carrying a tray of dishes and stopped when she saw that I was looking through her kitchen cupboards.

'Can I *help* you with something?'

I closed them quickly. 'Just looking.'

'Do you always make yourself this much at home?'

'Just with friends.' She smiled and let me take the tray off her. I said, 'I'll wash, you dry,' but she waved me away, said there was a woman who came in. She left the dishes by the sink then led me back through into the main lounge. I was pleased to see that the last of the mourners had departed. There were things I needed to know, but as we stood at the window and watched the last car descend the driveway, I couldn't think of one of them. She spotted a half-drunk glass of whiskey by the window and lifted it. She sniffed it, took a sip, then nodded down towards the gates. 'Well thank Christ they're gone. Never heard so much nonsense.'

I scouted along the windowsill for a glass for myself and managed to find one. I turned the scarlet lipstick marks on it away from me as I drank. I made a mental note that this wasn't for pleasure. It was research. It was work. It was almost certainly one hundred per cent Polish vodka. 'What do you mean . . . ?' I began.

'Oh . . .' She waved her hands again, although she was careful not to spill a drop. 'Hardly a one of them knew him really, those that did thought he was a low-life. Y'know, a gambler, as a breed they get rather bad PR. But I tell you, he was one of the finest I ever knew, and I knew most of them, believe you me. Do you gamble, Mr Starkey . . . ?'

'It's more of a steady stroll.'

She gave me a resigned kind of a smile, but passed no comment. 'I've been gambling all of my life. As you must suspect, I was not actually born to all of this . . .' She raised her glass to our surroundings. 'The Falls Road, outside toilet and a change of floorboards every few months when the Brits used to tear the place apart looking for arms.'

'Arms, legs . . . did they ever find any?'

'No, of course not. My dad had no time for any of that cak. He was a greyhound man, least he was at the start. Didn't keep them. Just liked a wee flutter. Used to be I'd go with him most nights: Dunmore on a Saturday, Celtic Park on a Monday . . . of course they're gone now, thank God, used to freeze your balls off standing there . . .' She smiled sadly. 'Used to be great. Y'know, me only ten or eleven but m'dad and I discussing the form together, him taking me seriously . . . that was a great feeling. So good.'

'Your mum?'

'Dead. Heart attack. Only twenty-eight when . . . Anyway, me and Dad, we moved on to horses then. Never betting much, never losing much, never winning much, just enough to keep us going. I remember it was such *fun*. Most people would be happy just going down to the bookies, studying the form in the paper, putting their dole on, but not us, no; we had to be there, see them in the flesh, make our call then. So off we'd go in our beat-up wee Anglia, down to Fairyhouse or Leopardstown, or across on the ferry to Cheltenham, Aintree, y'know, the big ones, hundreds of little ones as well. We'd bunk up at some B and B, get up early in the morning, watch them gallop . . .' She trailed off. 'Sorry. This Is Your Life.'

'No. It's okay. Go on. I still don't know how you got from that . . . to this.'

'Luck. Love. I was getting on for sixteen and I fell

for a jockey. Local lad we used to meet on the ferry going over . . . You remember Vincent McPeake?'

'I don't remember a *jockey* called—'

'Well he never really set the world on fire in the saddle. But *out* of it: now my Vincie was a man who could work *magic* with horses. He studied it hard, mind, and those early years there wasn't much money about, but he studied at the horseshoes of the masters and when the right time came he went for it: he got some financial backing, he got a licence out of Lambourn and off we went. Ten years we were, building up our stable. We'd one hundred horses at the height of it – eighty of them two-year-olds, would you believe that?'

'I'm sorry, it doesn't mean any—'

'Doesn't matter. It was just so great. I still remember our first winner. Bought Vain Glorious as a yearling. She won seven hundred and fifty pounds at some obscure race in Scotland, but we were off. The final year, oh the final year – our horses won seventy-five races on the flat, home and abroad. And then came Royal Tapestry.'

'I think I remember some—'

'Now that was a filly and a half . . .' She stopped, staring into nothingness or the garden. Then she slowly raised her free hand and pressed the tips of her fingers against the window. Her knuckles and joints began to redden with the pressure. For a moment I feared that the glass would give way, but she abruptly dropped her hand and focused her attention on the moist prints she had left behind. When she spoke, her voice had hardened again. 'Royal Tapestry. We Republicans should have known better than to trust anything with *Royal* in its name . . . She was a beauty, and she ran like the bloody wind. We'd been successful before, but she was to be our first real crack at one of the classics . . .'

'The . . . ?'

She let out a little sigh. 'Oh . . . Mister Starkey . . . what I have planned for you, and you just don't know anything, do you?'

'I . . . *Plan?* . . . Well no, not much.'

'There are five classic flat races – the Two Thousand Guineas, the One Thousand, the Oaks, the Derby and the St Leger. We'd Royal in mind for the Oaks and there were a lot of people reckoned she had what it took. Except one day, out for a gallop, she just had a buck and a kick along the way and she managed to shatter her shoulder. And that did for her. Believe me, they just don't break that bone. We had to put her down.'

'Sad. But surely one horse—'

'Ah but there's more. There was an inquiry. There was such a buzz about her for the Oaks that they had to know what had happened, and what do you know but they found dope in her. Don't ask me how. Vincie would *never* have dreamed of stooping to doping. I know that from the bottom of my heart. And doping *that* horse! It would only have messed her up, she was that *perfect*. Yet in its grand wisdom the Jockey

Club dragged Vincie in and took his licence off him. Took his *life* off him. He appealed of course, but they're such a tight little Mafia that Vincie knew they weren't going to give it back to him. He'd become too successful too quickly. They were jealous. They wanted to . . . Oh *fuck*.' There was a tear in the corner of her eye. I offered her a napkin sitting becrumbed on the sill where she'd lifted her drink. 'With no licence, no income, things were hard, but Vincie was convinced our appeal would work. The night before we were due to go up for it he went out to check on what horses we had left. When he didn't come back after a while I went out to see what was keeping him. Found him hanging from a rafter.' She took a deep breath. She fixed moist blue eyes on me. 'It all just got too much for him. Affected his head. I mean, you have to be off your trolley to hang yourself *before* the verdict, don't you?'

I shrugged. It wasn't the place to say *Unless you know you're guilty*. 'How did . . . ?'

'How did it go? Well *of course* they gave him his licence back. And it wasn't *ironic* if that's what you're thinking. It was just twisting the knife a little further. Believe you me, if he'd turned up, they would have burned that flaming licence in front of him. They had it in for Vincie, no two ways about it.'

We sat silently for several minutes. On first hearing, I found it difficult to believe that there could have been such a vendetta against her husband. The Jockey Club was, as far as I could determine, a highly regarded and much-revered body. Why stoop to . . . Well, it didn't matter. I was here to pay my respects and find out what had happened, not to take on the great British racing establishment. I noticed a half-bottle of whiskey sitting on a table on the other side of the room. I nipped across and retrieved it. I poured her another glass, then a smaller one for myself. I was pacing myself, like a thoroughbred.

'Cheers,' I said.

'Cheers.' We clinked glasses.

'So,' I said, 'you applied for a licence, took over the training, reared a stable of winners and retired to this mansion on the profits.'

'*What*?' She laughed. 'I *don't think* so. We were bankrupt – *I* was bankrupt. I was closed down almost before he was the full six foot under. The bailiffs came in, I was lucky to get out with the shirt on my back.'

'I thought . . .'

'I came home on the ferry, same ferry my dad and I used to get, same ferry me and Vincent met on. Except there was I coming home without a penny in my pocket, husband dead, father dying, back on to a little terrace on the Falls like none of it had ever happened, except the neighbours gave me a hard time for having picked up an English accent along the way. Though I soon lost it again, as you can tell.'

'I . . . yes . . . but I don't understand . . . There must have been some colossal pay-out on the insurance . . .'

'They don't pay out on suicides. There was nothing.'

My hands were in the air, waving vaguely about, but meaning the room, the *wings*, the stables, the tennis courts. 'But all *this* . . . how on earth did you manage to . . . ?'

She laughed suddenly. '*This* . . . *!* This isn't *mine* . . . it's Corkey's.'

'*Corkey's!*'

'I told you he was one of the finest gamblers I ever met. He won it on a horse.'

'Fucking hell!'

'Exactly. And the house used to belong to a guy called Geordie McClean.'

5

She led me up the stairs and into a bedroom.

Well, I say bedroom on the understanding that most rooms that are upstairs in a house are generally referred to as bedrooms no matter what activity takes place within. This one was large. The curtains were closed. There was no bed. There were several television sets, all of them switched on and all of them showing different channels of racing. There were three computers set up. From each came a steady bleep . . . bleep . . . bleep of messages arriving via e-mail. Across the room there were two fax machines, both of them in the midst of receiving data. She sat down in one of two large leather executive chairs and swivelled round to face the computers. Then she tapped the arm of the other one and I joined her. She glanced across.

'That's where Corkery used to sit.'

'Ah.' I shifted a little. 'This . . . all this, it's like NASA.'

'Well, not quite. The nerve centre. Where all the whispers converge. Wouldn't Geordie McClean just love to see this?' She gave a sweet little laugh. 'I take it you're like Corkery then, most of youse are. Journalists, I mean. Can ferret wonderful stories out of people, but new technology scares the shite out of you.'

'You might say that.'

'Mark, God rest his soul, was a people person. He acted on the tip-offs, he chased the leads, he was the man on the ground. I handled this end of it.' She patted the side of the computer sitting on the desk before her. 'We track practically every race meeting in the world, all of the bloodstock sales, we have an inside track on every stable, every trainer, every jockey . . . Look . . .' She pushed her wheeled chair across the floor to the fax machines and ripped a sheet off the first. I followed. 'Let's see what we have . . . Here's a jockey, Davey Scott . . . failed a random drugs test at Uttoxeter in 1997, Jockey Club took his licence away, soon afterwards he announced he was going back to the building trade . . . and this is a fax from an insider at the Victoria Racing Club in Australia reckons the young fella applying for a licence there under the name of Rodney Carstairs might be one and the same as our man . . . Could be, we'll make some enquiries, or we'll just post it on our page . . .'

'What if you're wrong?'

'It's all in how you phrase it. The Horse Whisperer merely remarks on the astonishing similarity between two jockeys, nothing libellous about that.' She moved to the next machine and tore off another page. 'Okay. Here we go. How much do you reckon a hundredth of a second would be worth at one of the top two-year-old sales in the States, eh?'

'Worth? I . . .'

'Could be as much as two hundred thousand dollars. See, we've been following this lovely wee chestnut for a while, he was clocked in at 21.61 seconds over a quarter of a mile during the pre-sale breezes. He goes up for sale in Pomona in California, tomorrow, could make his owners two million off a hundred grand investment. Except this guy . . .' and she waved the fax, 'reckons he has video evidence of an electrical device being used to speed her up, caught it on tape falling from the jockey's hand after he'd pulled her up. Of course when he went to check it was gone . . . still, we might put that out on the Whisperer and I wouldn't be surprised if we saw a million wiped off her price by tomorrow. Now do you see why a lot of the bad guys out there don't like us?'

'*I* don't even like you, and I don't know a thoroughbred from a donkey.'

She smiled widely. 'Of course you like us.'

'Us?'

'I know. I keep saying that. It's hard to . . . *Okay. Me.*'

I couldn't quite picture the two of them in bed, but I could certainly see them working together on the Horse Whisperer.

'I like to think we've done a lot of good, Dan. Occasionally we get it wrong, but ninety per cent of the time I reckon we're right on the nose. And if we can make racing – hell, the *world* – a better place, sure isn't it worth it?'

'It certainly is.'

'Good, I'm glad you feel that way, Dan. Because I want you to become the Horse Whisperer.'

We went back downstairs. A troop of cleaners had arrived and were setting about cleaning up the mess. As we passed through the house two of them were trying to evict a mourner who'd locked himself in one of the toilets and was refusing to come out. One was calling through the door, 'Now, Jimmy, just turn the key,' but Jimmy was intent on completing what sounded like a rendition of 'The Star of County Down'. I wasn't sure because he was banging his foot against the door and pulling on the chain in time to his wailing. At the sound of our footsteps on the tiled hallway the cleaners turned and looked helplessly towards us. My host wasn't the least bit fazed by it. 'Just leave him,' she said.

'But Missus, there's a powerful smell of boke . . .'

'Then let him stew in it, then give him a mop the instant he comes out.'

We walked back through the kitchen and out into the cobbled yard behind. The two spaniels I'd spotted earlier basked in the late afternoon sun. She led me across to the stables. She introduced me to half a dozen horses. Brown ones. I patted them and made *there's a good fella* sounds.

'Have you ever even been on a horse, Dan?'

'Only in my dreams. When I was about eight. Cowboy stuff. But my wife rides all the time.'

'Really? What stable?'

'Oh, she's not faithful to any particular one.' I patted a nose, and decided to get off the subject. She'd moved on to first name terms somewhere between NASA and the stables, while I was thus far too embarrassed to admit that I didn't even know her surname. 'Tell me about Corkery and Geordie McClean,' I said. 'I'm not really following what . . . I mean, Geordie was trying to shut down the Horse Whisperer thing, but he didn't know that it was Mark who was running it . . .'

'And me . . .'

'Sorry. Of course . . .'

'Yes he was. And if he wasn't getting anywhere with the law, then why not without it?'

I shrugged.

'Dan. Look, if we discount the freak accident theory, then Mark was killed because someone found out he was involved in the Horse Whisperer, and the one who's been our sworn enemy these last few months has been Geordie McClean. If you add in that McClean also had a grudge against him because he won this house off him in a bet, then *everything* points to him being involved.'

I patted some more horse. 'I know. But I also know

Geordie. He's slippery, but I wouldn't say that he'd be up to murder.'

'Nobody's a murderer until they commit the deed. And I'm quite sure he didn't drop the car himself. He might have sent someone, he might just have given a hint and somebody did it for him. He mightn't even have meant for him to die. But he was involved. I know he was involved. Every bit of my body *screams* that he was involved. Either it was because of the house, or the Horse Whisperer, or both, but he's the man.'

We walked on out of the stables and stood on the brow of a small hill which sloped down towards the tennis courts. Now that we were closer I could see that the net was sagging and although the grass on the court was closely cropped the white lines were badly faded. I couldn't imagine Corkery in tennis whites. He was more a duffel coat and Guinness man, more interested in rackets than racquets.

I turned and looked back up at the house. What a windfall. Geordie McClean would have been kicking himself at having to hand over the keys to the likes of Mark Corkery. And all because he'd overstretched himself.

Geordie made his money in the seventies in the insurance business when Belfast was literally booming. He soon branched out into retail and property. He was always a bit of a risk-taker, and that inevitably led him into gambling. He bought over a small chain of 'turf accountants' in East Belfast. It was just his bad luck that within a month of opening Mark Corkery placed an accumulator covering six different race meetings, a million-to-one shot really, the sort of crazy bet only a lunatic or the truly inspired could ever come up with, and one that threatened to bankrupt Geordie's whole newly acquired chain. He should never have accepted the bloody thing in the first place, but he was new in the business and some fresh-faced eighteen-year-old in his first year as well took it on without referring it above. Most bookies are insured against such freak results, but again there was a slip in the paperwork somewhere and McClean had to face the fact that not only did he have to pay out, but also that he *couldn't* pay out. He had the money, but it wasn't liquid. He could have realised it in a few weeks, but Corkery wasn't prepared to wait. McClean had a choice, of course, because the one thing the Government has never done is make betting debts enforceable under law. It is left as purely a matter of honour and trust between the bookie and the punter. And fair play to him, McClean fully intended to make good his debt; besides, without public confidence he'd have no business. So he offered Corkery the house as a stopgap and they agreed on a handshake that he could buy it back as soon as the cash was handed over; except Corkery fell in love with the house and reneged on the deal, and there was nothing McClean could do about it.

Except drop a car on him.

'Dan, my man was killed. I want whoever did it punished.'

'I understand that.'

'The Horse Whisperer will not die with Mark. What they don't understand is that it's now largely self-perpetuating. You saw those e-mails, the faxes, it's like that *all* the time. There's so much horse shit out there, it just has to have an outlet. If Mark was killed because of the Horse Whisperer, then Geordie McClean is one confused fella right now, because the Horse Whisperer just keeps appearing.'

'Or he's going to keep coming back until the job's finished.'

'Not if we nail him first. And for that we need proof and I've a nasty feeling it's not something that's going to land in my e-mail basket, or come through the fax. I need *you* to do what Mark used to do best.'

'I take it we're not talking sex here.'

'Stop it. Will you go down there and stick your nose in and see what he's up to? Will you do it for Mark?'

'Of course I will.'

'Thank you.'

We looked at each other for several moments. Then she said, 'Oh fuck it,' and came forward to hug me. I hugged her back. We released each other after a little and she wiped at another tear.

'There's just one crucial piece of information I need to know,' I said.

'Anything.'

'What's your name?'

She let out an involuntary laugh. 'Why, I presumed . . . It's Hilda. Hilda Abernethy.' She put out her hand and I grasped it. 'I'm very grateful, Dan.'

'Yeah, well, you might not be. Let's see what happens.'

I got a cab down to the King's Head.

Mouse looked up as I came through the door. He was sitting by himself at the bar. He nodded and ordered me a pint. 'I KNEW YOU'D TURN UP EVENTUALLY.'

'Shhhhh,' I said. He rolled his eyes and left a fiver on the bar for the drink. 'Everyone else gone home?'

'Aye,' he replied, a little more quietly, 'soft shower of bastards. Used to be an occasion like this they'd be throwing us out at closing and then we'd head off to a party . . .'

'Usually at my house . . .'

'. . . usually at your house. But half of them spent the whole friggin' afternoon on their mobiles making sure—' His mobile beeped. Without a blink he answered it. 'No,' he told it, 'page *seven* . . . he's never been front page in his life . . .' Then he clicked it off and turned back to me. 'Sorry,' he said, 'where was I?'

'Bastards with mobiles.'

'Oh aye, and it was all mineral water this and iced tea that. The cunts.'

I nodded and sipped my pint.

'How was the old girl?' he asked.

'Corkery's?' He nodded. 'Okay.'

'What's your interest up there?'

'Nothing. Paying my respects.'

'You? It's not your style. What're you after, Dan?'

'Why do I have to be *after* anything?'

'Because I know you.'

I shrugged and looked at my pint for a while. Mouse looked at his. There was racing on the TV above the bar but I tried not to show any obvious interest. The brown horse seemed to be leading. I said, 'You ever hear of the Horse Whisperer, Mouse?'

He kept his eyes on the screen, but nodded slowly.

'What do you think?'

'I think Redford's starting to show his age.'

I took a sip. 'I'm thinking of going back to work.'

'I thought you might be.'

'I'll be looking for some freelance shifts.'

'Shouldn't be a problem.'

'But first I'm going south. Dublin way.'

'Is it something to do with Corkery?'

'Yeah.'

'Anything I can do?'

'Keep an eye on Trish.'

'As ever.'

'She's living on Windsor Avenue with some bloke. She seems happy. We have to break it up. See if you can find out anything about him. There's bound to be something, he has a beard. His name's Clive.'

'Beard and Clive. I hate him already. Any chance of a surname?'

I shook my head. 'She's playing her cards close to her chest.'

'And what a chest it is. In a strictly not-interested-in-my-best-friend's-ex-wife's-chest kind of a way.' He cleared his throat. 'So where should I start?'

'By checking a list of all those recently released from institutions for the criminally insane.'

'Are you serious? You think he's . . . ?'

'Well of course. He'd have to be fucking mental to take on Trish, wouldn't he?'

6

There are one-horse towns, and there are thousand-horse towns, and Ashtown is a combination of the two. Twenty minutes north of Dublin, three pubs, one victualler's, a post office with a green postbox outside and a video store. Its claim to fame is having the Fairyhouse Racecourse, home of the Irish Grand National, a stone's throw away. Beside the course stands the Irish base of Tattersalls, the world's first bloodstock auction house. Ten thousand horses a year pass through its books and parade rings, millions upon millions of dollars. Horses are to Ashtown as dope is to Amsterdam, and the business can be just as murky.

I drove down on Easter Saturday. It was a relief to get out of Belfast, partly because there was a hiccup in the peace process and all sorts of trouble was threatening to break out, but mostly to get away from me. The old me. The memories and the broken heart. I put them into a shoebox and pushed them under the bed in my little palace. Out of courtesy I called the landlord and told him I'd be away for a few days. I'd the feeling it wouldn't have worried him if I dropped dead, decomposed and started dripping through to the slum flat below as long as the Government rent cheque kept filtering into his bank account.

Hilda had given me the lend of a car and the keys to the house in Ashtown that Corkery had rented for the duration of the Easter races at Fairyhouse. She drove round to hand the car over personally. I took one look at it and said, 'This is the car that flattened Corkery.'

She nodded. 'It's okay. It's been cleaned.'

I took her word for it, but it seemed to me that at least some of her late boyfriend would still be going to the races. Perhaps his soul had transferred into the car. Maybe my life was turning into *Herbie Goes to the Races*. Or possibly *Christine*. I had my laptop and an e-mail address for the Horse Whisperer. She handed over Corkery's ATM card and his bank card and said there was around a thousand pounds between the two accounts and I was welcome to use it as expenses. I said I wouldn't abuse her trust, and she laughed, although I think she meant it kindly. I promised her I would do my best; I also pointed out that my wife usually said that my best wasn't good enough. She said she had every faith in me and gave me an Easter egg. I looked at it and thought about my dead son, then gave her a hug. If she'd been twenty years younger

I'd have invited her to come along, and she'd have said no.

I drove south. I filled up on petrol before crossing into the unoccupied twenty-six. Not that it was any cheaper, but just so that I wouldn't be contributing to their economy. It wasn't much, but it was something. Then on across the border, or lack of it. There's nothing *physical* any more, just a sense of time warp and the grass seems a little less green. I drove through Dundalk, still home to hundreds of terrorists, then turned right at Drogheda. I passed through Slane, where I'd once seen Bruce Springsteen play a massive open-air concert, and then across the Boyne river, where King William of Orange had co-headlined an even bigger gig with King James three hundred years before, so successful that people were still talking about it.

I arrived in Ashtown in early evening. It took me a while to find the house, and sixteen seconds to move in my worldly possessions. It was recently built and had five bedrooms, which was four too many. There was a television and an ensuite shower and a kitchen I could have swung a whole family of cats in. There was an intercom system for fending off unwelcome visitors. There was a Spar around the corner. I bought groceries and a bottle of Ribena. I was pleasant and they were pleasant. They asked me if I was down for the races and I said yeah. I refrained from asking if the murder suspect Geordie McClean was a regular. I returned home and made myself beans on toast.

Before I could launch into them there was a knock on the door. When I opened it there was a man in a smart suit standing there with three oil paintings in his arms.

He smiled pleasantly and said, 'Would you like to buy an oil painting?'

'Excuse me?'

'Would you like to buy an oil painting?'

'I don't think so.'

'They're by some of Ireland's finest artists. I've been selling them for twenty years.'

'And you still haven't got the message.'

'Sorry?'

'I said, I don't need an oil painting.'

'Okay. Do you mind if I call again?'

'I'm only here for the weekend.'

'Oh. Right. Fair enough then.'

If he'd had a cap, he would have doffed it. Off he went back to his car. I watched him load up his paintings and drive off. Across the road kids with hurley sticks were staring at me. I closed the door and went back to my beans. I reheated them.

Five minutes later the doorbell went again. When I opened up there was a man standing there with a coat on a hanger and a receipt book under his arm. 'Do you want any dry-cleaning done?'

'What?'

'Do you want anything dry-cleaned? I've been dry-cleaning in this area for twenty years. I call every Monday.'

'This is Saturday.'

'I know, but it's Easter Monday on Monday, there'll be no dry-cleaning done that day. So I'm calling today. Do you want anything dry-cleaned?'

'No, I don't think so.'

'Right-oh, then. Good afternoon now.'

I watched him go down the path and climb into a small van. As he drove away the boys with the hurley sticks stared across at me.

I returned to my beans. I microwaved them again because there are few experiences in life more depressing than eating cold beans. They'd already soaked through the toast, turning it to mush. I finished them, then cleaned and washed the plate. I tried to watch something on the TV but I couldn't concentrate. I was a stranger in a strange land, even though it was only down the road. I couldn't relax. There was a crack against the window and then a boy came over the garden wall to retrieve a ball. He didn't look up at me standing glaring down as he lifted it.

I unpacked. Another twenty seconds. There was a knock on the door. A young fella in a white coat said: 'Ice-cooled chicken breasts?'

'Excuse me?'

'I've ice-cooled chicken in the van. I call here every Monday.'

I looked beyond him to a plain white van, then back to him. 'Are you having me on?'

'What?'

'Are you taking the piss?'

He blinked several times. 'Do you want to buy some ice-cooled chicken breasts?'

'No, I'm a vegetarian.'

'I also do frozen vegetables.'

'No. Thank you.'

He nodded. 'I can call again. I'm always in the area.'

I said, 'Please do.'

As he walked back down the drive the ball came into the garden again. The boy came over the wall and had picked it up and was already climbing back out when I shouted, 'Why don't you go and play outside your own house?' like my father.

He glanced back, his brow furrowed. 'I was,' he said.

I looked across the road to where a middle-aged man was scraping birdshit off his lounge window. He glanced round at me and I waved across. 'Well just be careful of that wall,' I said and closed the door.

I switched the TV off and paced. I had an address for Geordie McClean's stables but it was getting into early evening and there didn't seem much point in driving out immediately. That left the option of more TV and an early night or checking out the pubs in town. I went upstairs and had a shower. I dried my hair and had a think about what to wear. I decided on black jeans and a green tartan shirt. Black trainers and a smile. Friendly. Ingratiate. See how they are about strangers. The doorbell sounded again. There was an intercom by the master bedroom. I pressed the button and said, 'Whatever the fuck you're selling, I don't fucking want it, now fuck away off and don't come fucking near me again.'

I combed my hair and cleaned my teeth. When I went back downstairs I looked out of the front window at two nuns standing with collecting tins talking to the man who'd been cleaning birdshit off his window. One of the sisters saw me, then quickly pointed me out to her colleague. They both glared at me, then turned their backs and hurried along to the next house. The birdshit man fixed me with a steady gaze, then darted back inside.

Third pub. Third pint. The first two had been dead but the third was much better. It was called Muldoons, and like the others was decorated with photos of previous Fairyhouse winners. The barman was big and jolly and I didn't understand a blind word he said, his accent was that thick. Maybe he had the same problem. Every time I asked for a lager he poured me a Guinness. I can't stand Guinness, but seeing as how I was undercover it was important for me to blend in, so I accepted it without complaint and drank for God and Ulster. There were a couple of dozen people drinking, enough to give it a nice buzz. I'd brought a newspaper with me. I sat on a bar stool, reading some, pausing, looking, then reading some more. I'd thought about cutting eyeholes in it to simplify the process but I resisted on the grounds that it was getting a bit close to being origami, and origami sounds a bit like orgasm, and I hadn't had one of those for months and I didn't want to get depressed, first night on the job. The talk around and about me was not of horses, but of life in general. *EastEnders*, *Brookside* and Manchester United. I could have launched into a diatribe on British colonisation by cultural stealth but thought it would be better to ingratiate myself by volunteering to make up the numbers on one of the teams when the barman announced that a pub quiz would be starting shortly. He took a note of my name, pronouncing it slowly to himself, then added it to a list of three others. He pointed to a corner which had thus far been shielded from my field of vision by a cigarette machine. 'Yucan joinem,' he said.

I lifted my pint and walked over. Sitting at a table, looking depressed, were the oil paintings salesman, the dry-cleaner and the chicken man. They looked up, but if they recognised me they gave no hint of it.

'Hi,' I said, 'I've been drinking alcohol in several areas for more than twenty years, but you three are without a doubt the saddest-looking individuals I've ever come across. I think I'm absolutely perfect for your team, if you'll have me.'

They looked at me, then gave me a collective 'What?'

'Speak slower,' said the chicken man.

'What're you on about?' said the dry-cleaner.

'You're no oil painting yourself,' said the oil paint-ings salesman.

'I said,' I said, 'what can I get you to drink?'

'Guinness.'

'Guinness.'

'Guinness.'

'Okay then,' I said.

We weren't the worst team on the night, and we weren't the best. I excelled at the movie questions but was found rather wanting on the silage round. Bloodstock left me bloodied and I won no points on the point-to-point. But they weren't a bad bunch of lads. They worked on the farms there and about and tried to earn an extra punt or two in the evenings with their various franchises, scrambling into action every time word went out that somebody new and innocent had moved into town. But none of them made any money at it and they were all in debt to their shark of a supplier in Blanchardstown.

'We hate that cunt,' said the oil paintings man.

'We should kill him,' said the chicken guy.

'And I could get the bloodstains out,' said the dry-cleaning man.

It was a plot that was never going to get beyond the pub, and they knew it. The Celtic Tiger was creating superwealth for the chosen few in Dublin, while the likes of them were wallowing in the tiger shit, earning fuck all in the fields and fuck all calling cold with disinterested and similarly strapped householders. I asked about the upcoming races at Fairyhouse and they all said they were involved in the catering end of it. I asked for more detail and they said they'd be selling sandwiches and hot dogs on the road outside on Easter Monday.

We stayed drinking until closing time. I'd heard tales of marvellous country Irish pubs where the landlord never called time and you drank until you fell over, but incoherent fat lad behind the bar suddenly started grunting on the stroke of eleven and by a quarter past we were standing on the pavement outside. I felt quite sorry for them. They didn't seem to have any other friends and they looked shiftily away when I mentioned my wife in passing, though I doubted if any of them had slept with her. I invited them back to the house and then stood tapping my foot while they pleaded with the landlord to serve them a carry-out.

Eventually he caved in. He disappeared back inside, then reappeared with four bags packed full of tins of Guinness. He was wearing a blue Dexter and Hush Puppies and appeared to think he was coming to the party as well.

We set off down the winding road back towards my empty, spacious house. The oil paintings salesman, the chicken man, the dry-cleaner and the fat incoherent landlord. As we walked I reflected on the fact that although I had learned nothing, it hadn't been a bad first night south of the border at all.

7

At first he didn't have a clue who I was, walking across the damp grass, six a.m. and the sun just a dull glow behind dark clouds to the east; one minute he was watching horses galloping past and the next there I was smiling as I came towards him, cupping my hands against the diminishing sound of thunderous hooves and shouting didn't he think it was cruel to get horses up so early.

As Geordie McClean eyed me curiously, two guys carrying shotguns rushed up to intercept me.

'What are you doing here?' one snapped.

'What the fuck do you want?' followed the other. Their accents were northern, and so was their attitude. I didn't reply, I just kept my smile in place and my eyes on Geordie. Their hands ran over my denim jacket, probably searching for a designer label.

They continued to shout questions, but I ignored them and concentrated on McClean, coming across the chewed-up ground towards us. It had been several years since we'd met, but if anything he looked younger, fresher. He was wearing a Barbour jacket, a flat cap, wellington boots and a look of surprise that slowly transformed itself into a smile. He was puffing on a thin cigar which he removed as he approached and extended his hand. As he did the two gunmen glanced at each other, then let me go. 'Dan the Man!' McClean exclaimed. 'Dan the Man – how the hell are you?'

'Cold, wet and intimidated, thanks. Can't even go rambling without—'

'It's private property, son – but Jesus! Dan the Man! In the flesh. Jesus, Dan, appearing out of the mist like the fucking Grim Reaper! What are you doing here?'

'I got redirected from your stables.'

'No! What are you doing here at all? I haven't seen you since, like, New York.'

'I know. I heard you named a horse after me. I'm here to collect my royalties.'

He grinned widely. 'Dan – you should have called. I could have had you barred.'

'You probably would too.'

I glanced at the gunmen, who'd now retreated several yards but were still keeping an eye at me as they leant against the side of a Land Rover emblazoned with an angular green *IAR* logo. I looked back to McClean. 'I was just passing, y'know. Thought I'd look you up.'

'You never call me, you never write, and here you are – Dan the Man.'

'Yes, I think we've established who I am. Now who are you? Sheikh Abdul Lottsahorses or what?'

He took another puff on his cigar. 'I'm the man who's giving racing a fucking good kick up the arse, that's who I am, Dan. As you no doubt know already.' He gave me a serious look, and I shrugged. 'So what're you really doing here, Dan? You don't strike me as an early bird. You don't look like you've even been to bed.'

'It's the new look. Hangover chic.' I smiled. 'I want to write a book about Dan the Man. And about the business. About you. How you can switch horses midstream, boxing to geegees, and still make a mint. You know the kind of book. Like the last one.'

'The last one, indeed.' He nodded for several moments. 'You know, my lawyer wanted to sue.'

'I didn't even mention him.'

'You know what I mean. But I said no. Because I thought it was bloody good work. I'm not much of a book man, Dan, and I'm not sure I emerged smelling of roses, but then maybe I don't – not these days anyway, eh?' And to emphasise the point he kicked at a lump of horse shit which managed to splatter across the front of my jeans. We looked at each other for several moments before he said, 'Sorry about that.' I shrugged. I'd been knee deep in it before, and would be again. McClean took a deep breath and nodded towards the horses that were now galloping back in our direction. 'Ah now, Dan, I thought boxing was the thing for me, but this, it's an entirely different ball game.'

I nodded encouragingly.

'And I'm not sure it's one I want written about. But let's talk about it. Come up to the house for lunch. I've some business first, but sure, let's talk. It's good to talk.'

I nodded again. It had been much easier to make a connection than I thought. Maybe he was a changed man. Maybe he had mellowed. Maybe *I* was nicer, better with people, maybe I should stay up all night drinking more often.

As the horses came thundering past, a dozen of them, chucking up muck and grass, their diminutive jockeys with legs clamped to flanks and their arses in the air, I glanced at McClean, his eyes narrowed, a picture of absolute concentration.

'Ah, now, Danny boy,' he said when they'd passed, 'there's no substitute for this, getting up at dawn, coming down here. For all the science involved, the blood tests, the weighing, the working on the split times, it can all still just be down to watching the horses, like this, having that knack for knowing when they're going to hit the top of their form.'

'And you have that knack?'

'Sometimes. And when I haven't, I buy a man that has.'

I nodded after the departing horses. 'Which one was he, then? Dan the Man.'

'The fast one.'

I'd not noticed, but I nodded anyway. 'Did you really name him after me?'

'Somebody told you that?'

'I heard a whisper.'

There was no reaction; I didn't really expect one; he was an old pro. He gave a little shrug. 'Well it must be true then,' he said, turning and nodding to the men by the Land Rover. They pushed themselves straight and pulled open the doors. McClean put his hand out to me and we shook. 'I'll see you up at the house around one if it suits, Dan. You can have a proper look at Dan the Man and we can have a chat about the book. Good to see you.' He climbed into the vehicle. One of his men was behind the wheel and the other in the back. The passenger window was already rolled down. As the engine was started I said, 'Why the guns, Geordie?'

He flicked the end of his cigar out of the window and it landed at my feet. 'Dan, remember the boxing? You thought it was full of sharks? Well they were fucking goldfish compared to this.' The Land Rover moved forward. He winked and said, 'Toodle-pip then.'

I watched him speed off down the lane and thought for a moment about what I might be getting myself involved with. It wasn't the thought of shotguns, sharks or goldfish, or even the horse shit on my trousers. It was dealing with a grown man who said *toodle pip*.

*　　*　　*

I stopped off at a diner in the village that was advertising a full Irish breakfast. The woman serving didn't give a second glance to my shit-spattered trousers but she looked confused when I asked for an Ulster fry. 'Sorry,' I said, 'I forgot I was south of the border, down Mexico way.'

Her brow crinkled like the bacon she brought. And the egg and the sausage. It was nice, but it lacked what makes the northern fry special: potato bread, soda bread, pancake, and I pined quietly for it. I shouldn't have been eating *any* of it, of course. It is not the modern way. But then I've never been particularly modern, you only have to look at my record collection to see that. In my book, if it's not fried, battered or covered in chocolate, it's not worth eating.

The thing is, I've never been Mr Fatty. Quite the opposite. I'm dead thin. This occasionally helps me to delude myself that I'm actually quite healthy, but deep down I know that cholesterol gathers just as handily in the arteries of a thin man as a fat; that if I continue the way I'm going the day will come when I'm sauntering down to the pub for lunch and I'll just explode. Like a lot of fools, I have conned myself into believing that anything with the word *Diet* on the side must naturally be good for you, and that the more of it you take, the healthier you will be. It amazes me that the marketing people haven't yet devised Diet Benson & Hedges as a marketing ploy, because they do make you thinner, eventually.

I picked at my fry. I'd gotten out of the way of healthy eating in the past few months – being sad and lonely was enough without being hungry – but when I was properly married Patricia used to sit me down and say, right, healthy eating begins on Monday. That was generally on a Tuesday, allowing me the best part of a week to stock up on my supplies of sugar and fat, culminating in a Sunday night visit to McDonald's, where I'd discovered the delights of hot apple pie and ice cream smothered in caramel sauce. And all for just 90p. Or two for £1.80.

'I said, are you finished?'

I looked at my plate. It was clean. It was a stupid question unless down here they ate plate as well. But I nodded and smiled, because I had to live with these people, at least for a weekend. She was middle-aged and her hair was tied back in a hamburger bun. Her skin was yellow, or it might just have been batter. I glanced at my watch. It was still only seven thirty. Staying up all night to meet McClean had paid off, but now I could go back to bed and sleep off the drink.

Or I would have done if the party animals had not still been boozing and singing along at the tops of their voices to some country cak on the radio, with the birdshit neighbour across the road staring in with a face like a bag of spiders.

I roared in and smacked off the radio. 'Stop it!' I yelled. 'It's eight o'clock in the fucking morning! Grow up! Tidy up! And if you have to throw up do it somewhere else! Haven't you got jobs to go to?

Haven't you got homes, you sad fucking wankers! And even if you haven't, I don't fucking care, just get out of my fucking house, okay!'

They stared meekly at me as they gathered up their meagre belongings. I moved to let the dry-cleaner get his coat from the chair behind me. When he'd pulled it on he shyly gave my arm a little squeeze. 'We understand about Patricia, Dan, and your son.'

I looked from one sympathetic face to another, and wondered what I'd said, and why. 'You know nothing!' I snapped. 'Now you better be fucking out of here by the time I wake up!'

I practically ran out of the lounge and up the stairs. I tore off my jeans and crawled beneath a quilt. For some reason there were tears rolling down my cheeks and I couldn't stop hugging myself. It was the funniest thing.

I woke just before noon. The house was quiet. I had a quick shower and shave and soaked myself in anti-perspirant and aftershave, but I could still smell horses, and I'd the feeling that I would do for some considerable time to come.

I dressed in my idea of smart casual. Black jeans, red sweatshirt, black sports jacket, Oxford shoes. If I was going to spend much longer around horses I would certainly have to do something about the shoes. It would mean investing in wellington boots or at least investigating if they did a lace-up version. When I went downstairs there was an oil painting of a little girl picking flowers hanging in the lounge. There was chicken in the freezer and a bag of Guinness cans in the fridge. On a hanger perched on the open door to the utility room were my stained jeans, now washed and pressed.

There was no note anywhere, and there was no need for one.

Geordie McClean's stable was about twenty minutes out of Ashtown. As usual I was running behind schedule. The windy roads and the cows in the way didn't help. When I finally pulled up to the gates it was nearly half past one. It had been Hilda's idea to try and meet Geordie face to face on the gallops, rather than risk a brush-off from some underling at the house, so I was hoping he hadn't checked out my lie about being redirected there by his staff. But as I looked up at the gate and the security cameras watching me I knew that he knew, and just hoped that it wouldn't make any difference. I gave my name and my business and after a thirty-second wait the gates swung inwards.

I drove up towards a large whitewashed bungalow. Large, but it wasn't a mansion. It had nothing on Mark Corkery's place. There was an IAR Land Rover sitting outside and I could just see the red roof of what I presumed to be the stables beyond. As I parked, the front door opened and the two guys who'd admired my jacket earlier came out, though this time neither of them were packing lead. They were much friendlier. They introduced themselves as Derek and Eric and asked me what part of Belfast I was from. They said they'd grown up around the corner from there and asked me if Lavery's bar was still in business because it had been a while since they'd been back. I said it was and always would be. We were getting on like old mates, but there was no doubt in my mind that no matter what corners we might have passed each other on years before, they would still break my legs if McClean asked them to.

'Is the man in?' I asked. 'I got delayed.'

'Nah – he's running late. He sends his apologies and would you wait.'

I nodded. They invited me inside and I said I'd rather take a look round, if they didn't mind.

'Not at all,' said Eric.

'He said you'd want to,' said Derek.

'Feel free. We've no secrets here.' He laughed as he said it and I grinned back. Then they searched me for a camera.

'Sorry,' said Eric, 'we have to be careful.'

'In this business,' said Derek, 'information means money, and money means information.'

'It's a bit wasted on me,' I said. 'I wouldn't know a thoroughbred from a pantomime horse.'

I winked like a professional and wandered away, absolutely convinced that as soon as I was out of view they'd be scurrying back inside to watch my every step via one of the many security cameras mounted about the property.

8

I had taken the precaution of bringing sugarlumps, pilfered from the home of the Irish all-day breakfast. I was going up and down the stalls patting heads and feeding cubes and thought I was getting on rather well when there was a shriek from behind and a girl came powering out of the afternoon brightness into the rather pleasant gloom of the stable.

'What the bloody hell do you think you're doing!' she yelled as she approached, her voice English plummy.

Naturally I assumed someone else had done something awful. A stable lad had stuck a pitchfork into half a million's worth of prime horseflesh or a carelessly dropped hand grenade was about to blow; but no, when I turned she was certainly shouting at me. Her cheeks were red and her nostrils were flared and her big brown horse eyes were mad as hell.

'Nothing . . .'

She let out another shriek, this time generously

soaked in derision, and grabbed hold of the hand I was now holding tightly closed. 'Open it!' she screamed.

She had a more than decent grip, so fearing for my safety, I reluctantly uncurled my fingers. 'Sugar . . . horses . . .' I stammered.

She glared at the half-dozen sugarlumps sitting on my palm, then slapped them wildly out of it. 'Are you *insane*?' she hissed.

'I th-thought . . . horses loved . . . Trigger . . .'

'Have you any idea what . . .' Then she let out a frustrated grunt and stamped her feet down on to as many of the cubes as she could find. She was slim and somewhere around the twenty mark; her hair was mousy brown, cut short so that she wouldn't have to bother with it, but obviously did. It didn't seem the time to ask what a fine young filly like her was getting so upset about. So I just continued to look hapless while she opened the first of several stall doors and began to urgently examine the creatures within.

'Sorry,' I said.

'Who the hell are you?' she snapped. 'What the hell are you doing here? Who told you you could come in here? Didn't you think to *ask*? Have you any idea what this can do to their blood sugar? How it can affect our readings? How do I know they're not full of dope? Don't you know never ever *ever* to give a thoroughbred something to eat without checking first?'

'I'm sorry,' I said again.

She gently slapped the side of the horse, then came out of the stall towards me. The first assault had made her seem quite tall, but now that she was standing head to shoulder before me it was clear that she wasn't really. 'Who are you?'

'I'm Dan the Man.'

'What?'

'Dan the Man.'

'What on earth are you talking about?'

'Dan the Man. The horse.'

'Yes, I *know* the horse.'

'Geordie McClean named him after me. Dan Starkey. Dan. The Man.' I smiled proudly.

'Dan the Man was bought in as a juvenile last year from the East Coast. He wasn't named after anybody, at least nobody on this side of the Atlantic.'

'Oh,' I said.

'So who are you, and what do you want? How did you get past security?'

'I'm a journalist.' Before her mouth could fully form up into a sneer I added, 'Or was. I'm hoping to write a book about Dan the Man. And Geordie's move into the horsey world. I'll interview you if you like, as long as you promise not to break my pencil.'

She wasn't instantly won over by my rapier-like wit. She looked at me coolly. 'I don't talk to journalists.' She moved along to the next stall. 'You shouldn't be in here.'

I went with her. 'Geordie said it would be okay.'

'*Geordie* said it would be okay,' she mimicked. 'Do you know him well enough to call him *Geordie*?'

I shrugged. 'Who really knows him?'

'I do.'

'What do you think of him?'

'I told you I don't talk to journalists. Go outside. Go *away*. These are sensitive creatures, they don't need to be disturbed.'

'Sorry. Perhaps I missed something. Which of us has been causing the disturbance?'

I didn't wait for a response. I turned and sauntered out of the stables. Something behind me was blowing hot air out of its nose, and it probably wasn't a horse.

When I returned to the front of the house there was a gleaming red Ferrari sitting beside the IAR vehicle. There was an Irish number plate with this year's date on it. There were no furry dice. I admired it as a nice car and swore that if I ever got to be as old as Geordie McClean I wouldn't embarrass myself by driving around in a Ferrari. I stepped up to the front door and rang the doorbell. Derek came and let me in. He was wearing a pinny with the same IAR logo on it. 'Go on through,' he said, 'I'm just fixing lunch.'

He pointed me down a corridor and I followed the sound of Van Morrison into the lounge. Not that he was there himself, but his mellow voice seeped out of an expansive and expensive-looking music centre which would have dominated the room if it hadn't been for the enormous snooker table which did. Geordie McClean was enjoying a pre-lunch cigar and potting a few balls.

I stood in the doorway. 'Who's winning?' I asked.

He looked up, smiled, then potted the brown. He straightened, then stood the cue on its end. 'Y'see, Dan, you come into money and you go out and buy all the things you ever wanted. Like this monster. Then you realise you haven't any friends to play with.'

'What about Derek and Eric?'

'You don't play with employees. They always lose.'

'They might just be crap.'

'No, *I'm* crap, that's how I know.' I raised an eyebrow and came into the room. He didn't look that crap to me. 'Do you fancy a game?' he asked. 'Say, five hundred a ball?'

'No.'

'One hundred.'

'No.'

'You're no fun, Danny boy.'

He stubbed his cigar out into an ashtray sitting precariously on the edge of the table then waved me through into the lounge next door. It was luxuriously appointed and afforded great views over the Meath countryside. The leather seats creaked as I sat down. He stood looking at me to the point where it got embarrassing.

'Penny for your thoughts?' I said, eventually.

'I was just thinking about New York. We went

through some shit there, didn't we?' I nodded. 'How time flies, eh?' I nodded again. 'What're you up to, Dan? Please don't fuck me around.'

'I wouldn't do that.' He kept looking at me. I reconsidered. 'Okay, yes I would, if I'd any reason to. But I just want some cooperation. To write this book.'

'I heard you had a kid die on you.'

'Yeah.'

'Kidnapped and he starved to death.'

'Yeah.'

'That's dreadful.'

'Yeah. It was.'

'And you've dropped from sight ever since.'

'You've been checking.'

'Of course. Dan, I know you've been on skid row. I had someone look over your apartment, if that's what you call it. He'd never seen such a dive. I spoke to somebody in the sports department at the *Belfast Evening News* who nearly broke a rib laughing when I told him you were writing a book about horse racing. He said you wouldn't know a filly from a fire exit.'

'I'm gratified that you would go to such an effort checking me out. You've obviously got too much time on your hands.'

'Don't get defensive, Dan. I do care. I know what you've been through. I know your wife left you. I know you haven't been working. I'm sure you do want to get back to it, but believe me, this isn't the way. I was serious about the sharks and the goldfish and the guns. You had some knowledge of the boxing and you did a good job with it, we had great crack together while it lasted. But this is different, you can't swat up on it in a week; you try to write an insider book on this sport and you'll only embarrass yourself. It's not two men punching the living daylights out of each other, it's an industry, it's a multinational. I've been following it all my life, I'm doing well out of it, but it's a minefield, Dan, and if you try to walk through it without a detector you'll only get blown up. There are secrets, and there are secrets about secrets, and people do not want them revealed.'

'So I've heard.'

'I know you, Dan, you'll sell me on a nice book about a horse and how wonderful I am but you'll want to dig and look and dig and look and write it all down and fuck the consequences, but you don't fuck the consequences in racing. You don't want this in your life, Dan, believe me.'

I looked at him, and then I shrugged and looked out at Meath.

Then he was sitting beside me. 'Dan – come with me to the races tomorrow, I've half a dozen horses running. Be my guest, come into the Members' Room, we'll down a hot whiskey or two and I'll give you a few hot tips on the runners – Jesus, Dan, I've a nose for them, stick with me and you can go home this weekend with more money than you'd ever earn from a bloody book.'

I sighed. 'I don't know. Y'know, I thought it was a good idea.'

'Besides, you ever heard of a racing book that actually *sold*? Unless you're fucking Dick Francis.'

'I'd rather not.'

He smiled at me. 'Down but not out, Danny boy, sharp as a tack. Well think about what I said. Now then, can I get you a wee drink, or is that a sore point?'

'Yes, and yes.'

He got me a beer. Derek called us for lunch a few minutes later and we trooped into the kitchen. We sat around a large enamelled dining table, me at one end, McClean at the other and Derek and Eric opposite each other in the middle, once they'd finished serving. There was one other place set, but nobody remarked on it. Derek had prepared a roast turkey meal, which was lovely. McClean said grace, almost literally. The talk throughout was small. Derek and Eric, although they were only in their late thirties, talked wistfully about old Belfast, bits of Belfast that I had not found wistful at all.

'We used to be cops,' Derek said.

'CID.'

'Then the Troubles finished.'

'And they scrapped overtime.'

'We couldn't afford our mortgages.'

'So we came to work for Mr McClean.'

'He cooks,' said Eric.

'And he cleans,' said Derek.

'They're a formidable team,' said McClean. 'The hob shines, the turkey's tender and either one of them could shoot you between the eyes from two hundred metres.'

The back door opened suddenly. Derek and Eric's hands shot under the table, but then they relaxed when they saw who it was. Conversely I stiffened, although in a sense it was inevitable that the girl who walked through the door was who she was, because that was the way my life ran.

'Ah – Mandy,' said McClean, 'late again. Dan – I don't believe you've met my daughter.'

I cleared my throat. 'Actually, yes. We bumped into each other earlier.' I smiled across. The temptation was to say 'Hiya sugar,' but I've never been one to give in to temptation.

McClean looked at her, looking at me, his brow furrowing, then burst into laughter. 'Now youse didn't get off on the wrong foot now, did you?' He shook his head at his daughter. 'That's not like you, Mandy love.'

She transferred her glare from me to him. 'He was feeding the horses. You know no one feeds the horses unless I say so.'

'Yes, dear, I know.'

'Okay.'

'Your dinner's in the microwave,' said Derek. 'Two minutes forty-five on reheat.'

'I'm not hungry.'

'Now now,' said Derek, 'let's not be petulant.'

'I'm not being *petulant*. I'm not *hungry*.'

Eric tutted, and she glared at him. Then she walked

out of the kitchen. Her footsteps echoed along the varnished hall floor. A door opened, then slammed shut.

'Sorry about that,' McClean said. 'She always gets like this before the big meetings.'

'She's watching her weight,' said Eric.

'She still has to eat,' said Derek.

'Once the racing's over, you'll see her in a better light,' said McClean.

I nodded, and continued eating. There wasn't much more to the afternoon. Derek and Eric lingered over their dessert, so McClean gave me a personal tour of the yard and a run-down on the runners he would have at the Easter Monday meeting at Fairyhouse. I got to meet and stroke Dan the Man, a big brown horse with a sleek look and intelligent eyes, or maybe I was biased. I said I'd put a tenner on him tomorrow but McClean said it would be a waste of time, he wasn't running.

'But I thought . . .'

'Saving him for bigger things. Tomorrow will be fun, and profitable, but Dan the Man goes in *the* Grand National, this Saturday in Liverpool. He can't do both, and it'll mean more at Aintree. That's when they'll all really have to sit up and pay attention.'

Back at the bungalow McClean waited by the Ferrari while I popped inside to get my jacket. I put my head round the door to say goodbye to Derek and Eric, just in time to see them swapping Cadbury's

Creme Eggs. I didn't like to spoil the moment, so I just backed away.

Outside, I climbed into Hilda's car while McClean held the door open for me. 'Take it easy, Dan. Think about what I've said. If you want to come along tomorrow, feel free. I'll leave your name on the gate and there'll be a pass there for you for the private members' enclosure, okay?'

'And what if I decide to do the Dan the Man book?'

'Well that's up to you. Horses can't sue for invasion of privacy, but they can give you a bloody good kick between the legs.'

I smiled. He closed the door firmly and I started the engine and drove out of the yard. As I went back down the lane towards the open road I could see him watching me in the mirror, arms folded, thinking, thinking.

'Well what do you think?' I asked the car, or at least that bit of it which retained an essence of Mark Corkery. 'Did he kill you? Does he know what I'm up to?'

There was no response. I hadn't really expected any. But hello would have been nice, or thanks.

9

I spent a relaxed night in front of the television, then had a nightmare about opening a giant Easter egg and finding the mummified corpse of my son inside. I lay in the dark waiting for my heart to slow and wondered whether Patricia shared similar night terrors. I also wondered what it was like to kiss someone with a beard, and hoped that I would never have to find out.

I finally dropped off again towards dawn and didn't wake until near lunchtime. When I opened the curtains downstairs there were twenty-five thousand people in my front garden.

Well, perhaps not that many. But there were hundreds walking past the house; there were cars parked bumper to bumper on both sides of the road. It was Easter Monday, it was the Irish Grand National. I was going to put my new-found insight into horse racing to good use and win myself a fortune. Before I left the house I called up the Horse Whisperer on my laptop and perused that morning's breaking gossip. A Scottish jockey was in hospital after suffering a heart attack when a trainer locked him in a sauna to force him to lose weight. A horse that had twice been named US Horse of the Year was rumoured to have proved sterile when put to stud; the Horse Whisperer was predicting it would cost his owners up to $25 million. There were a dozen other reports that were a little too technical. As I locked up the house I thought about the possibility that McClean might be right. That horse racing was a different ball game. I'd had a feeling for the boxing, but this I couldn't get to grips with at all. How was I ever going to investigate his dirty dealings without *some* understanding of what was going on?

By blind faith, dogged determination and drink.

It was a combination that had worked before. It was getting them in the right order which was usually the problem.

I walked the half-mile to the course, joining in with the happy throng. I knew enough to know that the Irish Grand National was the social event of the horsey year. There would be big floppy hats and leggy models, and there would also be gnarl-faced old men with nicotine fingers pissed off about having to share the racecourse with big floppy hats and leggy models. Hopefully, in the members' enclosure, I would see more of the models and less of the gnarlers.

Sure enough, there was a ticket waiting for me on the gate and a pass to the members' enclosure. Before

I attempted to find McClean I took a walk around the course. There were three or four public bars dotted about, and also several kiosks set up to serve only hot blasts of the sponsors' whiskey, Jamesons. The bars were bunged full, so I concentrated on the whiskey. Only three or four, enough to give me the edge, not enough to knock me over it.

It was still two hours before the big race, but there were half a dozen others on the race card. I could see people pressing in around the parade ring to see the runners go by, so I went along to cast my eye over them. I nodded and tutted as each went past, then made tiny little shorthand notes on my race card; it didn't amount to much more than writing *brown*, and *browner*, but I hoped it made me look at least vaguely competent. I was watching out for Paper Lad, the first runner of the day from McClean's stable. His colours were listed as red, white and blue, although not in that order. He came into the ring last, which I presumed wasn't a reflection of his chances. As he passed by before me I noted sagely that he looked suitably athletic, and brown. I made a note.

The jockey was . . .

Familiar.

I'd been concentrating so much on the horse that I'd barely spared a look for the jockey and now he was past, but there was *something*. I made my way out of the crowd and hurried round to the other side of the parade ring so that I could take a closer look.

I was right.

He was Mandy McClean.

And she looked absolutely *stunning*. Sitting up on Paper Lad with her cheeks flushed pink and the peak of her cap pointing straight up and her slim, boyish figure encased in gaudy silks. Geordie's angry daughter. Her jaw wasn't square at all, but it gave the appearance of squareness, of jutting determination. Her eyes were set hard against distraction. Focused. It was no excuse for her behaviour towards me the previous day, but it was certainly an explanation. Pre-race nerves, fighting with her weight. I had a sudden desire to shout, 'Your turkey's in the microwave!'

I restrained myself.

I hurried up to the tote window and placed a bet on Paper Lad. Five pounds. I wasn't sure why. When I passed the fiver across I noticed that my hand was shaking slightly, and I didn't know why either. As far as I can recall, my only previous hand-shaking moments have been in the presence of gunmen or my wife. The first time I'd met Patricia *all* of me had started to shake involuntarily and I'd had to make my excuses and leave, although in retrospect it could have been the magic mushrooms. I didn't see her for another three months after that and then she was snogging someone else. It had been a long battle to win her, and a short war to lose her. How women affect you. I have occasionally fantasised about a combination of a beautiful young woman, silk, and a nice bottom raised invitingly towards me, but a jockey on a smelly brown horse parading her arse to twenty-five thousand drunken punters on a windswept racecourse south of the border suddenly seemed somehow more erotic than almost anything I could imagine.

How can sudden animosity transform itself into . . . into what? *Fuck*. It was the whiskey. That was all.

You just haven't had sex for a long time. Don't even think about it.

I hurried towards the members' enclosure, feeling foolish and excited.

There was a young fella in a blazer checking passes. As he let me through I noticed a hand-written poster attached to the gate on which he was leaning; it said, *Members' Passes £5*. I'd imagined a degree of exclusivity, a nice quiet place from which to enjoy the spectacle of the National, that McClean had had to pull a few strings to get me in, but everyone and his granny were already inside. It was as smoke-filled and boozy as any smoke-filled boozy place on the occasion of a great sporting event. Leggy models and wavy hats were nowhere in evidence.

It took me five minutes to locate him. I checked my watch. The race. The race with *her* in it was due off in another five. McClean was standing up against the window, binoculars in hand, observing the course. Like practically all outdoor events these days there was a giant video screen situated opposite the finishing line, which most people would end up watching. Below me was the main stand, packed to the rafters. In the distance there was a ferris wheel and beyond it fields packed tight with parked cars. On the screen I tried to pick out Mandy from the field of runners. As McClean lowered his glasses I said, 'You didn't tell me your daughter was a jockey.'

He turned and fixed me with a steady look. It seemed to me to be one half pride, one half worry. 'Aye, well. Anyway, Dan. I'm glad you could come. Can I get you a drink?'

I didn't think for one moment that he would physically push through the throng on my behalf. He nodded down to his left; there, hidden by his boss and sitting behind a small table, was Derek. He slowly raised himself. I smiled. 'Where's . . . ?'

'Keeping an eye on Mandy. What'll you be having?'

I asked for another whiskey and he hurried off. 'You don't sound like you approve.'

McClean shrugged. 'She's my daughter.'

'Is she any good?'

'As a jockey? She's excellent.'

'I put a fiver on her.'

'Good man. Paper Lad's a fine horse. You should turn a healthy profit on that one.'

By the time Derek returned, the horses were lined up at the start. There was a roar from the crowd as the starter set them off. Two laps of the course. Fences. I watched the big screen, troubled, and sipped my whiskey. Derek stood by McClean's side roaring Mandy on. McClean himself stood stock still, the binoculars clamped to his eyes, but his knuckles showed white from gripping them too hard. The runners were still on their first lap when I asked McClean if he had much money on the race.

'Not directly,' he said, his eyes never leaving the course.

'I heard you once lost a whole house over a bet.'

'Not directly,' he said again.

There was commentary relayed across the members' lounge but it was drowned out as the riders came back round for the final time. I sipped on my whiskey and watched as Paper Lad approached the third fence from home. He jumped it without difficulty and was third going into the second last. He jumped clear again. There was another yell from Derek to my left. McClean remained motionless. My leg was shaking. I thought: *what the fuck is this about?* Paper Lad was gaining ground on second-placed Evil Intent as they came to the last; all three went over it and began the sprint for the line. Mandrake, in the lead, was clearly going to take it, but Mandy and Evil Intent were sweating it out neck to neck for second; Derek was screaming hoarse in my ear and McClean's knuckles looked set to burst out of his skin.

The roar from the crowd was for Mandrake, but the smile from McClean was for his daughter, pulling fractionally ahead of Evil Intent to take second. I said, 'Well done.'

The smile faded. 'Could have been better.' McClean made a point of studying his race card for the next race. It seemed a bit churlish. I looked at Derek, sweaty-browed with excitement. He gave a little shrug and said, 'She was *soo* close!'

I smiled and looked back down to the track. I took a sip of my whiskey. McClean turned from the window. 'So you heard about the house.'

I nodded. 'It's kind of entered Belfast folklore.'

'I'm sure you're all having a bloody good laugh.'

'Not exactly.'

'That fucker Corkery. I'm glad a fucking car fell on him. Couldn't have happened to a nicer man.'

'There are those,' I said, keeping my eyes on the advert for Harp that was running on the big screen across the track, 'who say you might have dropped it.'

McClean's eyebrows rose slightly. 'And what do you think?'

'I'm not paid to think. Come to think of it, I'm not paid at all.'

'Never a fucking straight answer with you, is there, Dan?' He nodded for several moments. 'Dan – you wouldn't be down here because of that, would you?'

'Are you joking?'

'Have you ever known me to joke?'

'Not intentionally.'

'Okay then.'

I shook my head. 'No. I'm not here about that.' He kept looking at me. I've never been one to let things sit. Always the last word. 'Although I have met his girlfriend,' I volunteered. 'She's a bit cooky. She's full of conspiracy theories.'

'That house you're staying in was rented out in a

fictitious name, one previously used by that bastard Corkery.'

I tried to be as nonchalant as possible. Normally when I'm lying my face goes red, but with the whiskey and the heat generated in the members' room by several hundred drinking punters it felt like it was already most of the way there. 'Yeah, it was, and nice place. Too big for me though. His girl offered it to me for buttons when she heard I was coming down. It was bugger all use to her with her man flat under a Volkswagen.' I took another drink, then tutted. 'I came down to write a book. Now I'm not even sure about that.'

That was it. He appeared to believe me. I hung around the members' room for another couple of hours. McClean suggested I put what money I had left on a horse called Prior Commitment, and right enough, it came in at five to one. I made some money, though not enough to buy my way into heaven. There was no sign of Mandy, and I didn't ask why. I said goodbye to McClean. As far as he was concerned it was the last he would see of me. There were no further invitations. He had had me checked out, he'd confronted me, he'd heard what I had to say; it didn't make any difference to me whether he believed me or not, he'd already indicated that he wasn't going to cooperate with my book and by extension my investigation into the death of Mark Corkery. I'd never expected him to throw open his files and say, here, do your worst.

I tramped home, tired and slightly drunk.

I tried to sleep but there was a racket going on out in the street; the kids across the road were playing camogie or hurling or gaelic or one of those stupid Irish no-rules sports. I felt sick and homesick. I felt lonely and confused because the glimpse of Mandy's silk arse in the air had affected me more than it should have. I knew what it was, it was delayed reaction, it was the shock of Little Stevie's death and Patricia's desertion, it was nothing to do with a pretty young girl who clearly despised me. It was me, me, me.

It's always you, you, you, that's what Patricia used to say when we'd storm about the kitchen. And she was right. I could see that.

I took a shower. I studied the television guide. Although not at the same time. There was nothing even slightly interesting on. It was Easter, there was *Ben Hur* and *ET*. There were tins of beer in the fridge. I drank three and thought of my new-found pals and how awful I'd been to them.

I pulled on my clothes and went back out to Muldoons.

It was heaving. It was Easter Monday, everyone was off work and pissed from the races. Big fat incoherent lad appeared not to remember me. I asked where the chicken man, the oil paintings man and the dry-cleaner were, but he just stared at me like I was mental. So I ordered a pint and squeezed into a corner and sat there for a couple of hours thinking about everything and nothing, hardly noticing or listening to what was going on around me. I only cheered up as an image of Patricia's man getting his beard caught in elevator doors and his head being pulled off flicked across my mind.

I phoned Mouse and related this. 'You're back on the sauce again.'

'Only for tonight,' I said. 'It's Easter.'

'Happy Easter,' he said.

'*Slainte*,' I replied. He had nothing to report, and less to say. He was with his family enjoying dinner. I said, *at least you have one*, and he put the phone down on me without establishing whether I was talking about a family or a dinner, or both. He was right.

A woman's voice, a million miles away, said, 'Ish anyone sitting here?'

When I looked up, it took several moments to recognise her. She was wearing make-up, her hair was slightly spiked, she looked fantastic and she was *smiling* at me.

I have encountered many smiling assassins, so I tensed and said, 'What?'

'I said . . .' Mandy stopped and rolled her eyes; on closer inspection her eyeliner was smudged and her eyes were glassy. She sat down. Or tried to. She missed the stool completely and sprawled away across the floor. She lay there for several long moments, giggling hysterically into the floorboards and ignoring completely the hoots of laughter coming from the table behind. I glanced slightly groggily across to see a crowd of a similarly diminutive stature roaring their heads off. Empty pint glasses stood precariously in leaning towers before them.

Mandy crawled back across the floor towards me. Her lipstick was smudged across her face from kissing the woodwork and it took some considerable effort to drag herself up on to the stool beside me.

I took a sip of my drink.

'I been watching you for an hour,' she slurred. Her accent wasn't so English now.

'Very good,' I said. I looked warily beyond her, but another of her company had fallen off *his* chair on the other side of the table and general hysterics had broken out again.

'I'm sorry for shouting at you yesserday, but you shouldn't, sugar.'

I nodded.

'My father, the bastard, told me all about you.'

I nodded again and took another sip.

'You and your dead . . . tod . . . toddler. I'm very sorry. I didn't . . . know.' She leaned forward and gripped my hand. It was the same hand that was holding the pint, and the suddenness of it sent a wave of lager up and over the edge. She was looking into my eyes. 'I *really didn't* know . . .'

'That's okay.'

'No, it's not okay, it's inex . . . scusable.'

'Don't worry about it. Good, ahm, race today.'

'You saw it? Awe. That's sweet. Excep' – that horse is a fucking donkey. I could have run faster than . . . Can I ask you something?'

'Yes.'

'Have you had much to drink tonight?'

'No.'

'Well I have. And so . . .' she pointed wildly behind her, 'have those fuckers. Could you do me a really, really, *really* big favour?'

I shrugged.

'Could you drive me home?'

'I don't have the car . . .'

'M . . . *my* car. Please. Daddy'll kill me if I don't get the F . . . Ferrari home.'

I looked at her. I had come south to ruin her father, to gain evidence of his murder of Mark Corkery. To reveal the sordid secrets he was trying to hide from the Horse Whisperer. I was single, sad, drunk and depressed. My only friends south of the border were an oil paintings salesman, a chicken man and a dry-cleaner, and they weren't really my friends at all. Friendless, hopeless and ultimately, reckless. Because it doesn't matter what state you're in, you don't turn down a beautiful drunk woman with a Ferrari.

10

You don't, but you *should*.

I knew from the second I took off that the Ferrari was too wild a beast for me. I was more a Fiesta and Metro man, with a nice rug in the back and a packet of Jaffa Cakes melted into each other in the glove compartment. The Ferrari is *power*. It went faster in first than I'd previously managed in fourth. We'd gone about three hundred yards when I lost control on a corner and ploughed through a hedge and up into the air before banging down into a ploughed field with me flailing at the controls, finally coming to a rest on the edge of a steep bank overlooking a stream. The noise was deafening, and that was just me screaming. But if anyone, apart from the fish below and the sheep behind, noticed or gave a hoot, it was not immediately apparent. Not even Mandy was aware. She was snoring as gently in the front as she had been before take-off. I had taken the precaution of fastening her seatbelt, although I hadn't envisaged that it really would be for take-off.

I got out of the car as gently as I could and walked round to the other side. The breeze was nice and fresh and the gurgling of the water lent a peacefulness to the night air as if nothing untoward had happened. If I'd been driving drunk, I was now standing sober. I inspected the damage by the light of a pale moon, and I was relieved to find that it didn't appear to be too severe. The headlights were broken. There was an indentation in the hood, and some severe scratching to the paintwork. Nothing that a few thousand pounds wouldn't sort out. I stood and surveyed my surroundings for several moments, breathing easily, happy to be alive, then opened her door, undid her belt and began to push her over into the driver's seat. She kind of flopped across it, murmuring wordlessly. I returned to the driver's door and pulled her over further so that her legs were in behind the wheel. Then I pushed her upright in the seat and secured the safety belt.

I removed one of her shoes and hurried down to the stream. I hunkered down and filled the shoe with icy water.

Back at the car I threw the water in her face, then started to shake her. 'Mandy!' I called. *'Mandy!'*

'Whad . . . whad . . . what?' she said blearily, raising her hands defensively.

'C'mon! Get out of the car!' I urged her. 'We've had a crash – c'mon now.'

I undid her belt and helped her out of the vehicle. She staggered. I held her up. 'But . . . but . . . you . . . Christ . . . *Christ!* Daddy'll . . . *Fuck!*'

'It's okay . . . it's only a scratch . . . come with me. C'mon.'

I led her across the field, then hauled her back up the bank and through the hole in the hedge I'd created only a few minutes before. We started to walk along the road. We made slow progress, Mandy moving sideways like a crab, holding on to me for support, talking gibberish about the car and horses and her dad and thanking me repeatedly for saving her life. At one point she sank abruptly to her knees and peed in the middle of the road. I didn't know where to look, except at her peeing in the middle of the road. It seemed to go on for ever. It was only when car headlights began to appear around the bend behind us that she finally staggered to her feet. She was weaving about in the middle of the road trying to get her knickers back into place as the car appeared. It slowed, crept past her like she was a dangerous wild animal, then sped away, Mandy firing curses after it. Somewhere along the way she'd managed to completely lose the English accent.

We finally made it back to the house. It was five minutes by car, but half an hour by drunk woman in one heel. I opened the front door and she fell through it. I picked her up off the floor and steered her into the lounge. I let her down gently on to the sofa and her head fell immediately on to the arm rest. She was snoring before her eyes closed. I lifted her feet up on to the cushions. I removed her shoes. Her short skirt had ridden way up to reveal her tanned, finely muscled legs and her knickers, again. There was a smidgin of pubic hair showing through where she hadn't pulled them up properly and I debated for several seconds what the gentlemanly thing to do was, pull the material back into place or get a felt pen from my pencil case and write *Kilroy Was Here*. In the end, of course, I chose neither. I went upstairs and got a quilt off one of the spare beds and placed it gently over her. I fetched a glass of water from the kitchen and two headache pills from my personal and vital supply and left them on the carpet where she couldn't miss them.

Then I went to bed.

I woke to the sound of hearty cursing from below. It was still dark and I was in the middle of another bleak dream. It took me a moment to get my bearings. Then I pulled on my trousers and hurried down.

Mandy was sitting in the middle of the carpet, blood dripping from her foot. 'Some stupid bastard left a glass on the floor!' she cried as I appeared. She was gripping her foot and there were tears on her cheeks and blood on her fingers as she gingerly tried to remove the little shards embedded in her sole.

'Sorry,' I said, 'that was me. I thought—'

'For fuck sake! How could you be so . . .' She let out a painful sigh. 'Never mind – can you get me a towel or something?' She winced again and I went to get one. I stayed in the kitchen long enough to take a drink of Diet Pepsi to clear the hangover throat, then hurried back in. She was still examining her foot. I asked her if she'd got them all out and she said there might still be one in there, but she'd probably only know when it made its way through her bloodstream to her brain and killed her.

'Okay,' I said and handed her the towel.

She gave me half an apologetic smile then pressed the towel against her foot. She winced. She looked up again, then nodded at the sofa. 'I was sick on your . . . I was in the middle of clearing it up when I stepped on the glass. I got kitchen roll from the kitchen. I think I got most of it.'

'It's the *most of it* that worries me.'

She smiled endearingly. 'I know. There's some gone down the back in under the cushion I couldn't get.' She winced again.

'Do you think you need a doctor?' I asked.

'I don't know.' She peered in at the wound. She pressed some kitchen roll against it, held it, then removed it. I could see several small lacerations, but nothing major, at least to a man. 'It should be okay,' she said. She looked up at me. 'I'm sorry, it was more the shock of it.'

I shrugged. I got her a drink of Diet Pepsi. We sat opposite each other, sipping. After a while she said, 'What am I doing here?'

'You don't remember?'

'I remember – the pub. A field? I don't really know.'

'You insisted on giving me a lift home in your car. You were drunk, but you insisted. Then you lost control and we flew through a hedge and across a field and nearly tipped up into a river. But didn't. It's still sitting there. Or should be. I wouldn't leave it there too long.' I looked at my watch. It was getting near six and was starting to brighten outside. 'How're you doing?'

'My head's going to explode.'

'Feel free. The sofa's already ruined.'

'I'm sorry.'

'I've only got this house for the Easter week. They'll be advertising it next week as five-bedroom furnished house with slight smell of boke.'

Her smile was nice, but it soon faded. 'I can't believe how horrible I've been to you. At the stables, nearly killing you in the car, then I'm sick down your settee and bleed on the carpet. You must hate me.'

'Hate's a very strong word, but perfectly adequate.' I shrugged. 'Don't worry about it. Just let me know where to send the bill.'

'I . . .'

'Don't worry. I know someone in the trade. You'll get a discount.'

'I . . .'

'Joke. He doesn't give discount.'

'I . . .'

'You have a hangover. You should sleep some more. Come upstairs. Uhm. There's a spare room.'

'Okay. What about the car?'

'We'll get it later.'

'Are you sure? It's worth nearly two hundred thousand.'

'Not now it's not.'

'Oh *shit*.'

'Relax. It's too early, we can't do anything yet. Let the blood-alcohol content reduce.'

We found a plaster in the bathroom cabinet and carefully applied it to her wounded foot. Then I showed her into the spare room. She thanked me and I closed the door. I returned to my room and tried to get over again. I was just dozing off when I felt the quilt go back and someone climb in beside me. Mandy said, vaguely, 'Warm,' then snuggled up beside me and fell asleep.

It was nice.

I didn't try anything.

I didn't even object to the boke in her hair, although that probably wouldn't last much beyond the second or third date.

The farmer was okay about it, actually, though a little bemused as to how we'd managed to miss the dead sheep mangled under the rear tyres. Mandy was charm itself. She asked him the sheep's worth, then doubled it and gave him the cash. He got his tractor and towed the Ferrari back from the edge of the stream, across the field and back up on to the road.

As he did, I said, 'That was very generous, the sheep.'

She shrugged. 'I killed it. Besides, it would cost me three times as much to get a garage to tow it. Once they saw it was a Ferrari you'd see the pound signs in their eyes. To him, it's just a red car.'

'Fair enough.'

'My dad'll sort it out. Though he'll probably take the time to kill me first.'

'His car?'

'His car. Fuck.'

'C'mon,' I said, 'let's get some breakfast.'

She looked at me oddly. 'Why are you being so nice to me?' I think she was just getting towards a smile, but then she stopped herself suddenly and frowned. 'You're writing that bloody book, aren't you? You're going to write about me and the drink and the crash and make it sound like we're all fucking Hooray Henrys pissing about at the expense of other jockeys who can hardly afford to feed their bloody kids. Well it's not like that! I swear to God – Daddy doesn't give me a penny. He didn't want me to go into the riding at all. He's done his best to keep me off of it. Do you have any idea how much I earn from this?'

'Enough to pay double for dead sheep.'

'Oh really? Oh really? Well take a look at this?' She brandished her open purse at me. Apart from a few coins, it was empty. 'I've bugger all. It was just the right thing to do. I killed his sheep. But I've nothing left! Do you have any idea how difficult it is for a woman to make her way in this business? Okay, so I'm lucky, my dad begrudgingly lets me ride the odd donkey, but for other owners? Once in a fucking blue moon. Even then – fuck, I get paid eighty-seven pounds a ride. Out of that I've to pay a tenner to my agent, another tenner to get my kit cleaned. I've to pay fees to the Jockey Club's accountants and to the Jockeys Association, I've to run my own car – it's a fucking Metro – and drive everywhere. What I'm saying is I don't make any bloody money at this game and I work my guts out, so if you're writing about me don't make me out to be some sort of pampered little daddy's girl. I give everything to this and I take nothing back, okay?' She was breathing hard, her cheeks had flushed and her eyes were narrow and intense.

I felt like hugging her. 'Is this a convoluted way of getting me to pay for breakfast?' I asked, instead.

She rolled her eyes. 'Okay. *Okay*. Sorry for getting on my high horse. *Literally*. I just need . . .'

'To be taken seriously?'

'Yes.'

'I'll take you seriously. But you can relax. Your father talked me out of writing the book. I'm just here to relax and try to get my own life back together.'

'Honest?'

'Honest injun.'

As we approached the Ferrari, now sitting forlornly

back on the open road, the farmer was just about to unhook his tractor. He stood, sucking on a pipe, while Mandy inspected the car again, and insisted he towed it back to the village.

I directed the farmer into the car park beside the diner. After waving him off, we went inside and ordered two unoccupied fries.

'This is a bit of a no-no,' she said when they arrived, looking down at the plates with glee. 'I'll be starving myself all week after this.'

'Another ride?' She nodded. I shook my head. 'If there's so much self-denial involved for so few rewards, why bother?'

'Because I love it. Because the greatest feeling in the world is coming into those final few furlongs with the crowd cheering you all the way and then crossing that finishing line in first place, knowing that that special bond between you and the horse is what's gotten you there. And because this Saturday it's all going to pay off.'

'Meaning?'

'Meaning that that special bond with a horse doesn't happen very often. But when you train him yourself, look after him night and day, ride him out in the gallops every morning come rain or shine, when no other single human being has anything to do with him but you, when he won't *let* anyone else on to him but you, and you know that he's something special . . .'

'This is beginning to sound a little . . . unnatural.'

She smiled. 'Maybe it is. But Dan ... it's just, y'know, some horses can be awkward to ride, part elephant, part camel, but on *him* it's like sitting in your favourite armchair ... There's like plenty of head and neck in front and those big quarters behind ... he's deep-girthed and a smooth walker and such a fearless but skilled jumper. He'll tackle anything you can throw at him, his footwork's amazing, when he jumps he just kind of arches his back and really goes for it, whereas half the others just blunder through ...'

She trailed off, looked down to her plate, a little embarrassed. 'Sorry,' she said.

'It's okay. I'm starting to fall in love with him myself. What's he called?'

She looked up, small smile. 'Dan.'

I smiled back, although it hadn't been a hard question. 'What?'

'Dan.'

'*What?*'

'Dan. It's Dan. Dan the Man. I'm riding him in the Grand National on Saturday.'

11

We lingered over our fry. She told me more about the stables and the state of the horses within them than I could ever possibly remember, so it was just as well I was taping it. I had to earn a crust and Hilda had promised me a whole loaf if we got any dirt on Geordie McClean. Mandy was beautiful and fiery, but she was his daughter, so she was completely and utterly off limits. We said a somewhat awkward goodbye. She was walking away when I asked her out to dinner.

She stopped, she thought for a moment, she turned round. Her face was glum.

'Sorry,' I said immediately, 'bad idea.'

'Good idea, but bad timing. I told you. I can't eat anything else because of the race. We could go for a jog tomorrow morning if you want.'

'Yeah. Okay. That would be great.'

She smiled and turned away again.

Jog.

What on earth was I doing?

Jog.

I had clearly taken leave of my senses. Playing football between ciders in the park was one thing, but *jogging*. Jogging *kills*.

I tried to shout after her, but there was only the roar of the Ferrari engine and she was gone.

Jog.

I tramped home from home, thinking about jogging and ways I might get out of it. She didn't have the look of someone who just went for a gentle little run either. She'd glide like a cheetah, barely breaking sweat; I'd be reduced to a puddle by the end of the road, if I made the end of the road.

Well, hell, she could stick to my pace or she could . . . not.

The birdshit cleaner's kids were out playing hurling or something in the middle of the road when I got home. 'Shouldn't you be at school?' I snapped as I put the key in the door.

They snapped back, 'At Easter? Y'heathen.'

'Well just . . . *just* . . .' I warned them conclusively and sloped inside.

I took one of fat incoherent lad's gift beers from the fridge, then sat and spent an hour transcribing the tape. There were a lot of cutlery and chewing sounds, but once they were edited out I e-mailed what was left to Hilda. Then I phoned her. That's the way e-mail works. Send it, then you make the phone call you would originally have made to make sure the e-mail has arrived. She sounded pleased to hear from me, but it faded slightly when I said I was thinking of going to Liverpool.

'Why for?' she demanded.

'Because the National's on Saturday.'

'I *know* that. What's it got to do with you?'

'McClean will be going. His daughter's a ride.'

'Excuse me?'

'I said, his daughter's riding in the National.'

'You did not.'

'I did too.'

'You . . . Oh Jesus, Starkey, have you been drinking?'

'Not really.'

There was a sigh, then a silence. Then a diplomatic 'Surely it would be better to take advantage of McLean's absence to infiltrate his organisation.'

'What're you suggesting, *burglary*?'

'Whatever it takes.'

'Hilda – please. I want to find out who killed Corkery as much as you do, but I'm not a burglar. I'd impale myself on something if I tried to break in anywhere. Besides, those stables are secure, I wouldn't have a chance. Anyway, I have an *in* already. His daughter's taken a shine to me. I'm getting it straight from the horse's daughter's mouth. Let me follow her to Aintree, you never know what'll develop.'

'I have an idea.'

'You don't even know me, you can't have an idea.'

'Starkey, I know *of* you. I looked up your name in the Belfast Who's Who and it says skirt-chaser.'

'You liar.'

'Well.'

'Was the information I've just sent you not first rate?'

'It will do nicely. But it's not dirt.'

'Well give me a chance.'

'Dan, we're running out of time.'

'How? I've got all the time in the world.'

'Well I haven't.'

'Meaning?'

'That they're closing in. McClean's got a team of hackers out there. The Horse Whisperer has crashed half a dozen times since Saturday. It doesn't take that long to get it up and running again, but he'll be paying top people to do it and he won't want to keep that up. What worries me more is my supply of information. If people can't find the page, or it keeps disappearing on them, they're going to lose confidence, they're going to stop *trusting* it. And if they can hack the page to bits, there's nothing to stop them with a little bit of extra work getting into my e-mails and finding out who exactly has been supplying information. Worldwide. If *that* gets out there'll be a lot of dead bodies turning up, I assure you.'

I sighed.

'Dan, I know it's asking a lot.'

'No, it isn't.'

'If you think going to Aintree is the right idea, then

go for it. But please don't go just because of some . . . girl, okay?'

'I won't. I promise.'

'And the info this morning was good. Well done.'

'But you need more. You need substance. You need proof.'

'That's what I need.'

'Okay. Let me have a think.'

'The time for thinking is over. It's the time for doing, Dan.'

How do you respond to that?

I responded by promising her the world, or at least Geordie McClean, then put the phone down without any better idea of how I might achieve it. Hilda had been making a list of jockeys, apprentice jockeys and trainers who had worked for or had business dealings with McClean, and promised to send it by the end of the day, but I wasn't convinced that it would be of much help. This whole world of horses and racing and gambling and breeding and blood and arses in the air was so alien that it denied me the chance to use any kind of direct approach, or even a subtle one, because they could spot that I wasn't horsey at a dozen furlongs, whatever the hell a furlong was. Even Mandy had creased herself laughing when I'd told her I'd always thought blinkers meant a horse was basically blindfolded and the jockey said *jump* as they approached a fence.

So I did what I always do in moments of stress, when there is no obvious path, when there are no pointer stones marked Arne Saknussemm: I called Trish. She had changed her home number so that I couldn't contact her and she'd also left instructions on the switchboard at work not to put my calls through, but it was Easter Tuesday and there was no one on the switchboard, and probably no one but Trish in the tax office. She answered the phone.

'You're not happy,' I said. There was silence. 'You always go into work on holidays when you're not happy. Tell me you're not happy.'

'I was happy, till about five seconds ago.'

'Not enjoying the sun with Clive.'

'He's away on business.'

'Where, India?'

'You're not funny, Dan. What do you want?'

'I've just won the lottery. Ten million. Can I buy you back?'

'I'm not for sale.'

'That's not what I heard.'

'Dan . . .'

'Okay. Sorry. How're you doing?'

'Okay.'

'Good.'

'I'm fine too.'

'Good.'

'I've met someone,' I said.

'Good.'

'She's really nice.'

'Good.'

'No beard.'

'I'm very happy for you.'

'You should get him to shave. It would make a new man of him. Or you could just get a new man.'

'Dan. You're calling for a reason.'

'Just lonely.'

'I thought you had a new woman.'

'Girl. She's much younger than you.'

'Dan . . .'

'I was thinking about Little Stevie.'

There was a sigh. 'What?'

'That he was beautiful, and I miss him.'

'I miss him too.'

'That even though I complained about his ginger hair, and he wasn't really mine at all, I did love him.'

'I know you did.'

'And I didn't kill him. I really didn't.'

'I know you didn't.'

'There was nothing I could do. I did my best. But then you always say my best isn't good enough.'

'Dan . . .'

'No. I could have done more. I could have done less. I shouldn't have got involved with film stars and drugs and gangsters, what have they got to do with me?'

'Nothing. But you always do get involved, it's your nature. What're you involved in now?'

'Horses.'

'And how're you involved?'

'Geordie McClean's become a big number in horses.'

'Never liked him. So what if he's become a big number in horses?'

'He might have had someone killed. An old colleague. Mark Corkery?'

'The creepy one?'

'He wasn't creepy.'

'Yes he was. He was always sidling up to people and asking impertinent questions. That's the word I think of when I think of him, *sidling*. I didn't know he was dead. What happened?'

'Car accident.'

'What'd Geordie do, fail to pay out on the insurance or something?'

'He might have dropped a car on him.'

'He doesn't look that strong.'

'Believe me. He is.'

'So what's your problem?'

'I don't know what I'm doing, is the problem. I know bugger all about horses.'

'It isn't about horses. A horse didn't kill anyone. It's about people.'

'I know more about horses.'

'No you don't. You're good with people. Women especially.'

'With the exception of you.'

'Yes, well . . . Who's the girl?'

'What girl?'

'The girl you're sleeping with.'

'I'm not sleeping with anyone.'

'Having sex with, then.'

'I'm not having sex with anyone apart from myself.'

'Then who're you talking about?'

'I was just trying to get you jealous.'

'Dan.'

'Okay. She's just a girl I met. We're going out for a jog.'

'Jesus. It must be love.'

'Yeah, well.'

'Who is she. Anyone I know?'

'She's Geordie McClean's daughter.'

'Oh shit.'

'Exactly.'

'I didn't even know he had a *wife*.'

'He doesn't. At least not any more.'

'And you're all confused because you don't want to be sleeping with the daughter of the man you're trying to do for murder.'

'I'm not sleeping with her, but yes.'

'You never go for anything simple, do you, Dan?'

'No. Not by choice.'

'I know. It's just the way you are. Well, if you don't want to go through the daughter, metaphorically speaking, why not go through the wife?'

'Because as far as I'm aware she's been off the scene for years.'

'Dan. Believe me. We're elephants. And I don't mean fat and grey, though no doubt I'll get there. We never forget. And if we don't know something, we make it our business to find out. Remember

129

Margaret, way back when? What started us down this shitty path? How do you think I tracked her down? Show me a wronged woman, and I'll show you Miss Marple. If there's any info to be had on Geordie McClean, an ex-wife is the place to start.'

'Do you know something?'

'What?'

'I love you.'

'I love you too.'

'Do you really?'

'Sometimes.'

'Why don't we get back together then?'

'Because the police are busy enough without another murder on their hands.'

We were silent for a few moments. I had a killer to catch and Trish had people to tax, but neither of us knew how to finish it. Perhaps neither of us wanted to. But then fate or providence stepped in; I heard glass breaking down below.

'Those hurley fucking bastards!' I hissed into the phone.

'*What?*'

'Nothing. Kids. I'll have to go.'

'Okay. Good luck.'

'Thanks. I'll be in touch.'

She hesitated, then said, 'Okay.'

It wasn't much, but it was something. I put the phone down and hurried along the hall. I'd murder in mind as I took the stairs three at a time, and it remained there, only turning 360 degrees when the man in the white suit stepped out of the cloakroom, raised a pistol and said something in Chinese which didn't require translation.

12

There were three of them, though thankfully only one wore a white suit. They were all of Oriental extraction. They all bore serious demeanours and callous mouths. One checked out the house, one tried to access my laptop, while the third, he of the white suit and pistol, tied me to a chair, which is a difficult enough thing to do with a pistol in your hand. I didn't put up a fight. I never do put up a fight if I can help it. I rely on the aforementioned rapier-like wit and a lot of tears.

When I was tied secure, White Suit stood back, glared at me some more, then said, 'Don't try anything stupid, Horse Whispara.'

There was enough of the kung fu's about his accent to suggest he hadn't just stepped off the ferry from Nanking. He was close enough for me to see a reddish spot dried into the lapel of his jacket. I was well acquainted with blood stains, and it wasn't one of those. Further down I noted several grains of rice on one of his fake Gucci loafers. In downtown Dublin, I suspected, there'd be someone waiting a little longer for lunch.

I looked at him blankly and said, 'Horse *what*?'

He cracked the barrel of the gun across my nose. I let out a yelp and started to bleed. One of his comrades came up with the laptop under his arm and said something in Chinese. White Suit snapped, 'Password, Horse Whispara!' at me.

'I'm sorry, but one never reveals one's—'

He hit me with the gun again. This time with the butt, to the forehead, and I toppled backwards. From my prone position I groaned, 'Dalglish.'

They looked confused.

White Suit stood over me. 'Spell.'

I spelled it, he repeated the letters after me in primary fashion, then allowed himself a smile of recognition. 'Ah. Dalg-lish. Inspector. Pee Dee James.'

'No. Dalg-lish. Liverpool. Blackburn. Newcastle. Celtic and God knows where else. *Football*.'

'Ah.'

They left me on the carpet while they set the laptop on the dining table and gathered around it. They chatted excitedly amongst themselves as the password was accepted, then took a few moments out to glare menacingly at me before returning their attention to my files.

'If you're looking for porn,' I said, 'I never take it across international boundaries.'

There was no reaction. They were scrolling through

my e-mails. Then my files. There was more jabber, though now markedly less excited. White Suit turned from the table while the others continued their useless search. I knew it was useless because there was nothing for them to find. I remained on the floor, bleeding, while he towered over me. He wasn't, in truth, very tall, but even a midget is tall to a tied man on his back on the carpet.

'Where you keep the money, Horse Whispara?'

'It's Whisper-*er*.'

'Tell us now, Whispara, save yourself trouble, you will wank us later.'

'I'd really rather not.' It was time to shut up, to leave them alone, and God knows I'd enough racial tics of my own, but I was on a panicky roll. It was an attempt to stave off impending doom, although with my luck it would probably serve only to hasten it. It was difficult to tell. 'It's all about *diction*,' I continued at speed, 'keep saying Whisp-*ara* and people will dismiss you as a Johnny Foreigner. You have to assimilate these days if you're going to get on in life and not get treated like a fucking boat person. And that's before I even get into the wanking.'

He hesitated, rapidly blinking several times while he decided whether he was dealing with a nut, which was the reaction I was hoping for, then kicked me hard in the ribs, which was the reaction I was not.

'You owe us big money, Whispara, and we gonna find it *now*.'

The other two turned from the computer, shaking their heads. I had a notion things were going to turn even nastier, and not a clue how to get out of it. They were welcome to all the money I had, but I doubted it would satisfy them. I had heard of Chinese water torture and didn't relish the thought of it. I'd already experienced Irish water torture. You just drink it, the limescale nearly kills you.

White Suit removed a blade from his pocket.

I said, 'I don't have any money.'

'You rip us off big style, you can't spend that much in two week.'

'I've never met you. I don't know who you are. If it's an unpaid restaurant bill I'll happily settle up.'

He kicked me again. This time to the head. To the ear, to be more precise. It was extremely sore. I managed to croak, 'I don't know what you're . . .' before closing my eyes and feigning unconsciousness.

They brought me round by holding a cigarette lighter to the sole of my right foot, having first thoughtfully removed the shoe and sock. I yelped and tried to pull my burning flesh away, but they held it in place. I yelped some more.

'Where the money?'

'I don't—!'

'Where the money?'

'Please . . . !'

'Where the fucking money!'

I was on the verge of blacking out. I screamed, 'Okay, okay . . . *okay* . . . !' and they finally removed the flame from my smouldering foot. 'Fuck, fuck, fuck, *fuck* . . . !'

'The money.' White Suit flicked the lighter again.

'The money . . .' I blinked helplessly at him. 'I'm not the Horse Whisperer. My name is Dan—'

I screamed as he held the flame back to my flesh. I flexed against the flex holding me in place. There were tears rolling out of my eyes and snot dripping down off my chin. 'For . . . Jesus . . . fuck . . . I don't . . . know . . .'

'You think you very smar', but I think differen'.'

'I don't . . . I don't . . . I don't . . .'

'We respec' Horse Whispara, ''cept he comes off fence now and tries to take us to the laundry. No wank you, Horse Whispara.'

'I didn't—!'

The doorbell.

Never was I so pleased to hear a doorbell. I would lick it in thanks next time I passed. The third Chinaman, the one who'd searched the house, produced a length of masking tape and stretched it across my mouth. I was trying desperately to look on the bright side, but I was never much of an optimist. They wanted money and seemed to think I had access to it, so they weren't going to kill me or inflict so much damage that I couldn't tell them. And even if I was able to tell them they wouldn't kill me until they'd retrieved the money. So really, I was fine. It was just that I wasn't able to get the message through to my quaking, aching, smoking body.

The doorbell again.

The police, alerted to the breaking window and hideous screams.

The neighbourhood watch, summoned in force by birdshit man and his annoying kids.

Anyone.

Anyone but . . .

'Would you like to buy an oil painting?'

'No,' my laptop enemy said.

'All by top Irish artists. I've been selling these paintings for twenty years. Are you new to the area?'

'Yes.'

'Only one hundred pounds.'

'No. Wank you.'

'That's awful decent of you . . .'

And then there was an explosion and the Chinese came barrelling back into the lounge; I watched horrified *through* his chest as the oil paintings man followed in after him with a shotgun held to his shoulder. The shot man sprawled on to the carpet as White Suit and his remaining comrade reached for whatever weapons were concealed within their jackets, but before they got near them there was another shot from Oil Paintings. A body splattered back against the lounge wall, leaving just White Suit, now with his gun out and suddenly in no apparent rush at all.

Double-barrelled shotgun. Two bullets.

Oil Paintings was out.

A grin spread across White Suit's face as he raised his pistol.

I closed my eyes.

There was a shot and my face was sprayed with blood, and a moment later there was a body in my lap. I fought against opening my eyes, but it was inevitable. Curiosity. And cats. The corpse lying across me was wearing what had formerly been a white suit.

I looked up, puzzled, shocked, as Oil Paintings smiled down. He winked once, then nodded across at the window. I followed his gaze to a gun-sized hole, and saw the chicken man grinning through the glass.

I managed a 'Thank Christ,' then directed a 'Can you get . . . him off me . . . ?' towards the oil paintings man. 'Then tell me what the fuck is going on.'

'Sure thing, Dan.' He rolled White Suit off me with his foot as the chicken man appeared in the doorway, paused, frowned, then hurried back out again.

'Do you think there's more of them?' I asked nervously. I tensed for more gunfire, but Oil Paintings didn't seem concerned. He strolled to the window and peered out.

He shook his head. 'I think he's just having a word with the neighbours.'

He turned back from the window and started to search the dead Chinese. He pocketed three guns and three wallets while I waited for an explanation. When it didn't come I said, still lying tied to a chair, 'Get me up.'

He paused, nodded, then stood up from White Suit's side and took hold of the back of my chair. He heaved me up into a sitting position. 'That better?' he asked.

'Yes . . . Jesus . . .' I began to struggle against the ropes, presuming he'd take the hint, but he remained where he was, looking down at me, and after a little, I stopped.

'You don't sell oil paintings, do you?'

He shook his head.

'How did you know they were here?' I asked, nodding at the dead Chinese.

Oil Paintings smiled and crossed to the canvas he had hung on the wall by way of thanks for the party. He lifted it off the hook and twirled it round, then ran one hand up the back. His fingers delved inside the frame, then a moment later emerged clasping a small, round, black object. 'Bug,' he said. 'Strategically placed. That girl sure knows how to vomit.'

'Who the fuck are you? Cops?'

'Doesn't matter,' he said. He looked back to the door, where Chicken had reappeared. 'Okay?' he asked him.

'Their phone's suddenly out of order.'

Oil Paintings nodded.

'Hiya, Dan,' the chicken man said, coming into the lounge. 'Close shave, yeah?'

I nodded. 'I don't suppose you're going to let me go either.'

He smiled and shook his head. He looked from one dead body to another and another. 'Fucking Chinese,' he said.

'I don't know what the fuck's going on,' I said. 'I don't know who *they* were, I don't know who *youse* are, and I don't know what the hell any of it has to do with me.'

'Well,' said Oil Paintings, resting for a moment against his shotgun, 'they're the Chinese bookies who've been muscling into our turf, and you're the cunt who ripped us all off. What we're going to do now is take you and that chair and we're going to put you in the back of our van. Then you're going to lead us to the money. After that we'll probably blow your knees off and throw you out the back of the feckin' van, then you'll be free to crawl to the Guards to explain how you have three Chinese carry-outs festering in your house. Is it any clearer to you now, Dan?'

'Crystal,' I said.

13

We arrived at the Superquinn car park across the road from the National Irish bank in Blanchardstown, a busy little suburb of Dublin, exactly fourteen minutes by battered Ford transit van from Ashtown. There were other cars waiting patiently for parking spaces to come free, but after some tasty threats were issued by the chicken man, we soon had a spot. I lay on the floor in the back, still tied to my chair. I'd started the journey upright, but two roundabouts had seen to that. I lay ignored amongst greasy overalls, a mechanic's tools, empty cans of Steiger and crushed boxes of Superkings Menthol. It all smelled of neglect and surveillance.

Chicken switched off the engine. He turned from the wheel while Oil Paintings slipped into the back to untie me. 'Okay,' the chicken man said, 'this is the way it works. You and me, we're going into the bank. You withdraw the cash, you put it in this . . .' and he raised a sports bag with *Head* emblazoned on the side.

'I'll be right there with you. You try anything funny I just pull out m'gun and rob the feckin' place, then you'll be done for your Chinese carry-out *and* armed robbery, okay?'

'Okay.' They'd found Corkery's bank card in my wallet and put two and two together. It didn't seem to matter to them that I'd never been near the bank in my life and had no other identification to prove that I was Corkery. But then I was south of the border and maybe they did things differently down here. I was to go in, introduce myself and ask to close my account.

'You reckon this bag'll be big enough?' Chicken asked Oil Paintings, who shrugged and looked at me. I shrugged as well. I didn't have the heart to tell them a medium-sized wallet would be big enough, or the courage. I was trying to come up with a plan, but as ever when you try to do that under difficult circumstances all you can really come up with is *I'm going to die* and *Isn't there a lot of traffic for this time of day?*

All I could do was play it by ear and hope that something happened that didn't involve any further pain to myself.

Oil Paintings knelt and examined my face. He shook his head, then removed from his pocket an opened packet of Kiddiwipes. He crushed one into my hand. 'Sort yourself out,' he said, 'Can't have you goin' in there covered in blood. You'll look suspicious.'

'I'll look . . .'

'Just do it.'

I wiped my face. I didn't have the benefit of a mirror, but the state of the Kiddiwipe told me all I needed to know.

'They're not going to . . .' Oil Paintings held his gun against my knee. 'On the other hand, I was captain of my school debating team. I can get blood out of a stone.'

It wasn't the most appropriate analogy, but he removed his gun. He pulled open the transit door and pushed me out. I stood on the tarmac and stretched. All around me happy families were going off shopping. Kids were crying and there was a grandmother struggling to release a shopping trolley from its moorings. I grunted and walked ahead of Chicken through the car park and on to the pavement. We paused at traffic lights. The bank was directly opposite. As we approached it a gnarled old gypsy woman sitting on a dirty blanket by the door raised a paper cup towards us for donations. Ordinarily I would have asked if she'd take a traveller's cheque. It was the place, it just wasn't the time. We ignored her. I pulled open the door. Just as we entered, the chicken man hissed, 'Careful does it.'

Inside, it was larger, busier than I'd expected. There was a queue of around a dozen people, with others already being attended to at one of the five windows. There was an unattended foreign exchange desk and beyond that, behind another glass partition, a balding man in a green shirt sat studying a computer screen. That would be the manager, then. I looked at the chicken man. He nodded at the queue, and we joined it. The young woman immediately ahead of me was straining under the weight of a large bag of coins. She had the russet cheeks of a farmer's daughter. She puffed them out as she shifted the bag uncomfortably from hand to hand. She noticed that I was looking at her. She looked away, slightly embarrassed. I said, 'Ten thousand pennies for your thoughts.'

She smiled and rolled her eyes, then moved the bag again.

Chicken whispered, 'Watch it.'

'I'm trying to act normal,' I muttered.

'Your normal is different from everyone else's,' Chicken said.

'And how would you know?'

He pointed at his eyes. I turned away. 'Awful weather,' I said to the girl with the money and the cheeks.

'Dreadful,' she replied.

'Still, nice for ducks. Unless your waterproofing has been ruined by pollution.'

She nodded thoughtfully.

Chicken jarred his elbow into my back and I gave a little jump. The girl, noticing, looked around me to him. He looked away. She kept looking at him, until he slowly turned back to face her.

'It's Jimmy, isn't it?' she said.

'What?' the chicken man said.

'Jimmy. You're Jimmy Farrelly.'

'No. Sorry, you must be mistaken.'

'No – Jimmy Farrelly. We went to school together. Plunketts. In Swords.'

'Nope. Sorry. Wrong man.'

'Ach, stop it, Jimmy. Don't I know you well enough. It's Deirdre. Deirdre Slevin.'

His voice faltered. 'I don't . . .'

'You went out with m'best mate. Roiseen. Roiseen Culcavey. It is Jimmy, isn't it?'

Jimmy sighed. 'Yes. Okay. I remember you now. Hoy-ya, Deirdre. Long time no see. How's it goin'?'

'Oh, y'know.'

Chicken, or Jimmy, nodded.

'So what're you doing round here, Jimmy?'

'Just a bit of business.'

'Last I heard you were running a bookie's in Tallaght. You still . . . ?'

'No – no. All closed down now.'

'So what're you doing now?'

'Oh – y'know. This'n that.'

'Still the horseys? You always loved the horseys, didn't you, Jimmy?'

'I . . . yes.'

'Do you remember when we all adopted that pony? Do you remember that, Jimmy? The whole gang of us. Everyone's got one these days, but back then—'

He cut in. 'Deirdre,' he said, his voice low and slightly strained, 'sorry – do y'mind? I've got a really bad head. I'm not trying to be rude – just, y'know, m'head.'

'Oh Jasus – sorry, Jimmy. There's me rattlin' on. Can I get you something for it? I've . . . hold on a minute . . .' She set down her bag of coins and pulled around a handbag from behind her. She flipped up the cover and began to root around inside. 'I've some Nurofen somewhere . . .'

'No . . . listen, I'm fine . . .'

'Hold on . . . there's nothing worse than a headache when you're trying to do business, Jimmy, I know that . . . Ah now . . .' She produced a crushed-looking box, then slid out a plastic press-out sheet. 'Och shite . . .' She held up the empty sheet.

'Never mind, I—'

'No, listen . . .' She stuffed the empty packet back into her bag then stepped out of the queue and across to the counter. There was an elderly man leaning into the glass, a hand raised to his ear as he struggled to understand what was being said to him by the plumpish girl behind the counter. 'Excuse me,' Deirdre said, shuffling in to make room for herself. 'Ailish?'

The bank clerk frowned momentarily, then smiled in recognition. 'Deirdre . . . how're you doin'?'

'Fine. You wouldn't have any headache pills now, would you?'

'What's wrong . . . Oh, stupid me! Headache, of course!'

'Headache . . . ?' the old man asked, leaning a little

closer to the glass, trying to prise Deirdre away from it in the process. 'I don't have a headache, I just can't *hear* . . .'

'Not you, Mister Brady – sorry,' the clerk said. 'My friend here. *She* has a *headache*.'

'No,' said Deirdre, 'it's not for *me* . . .' She glanced back to the queue. 'The man behind me has one. He's an old friend, I just thought . . .'

'Oh sure . . . hold on a minute . . .' She bent and retrieved a handbag from the floor beside her. As she began to look through it she smiled across at Jimmy. Then her brow furrowed slightly. She lowered her voice, but it was loud enough to make out. 'Isn't that Jimmy Farrelly?'

Deirdre leaned conspiratorially closer. 'Do you know him?'

'Oh sure, wasn't he in the year above me at Plunketts.'

Beside me Jimmy the Chicken cursed. Quietly.

'You get around,' I said.

'In all the banks in all the world, I have to walk into this feckin' one.'

Ailish was waving him over. She had a box in her hand. 'Hoy-ya, Jimmy, you got a headache? I've some Anadin here, will they do?'

'Yeah, great,' said Jimmy. The whole bank seemed to be looking at us. As he stepped forward his foot caught on Deirdre's bag of coins and tipped it over. Several thousand coppers spilled across the floor like a jackpot. Jimmy gave a strangled '*Feck!*'

Deirdre rushed across from the counter. As Jimmy and I bent forward to help scoop the coins back into the bag, Jimmy's gun slipped out of his jacket and on to the floor. Deirdre froze. Those around us who'd been coming to assist froze. My eyes locked with Jimmy's.

Then I cracked him with my head.

I have never been one for headbutts. It hurt me as much as it hurt him. We both reeled away clutching our skulls. There was a tremendous ringing in my head, and it took me several moments to realise that it wasn't in fact in my head, but in the bank, and that Ailish had sounded the alarm. There was already a metallic screen descending rapidly from the ceiling above her.

Jimmy made a grab for the gun. I managed to kick it away from him. As I went after it Jimmy dived after me and we both fell clinking on to the coin-covered floor. There were screams of panic from the customers as they scattered. There was a scream of pain from the counter where the old man had caught his hand under the security screen, which was refusing to fully close. Jimmy had me by the hair and was pounding my head against the wiry carpet. If I ever got the chance to check my skull again I would find a bruise to the front, carpet burns to the back and the imprint of dozens of Irish harps from the cold, hard coins cushioning my assault covering the rest of it.

Abruptly Jimmy let out a yelp and fell back. I

blinked up at Deirdre, holding the remains of the bag of coins in her hand, and then at Jimmy, sprawled out on his back, groaning. She looked pleased as Punch. 'He was always a bad egg,' she panted. 'He sold that feckin' pony on us.'

I pulled myself up to my knees, feeling groggy. Deirdre took a step back, still menacingly clutching the bag of coins. The customers hadn't hung around to get shot and the staff were safely ensconced behind the security screen, which had finally closed, separating the old man from one of his fingers. He was now slumped down against the counter, cradling his hand and sobbing. I looked at the gun. It was under Deirdre's foot.

'There's no point in robbin' it now,' she said, calmly.

'I never intended to,' I replied.

'What about him?' She nodded down at Jimmy.

'He intended to rob me. But you saved me. I love you.'

She smiled hesitantly. The alarm continued to shriek. 'I shouldn't trust you,' Deirdre said, 'but at least you were pleasant. Costs nothing to be pleasant.' She kicked the gun across the carpet to me. 'Now please don't let me down by shooting me.'

I lifted the gun. 'Thank you so much.'

Jimmy rolled back up into a sitting position. He was still pretty much out of it, but there was no way of knowing how long that would last. I stepped towards him. I turned the gun round in my hand, then stood over him, brandishing the butt. I wasn't quite sure where or how to strike him. It was quite easy in films. You'd just biff him and he'd fall over. But with a real person I'd probably have to do it repeatedly, until the blood started to spurt or his head caved in. Or I'd not have the strength and he'd just laugh, take the gun off me, and shoot me. I wasn't going to shoot him, that was for sure.

Deirdre solved it for me. She stepped up beside me and nodded disapprovingly down at Jimmy, holding his head in his hands. 'You go,' she said, patting the bag of coins again. 'Leave him to me.'

'I . . . you can't . . .'

'Believe me. It'll be a pleasure.'

I smiled. 'Thanks,' I said. I nodded around the bank. 'All this . . . difficult to explain.'

'It's okay,' Deirdre said. The alarm was joined by a police siren. 'Go,' she said.

I nodded again, then hurried to the door. As I pushed through it there came an ominous *thump* from behind and I glanced back in time to see Jimmy settling horizontally. I gave Deirdre the thumbs-up and stepped outside.

The police siren was immediately louder, and definitely closer.

The bank customers were gathered in a loose semicircle, waiting to see what would happen. Passers-by had stopped with them, curious. They all moved back a little further as I emerged and they saw the gun in my hand. I looked beyond them to the

Superquinn car park. There was no sign of the Ford transit.

There came a rattle to my left. I glanced down at the gypsy, extending her paper cup. I removed a pound from my pocket and dropped it in. Then I handed her the gun. She accepted it with a black smile.

'Shoot anyone that moves,' I said, then added, 'Except me, of course.'

Then I made my way through the crowd. They remained statue still and I didn't hear any shooting until some minutes later.

14

Where I can help it, I avoid sleeping in bushes, shop doorways and on park benches. There's nothing romantic about waking up with slugs on your face or dog pee in your pocket. The most important thing about being on the run is finding comfortable surroundings, getting your rest, a good night's sleep, and taking the opportunity to step back from it all and analyse your position in a philosophical light before coming to any major decisions. Of course, this isn't always possible. But I had the advantage of a little cash, clothes in reasonably good nick, the late Mark Corkery's cash card and an urgent desire to hide out until the Second Coming sorted everyone's problems out and left me in peace.

The facts remained: three dead Chinamen in my house and a starring role in a straight-to-video epic about a bungled bank heist, showing at a police station near you, or more probably me.

I needed a base until I could work out what to

do next. I walked the streets of Dublin for a while, keeping to the less salubrious surroundings of the northside, working my way out from Connolly station until I found a small bed and breakfast which looked about right. I booked in for one night. There are generally two types of B&B, and they've little in common. One is a small family affair aimed at tourists on a budget, nice fresh sheets on the bed, a traditional Irish breakfast, quaint, homely, playing to the stereotypes; the other's a doss house for the unemployed, the drink-addled or the drug-dependent, a hole where the owner supplies nothing but a room and a bed and a glare and everything else is left to you. This owner, in tracksuit, trainers and a Keegan perm, was firmly in the latter camp. He asked no questions and demanded payment in advance.

He didn't show me to my room. He took the punts then pointed vaguely up the stairs as he counted them. He mumbled *twenty-three* and something else that I took to be *keysindoor*. I creaked up the stairs. The carpet in the hall lifted a little with each step I took. I came to an open door with *23* written on it in thick black marker strokes. The room was spartan. It smelled of sweat and cigarettes. The sheets on the bed were thrown back and there was an indentation that, given time, might prove a major attraction in Turin. I took the sheets off the bed and stuffed them in an empty cupboard. I turned the mattress over. It didn't kill the smell, but it improved it a little. The glass in the window frame was loose and rattled in the breeze. I'd a partial view of the street outside. I sat on the ledge, sipping on one of the cans of Diet Pepsi I'd brought with me, one eye on the passing traffic and the other turned in on my troubled soul.

I was trying to come up with answers but there were only questions. Corkery, despite his crusading as the saintly Horse Whisperer, had evidently been up to mischief. Clearly the Chinese bookies and my more recent captors felt he owed them a large amount of money, but what if it wasn't stolen, but the result of another of his betting coups? If they were operating illegally as bookies they'd have had to be offering better odds than legal ones; if they'd been stung they had no legal redress. Whatever way Corkery had managed to get the money out of them, they obviously wanted or needed it back. The Chinese had clearly believed I was the Horse Whisperer; they were dead now, but that didn't mean that was the end of it. There would be brothers, and bosses, and *tongs*. They could have been friendless orphans, of course. But my history suggested they had ten thousand angry relatives thirsting for revenge. Oil Paintings, Chicken and the mysteriously absent Dry Cleaner, on the other hand, hadn't mentioned the Horse Whisperer at all, and didn't seem to care who I was so long as I came up with the cash. I'd been staying in Corkery's house, I was using his bank card, so I was connected. Simple as that.

Was either camp going to forget it now that I'd managed to give them the slip?

NO.

Was I brave, courageous and determined to out-wit them?

NO.

Was there anyone in the entire world who would give me a hug?

NO.

I had the Chinese and Irish bookies on my trail, the Garda would shortly be added. In my corner – a widow on the internet. There was Patricia, but I'd caused her enough pain. And Mandy . . . what of her? A beautiful, highly strung woman, who wanted to take me jogging. Tomorrow. If I collapsed after the first hundred yards I could truthfully explain I'd been running since the previous day. Her father stood accused in at least two minds of murder-ing Mark Corkery. Mark Corkery stood accused in McClean's mind of reneging on a gentleman's agree-ment that had grown out of another betting coup. Was there any connection between Corkery's coup with McClean, and Corkery's coup with the Chinese and Irish bookies?

No idea.

I needed to talk to Hilda. There was no phone, of course. There was a lounge downstairs with a television set. There were half a dozen down-and-ins watching coverage of the racing from Punchestown. If I'd stayed I'm sure I might have seen one of Geordie McClean's horses. Maybe the man himself. Mandy was keeping herself for Aintree.

I walked out into the late afternoon sun. At least it had brightened up. The *Evening Press* was on sale on the corner. The headline read *Traveller Runs Amok*. The strapline beneath said *Six Wounded*. I didn't know much about guns, but in Westerns there were only ever six bullets; if there had been that many in the weapon I'd given to the old gypsy, then it wasn't bad shooting. I flipped the pages to see if there was any mention of the Chinese, but there was nothing. It was early days. Birdshit man was probably still too scared to phone the cops.

I crossed a footbridge over the Liffey and wandered into Temple Bar, the booming bohemian area of the city that seemed the best bet for what I was after. Normally I refuse to ask directions, but I was in a hurry. A tiny girl in a tiny shop that seemed only to sell earrings pointed me the right way and I was soon seated with a Diet Coke in a smart and spartan internet café. The owner or manager, early thirties and balding, sat behind a counter, surfing himself, while two black-T-shirted waitresses dispensed beverages and smart-looking pastries. There were a dozen terminals, about half of them in use. There were eight other people just enjoying coffee. It seemed strange. Like going into a car showroom because it served nice cups of tea.

What I really needed was a one-to-one with Hilda. There was no point in leaving a message describing the mess I was in. It would only panic her. Without revealing any details of my adventures, I left e-mails for her at fifteen-minute intervals. I idled over four

Diet Cokes while I waited for her to respond. It turned into early evening; the sun vanished behind the shops and offices; the café began to fill up. All of the terminals were in use. People were waiting, patiently, it must be said, to go on-line. I was getting a little embarrassed. Like standing by a call box waiting for it to ring and not allowing anyone else to use it just in case they phoned while it was busy. I checked my watch. I'd been in the café for two hours. I was busting for a pee. There was a young man in a smart blue business suit standing directly behind me, waiting. I nodded apologetically at him. He smiled benignly back.

'Sorry,' I said, 'waiting for something.'

He nodded. 'That's okay.'

'Should be here any mo.'

He nodded. I drummed my fingers. 'What about you?'

'No rush. Checking for the new *Star Wars* release date.'

'Won't be long.'

But I was. Another ten minutes passed. His eyes weren't exactly boring into me, but. Hilda could be anywhere. Shopping. Snooping. But I needed to talk to her. It was *urgent*. People were *dying*. All she had to do was type. I sighed. I turned. 'Tell you what . . . would you be long?'

'Couple of minutes.'

'Well do you want to do your stuff while I go for a pee? If you promise to let me back on?'

'No problem.'

I stood. He smiled warmly and took my seat. I hurried into the gents. It was very clean. Lots of mirrors. The peeing wasn't the problem, it was the washing of the hands. There was no tap to turn on the water. I had realised, of course, that it was hi-tech, just not *how* hi-tech. Days were you could just go for a straight pee, but this was *ridiculous*. I tried holding my hands under the water spout to see if it would trigger automatically, but nothing. I moved the spout left and right, down and up, but nothing. I looked for a button on the wall. There was only one and that turned the lights off. I wasn't brought up to believe that cleanliness was next to godliness, but my dad did insist that my hands not smell of pish. It wasn't fair. I had fearlessly conquered my phobia of new things. I was no longer computer illiterate. I could surf without taking a bath. I was not going to be defeated by a tap. The only reasonable conclusion was that the tap was voice-activated. I steadied myself, took a deep breath, and said, 'Cold water.'

Nothing happened.

'Warm water.'

Nothing.

Perhaps I was getting too technical.

'Water,' I said.

There came a squeak from behind me. I turned to find the owner standing there, his feet grinding into the chequered linoleum, looking a little concerned that I'd been talking to his sink.

'Sorry . . .' I began.

'No . . . *I'm* sorry,' he said, coming forward, producing from his pocket the head of a tap. He began to screw it into place above the fountain. 'Should have done this earlier. Been cleaning the limescale.'

'I thought . . .'

'Yeah . . . sorry.' He looked at me. He cleared his throat. 'The internet's all very well,' he said as he turned the tap and water began to cascade, 'but we can't download a feckin' plumber. Or afford him.' He turned the tap off again. 'There y'go now, I'll leave you in peace.'

I nodded gratefully and resolved to stay in the toilets until the colour had drained from my face. It didn't take long. I had embarrassment down to a fine art. I could have bottled it and sold it. It would have tasted better than Bass and given half the hangover.

For a while I stared moodily at the paper towel dispenser. Then threw caution to the wind and ripped one off.

I returned to the buzz of the café. Beautiful young things stood chatting in a duller light. Someone had pressed the ambience switch. Three of the terminals now sat neglected. Muzak which had been playing subtly had been replaced with louder mus-*ic*. It was something trippy hippy hoppy. I wasn't altogether familiar with the new terms. I had grown up with the five chords of punk. That's three chords for the guitar plus the pair of my hippy brother's cords I'd thrown out of the window while he was sleeping. I pushed through the throng. A photograph of Ewan McGregor as Obi Wan Kenobi stared out from my screen. It had so excited the *Star Wars* fan that he'd fallen asleep on the keyboard, or perhaps collapsed in ecstasy, or from it.

I nudged the chair, but he didn't move. I gave him a gentle tap on the shoulder, but there was no response. I tutted and looked about me. Nobody else was appreciating my predicament. Friggin' kids today. Load up on drugs, plug into cyberspace, then can't cope with it. I tutted. On screen Ewan was staring at me. He looked kind of pleased with himself, and he'd every right to be. I put a hand on the fan's shoulder and gave him a shake. 'Helloooo,' I said, 'anyone in?' then tutted again because he'd managed to spill the remains of my Diet Coke and it was just starting to seep out from under the keyboard.

I put my fingers to it to stem the flow, and realised immediately that what had appeared in the reduced light to be Diet Coke wasn't. It was warm and thick and sticky. And red.

I froze.

Just for a moment. Just long enough for the devil to get an icy grip on my heart.

Then I slowly sank until I was level with the guy's face, until I could look into his cold, lifeless, staring eyes.

I'd been gone five minutes and someone had drilled a smart little hole in his throat.

May the farce be with you.

A scream.

A young girl in a black cocktail dress, pointing.

I stumbled back.

There was no point in a *It wasn't me!* because it was bleeding friggin' obvious that it was.

Blood on his hands, your honour.

I only found the corpse.

Murder weapon?

Who cares? Doesn't he have three dead Chinamen in his house and a *You've Been Framed* special from a bank in Blanchardstown.

The screaming was spreading.

'It wasn't me!' I yelled anyway, holding up bloody hands.

The lights went up. The hip-hoppy-trippy shit abruptly stopped.

'Call an ambulance!' I yelled, looking desperately around me, pleading. 'For Christ sake, don't just stand there!'

Nobody moved. They were a weird mix of computer geeks and bright young things ready for a night out. None of them wanted to be heroes, or villains. They wanted to surf and dance and drink and drug. They didn't want a wild-eyed Northerner with blood on his hands ruining their night out. I looked from cool eye to cool eye and I knew there wasn't one of them would stop me if I walked out of there. I knew just as well that whoever had killed the *Star Wars* fan, he was no longer amongst us.

I glanced at the ceiling.

Security cameras.

I stormed across to the counter. The sea parted. The owner took several steps back until he couldn't go any further. 'I . . . I . . .' he stammered, 'I'm . . . s-sure he'd . . . have given your ch-chair back if you'd a-asked . . .

I put my hands on the counter and tried to look menacing. 'The cameras,' I said, 'do they work?'

He shook his head. 'Show. We've only just o-opened, money's t-tight.'

'Fuck,' I said.

'I'm s-sorry.'

'I . . .' I looked down at the counter. Bloody handprints. 'I didn't do . . . Fuck!' I kicked the bottom of the counter in frustration. Why me? What did I ever do to deserve . . . I sighed. 'How much do I owe you?'

'What?'

'For the use of the computer.'

'I . . . no. It's okay. Just go.'

'No. I don't think so. I didn't do this. Just tell me how much and I'll be off.'

He looked warily at the rest of his customers, then stepped cautiously towards his computer and called up my terminal. I glanced behind. Still nobody moved. They just looked. Blood was now seeping across the floor.

'Five eighty,' said the owner.

'Okay.' I dug into my pockets. I produced coins and held them out. They were sticky red already.

'Plus three for the Cokes.'

'Diet Cokes,' I said. I turned my hand and the coins fell on to the counter. They didn't roll away. They stuck. 'Keep the change,' I said and walked quickly out of cyberspace.

15

I was certain that I was not followed. Nevertheless I spent the entire night by the fly-smeared window of my tiny bed-and-breakfast refuge, watching every car, studying every drunk, turning only to listen to every creak from the landing outside. Death was my shadow. A young man had been killed by mistake, in mistake for me. I was alive because I'd been accommodating, and needed to use the gents. It was Coke proving that it really did add life.

My stomach rumbled incessantly. There was nothing to eat. Kebab smells filtered through from a carry-out down the road, but I was too frightened to go out. Someone had stabbed the guy in the throat in the middle of a crowded café and nobody had noticed. I was not walking down a cracked-pavemented barely lit street to satisfy mere hunger. I would suck the hairs out of the manky sink for sustenance before I crossed the threshold of this matchstick fortress in the hours of darkness.

They, he, she, couldn't have followed.

I had crossed and crissed so much on the way back that even I got lost for a while.

I also tried to convince myself that I would not have been followed because there was no need for it. Whoever had killed the *Star Wars* fan had presumed it was me, and must thus have been satisfied that he had carried out his task. The only way he could have tracked me down was by somehow hacking into the messages I'd left with Hilda and backtracking them to the specific computer console I was operating in the internet café. A fortuitous slash and I was still alive. *Star Wars* fan's last view was of Ewan McGregor, his last thought of distant, equally violent galaxies.

Fuck.

I slipped out of the bed and breakfast shortly after eight the next morning. Not that there was any breakfast on offer, and the bed only just qualifed.

Traffic was already gridlocked. It was quicker, although scarier, to walk. He, she, they would probably be aware by now that the man they believed to be the Horse Whisperer was still alive. He, she, they would be looking for me. I was fairly certain that whoever had tried to kill me wasn't connected to either Oil Paintings, Chicken or the dry-cleaning man. Neither was he, she, they avenging the late Chinese bookies. *Their* interest was in keeping me alive. Their motive was money, and they were all still looking for me as well.

Popular guy.

There was a newsagent's on the corner with papers hanging up outside. The *Irish Times* led with it. *Internet Murder*, the headline screamed, and I felt like screaming back. There was a description of me, the killer. It was fairly accurate, but it could just the same have fitted ten thousand men in the city. Police had closed down the café and impounded the computers. I knew that they would track my e-mails back to Hilda, and perhaps beyond that to the Horse Whisperer, but there was nothing in either of them to specifically identify me. Hilda would claim ignorance or innocence or both.

On the other hand, I hardly knew her. She might sell me down the river. That was the way my luck was running.

Running.

Jogging.

Shit. I looked at my watch.

Jogging.

It was the last thing I needed.

She was pretty and lovely and prone to bad temper, but I was up to my eyes in trouble and the last thing I needed was to go busting a gut on a country road.

But then.

Why not?

Wasn't I trying to tie Geordie McClean into the death of Mark Corkery? Mandy was my only valid reason for remaining in his company. If he now believed he had killed Corkery in error, and was back on the trail of the real Horse Whisperer, right down to murder in an internet café, surely it was better to stick close to him; he wouldn't think the real Horse Whisperer would be foolish enough to hide out in his own back yard. If he was behind the internet café murder, then he had ordered the death of whoever was using that computer, not *me* specifically. If he did suspect me at all, then the likelihood was he wouldn't touch me with his daughter around, and wouldn't risk anything near his own property. Hiding in plain sight. Dangerous but . . . well, just dangerous.

I kept my head down, and walked.

Close to Connolly station I found a sports shop. I went in and bought a Liverpool top, a Liverpool tracksuit and a pair of Nike trainers. The clothes felt coarse yet frail and I could feel the linoleum floor of the shop through the trainers. They were clearly pirated. The Celtic Tiger wasn't really a tiger at all, just a big pussy cat purring as the cash registers rang. I left the shop wearing my sports gear. My ordinary clothes were in the small sports bag they threw in for a fiver. As I hurried into the railway station one of its straps broke, but there wasn't time to go back and complain. It was probably the only piece of my new ensemble that was authentic. I bought a ticket to Blanchardstown. From there, making sure to keep my head down as I passed the bank, I took a cab about half a mile out past McClean's stables and it dropped me by the hump of a small bridge which she'd picked out as the spot for us to meet. We'd agreed ten thirty for our jog. I was five minutes early. I checked the road, saw that it was clear, then climbed down beneath the bridge. There was a stream running beneath it, only about a foot deep, but there was plenty of dry undergrowth in which to hide my sports bag. I was back out just in time to see her jog around a bend in the road. As she approached I was running on the spot, looking eager, and feeling like death.

'Top of the morning to you,' I said.

She was wearing a blue and white tracksuit with grey slashes. She was devoid of make-up. She looked stunning, even while frowning. She didn't say good morning. She just kind of grunted in response, then added a terse 'Let's do it.'

Perhaps she wasn't a morning person. She took off again at speed and I used up what pitiful reserves of energy I had in catching up. From there on in it was a case of hanging on for dear life.

'How many . . . miles . . . do you . . . normally . . . do?' I managed. We were, of course, going uphill.

'Thirty-four.'

'Thirty-four!'

'Three *to* four!'

'Christ . . . that many?'

'I thought you ran?'

'I . . . do . . .'

'Uhuh.'

She upped the speed, I fell back, with a major effort I caught up, or maybe she slowed again. I gasped: 'You . . . seem . . . distant . . .'

'I will be if you keep up that snail's pace.'

'No . . . I . . . mean . . .'

'I know what you mean.'

She sped away again. *Fuck it*.

Within a couple of minutes she'd become not much bigger than a dot on the horizon. I was bent double, trying to get my breath. When I managed to look up the dot was getting bigger again. I steadied myself against a fence post as she continued to grow. As she closed in I pushed a smile on to my face and said, 'I must have pulled a—'

But she flashed past. 'It's all downhill now,' carried back to me on the wind.

Christ.

I started after her again. I could feel every friggin' ounce of gravel through my trainers, plus they were cutting the heels off me. I had sweated through my Liverpool top and was gratified to see that the colour was running; my hands were already dyed red.

Up ahead, distantly, she finally stopped.

She was on the bridge. When I finally got there she was sitting on the wall, hardly out of breath at all. I was gasping for dear life. I sat down beside her. She smiled at me. I smiled back. She put a hand on my shoulder. She smiled again. I smiled back. Her face moved towards mine. Mine moved towards hers.

I had a sensation of floating through the air.

No.

I *was* floating through the air.

She'd given me an almighty shove.

I shot backwards. It was only a drop of fifteen feet or so, but it seemed more. I plunged into the stream with a yell, when I should have kept my mouth closed. As I thrashed about I swallowed a lungful. The stream bed was relatively soft, small pebbles as opposed to sharp rocks, but it *hurt*. I was bruised and scratched and soaked and suffering from mild shock.

I stood up and yelled 'What the fuck was that for?'

She was above me on the bridge. She was no longer smiling. 'For telling me lies, you bastard.'

I finished coughing up stream life then ran a sopping hand across my face before responding with a suitably Wildean 'What're you talking about, you fucking stupid bitch?'

She raised an eyebrow.

I spat. I looked away. I dragged my feet out of the water and tried to pull myself up the bank. Where before I'd negotiated it with the nimbleness of a gazelle, now, wet, cold, heavy, my legs like lead, it was too much. I made several attempts and kept slipping down.

Finally I stayed where I was and glared back up at her. 'What did I lie about?'

'You tell me.'

I blew out. 'Okay! So I don't go jogging much! I used to run . . . all the time. I just . . . overestimated my capacity for—'

'Not about the running.'

'Then . . . what?'

'Where do you want me to start?'

'I don't know!'

'Well how about the car?'

'What car?'

'The fucking Ferrari!'

'Oh.'

'Indeed. I should have you arrested.'

I looked at my feet, hazy under the water. 'Sorry,' I said, glumly.

'The mechanic spotted it straight away. Are you fucking crazy or what?'

I shrugged helplessly. 'I really am sorry. I couldn't control it. I was embarrassed. I didn't think you'd notice.'

'Didn't think I'd notice! You tried to kill me!'

'I didn't! It was an accident!'

'You cut the brakes by accident?

'*What?*'

'You don't do something fucking lethal like that by accident.'

'I didn't cut any fucking brakes!'

'You just bloody admitted it!'

'I did not!'

'Well what the fuck were you saying sorry for?'

'Swapping . . . swapping seats with you after we crashed.'

'*What?*'

'I . . . I was driving you home . . . it was too fast for me . . . I crashed and you were still out of it . . . so

I put you in the driver's seat. I thought it might . . .
help your insurance . . .'

'*What?*'

'Or . . . or . . . more probably mine.' I blinked up at
her. 'It was stupid and churlish and I didn't think it
would matter because you'd been nasty and I didn't
think I'd ever see you again so I went and did it except
since then I've found out how nice you are and I'm
really really sorry for doing it.'

Her face was scrunched up. 'I . . . can't believe I'm
hearing this . . . You put me in the . . . you didn't cut
the . . . ?'

'No. Fuck! No! Somebody . . . ?'

'Yes they did. Beyond doubt they did. And it wasn't
you?'

'I swear to God.'

'Why do I not believe you?'

'I honestly wouldn't lie to you.'

'Like about the jogging?'

'That wasn't a lie, that was a fib.'

'Oh yeah. And what about the Horse Whisperer?'

'What?'

'You tell me.'

'I don't . . .'

'Don't fuck me around, Dan.'

'I'm not, I wouldn't, I . . .'

'Stop it. Do you think I'm fucking stupid? You
know, you're more to be pitied than . . . than whatever the phrase is.'

'I don't—'

'Dan. I *know*. You ask me all that shit about the horses and the stables and the next day, lo and behold, there it all is in the Horse Whisperer. Coincidence?'

'It *must* be . . . I wouldn't . . .'

'Dan . . .'

'You know, there's lots of spies out there. Lots of journalists. Just because . . . doesn't mean . . .'

She was at the edge of the bank now, hands on hips, confident, in control, *certain*. I was the drowned rat, shrinking by the second. 'And what,' she began triumphantly, 'if I had fed you a deliberately false snippet of information, just to see if it would turn up?'

Hook, line and sinker.

'Ah. Well. Then you'd be feeling pretty damn smug right now.'

She let out a sigh. 'Dan. You crashed my car. You tried to blame it on me. The only thing that makes me think you didn't cut my brakes is that you were in the bloody car as well. Then you sold information to the Horse Whisperer. Give me one good reason why I should ever, *ever* speak to you again.'

'Because.'

'Because what?'

'Just because. It's reason enough.'

We stared at each other.

'Why, Dan?'

'Truth?'

'Truth.'

There are times in your life when you have to make a decision. When you have to swallow your pride, stand up and tell the truth. It's the mark of a man. I took a deep breath.

'Because somebody is trying to kill your father and I'm trying to find out why.'

16

I retrieved my belongings from beneath the bridge, and then went back down the road towards her father's house. I was soaked but not chilled, warmed perhaps by her unexpectedly positive reaction to my strategic lying. We walked in silence. Deliberately. I had told her I wasn't going to reveal anything until I'd had a shower and the opportunity to change back into my clothes. She agreed quickly enough. The cutting of the brakes on her father's Ferrari had sown the seeds. I had merely added the fertiliser. I was bathed in a new and flattering light. I had gone from sinner to the Saint. I had a halo that glistened off my teeth.

Over the last hundred yards or so she took my hand. 'You're cold,' she said, although I was not. 'I'm sorry.' It was gratifying to see the red dye from the pirated Liverpool shirt soak into her skin as well.

It was the briefest of encounters. As we approached the gate, with its security cameras, she dropped my hand. She rang a bell, then waved up the drive towards the bungalow.

'Your dad's not going to be pleased to see me.'

'Even with your news?'

'He won't believe me.'

'Maybe not. Relax. He's probably not home yet.'

After a few moments there was a low hum from the gates and they began to swing inwards. I could immediately see the Ferrari, gleaming like new, sitting outside the bungalow. There was a Land Rover beside it. We walked briskly up the driveway towards where Derek, watching quizzically, waited just inside the front door. He only pressed the security buzzer to allow us in at the very final moment.

'Look what the cat dragged in,' was his greeting.

I smiled appreciatively. Mandy, without explanation, brushed past him then led me down a long, dark corridor to a bathroom. She showed me how the shower worked. There was really no need. I'd been taking showers for years. She got me a fresh towel. There was a bottle of Grecian 2000 and a set of pristine steel combs on the shelf above the sink. There were balms and moisturisers and gels in a straw basket. There was a half-squeezed tube of KY Jelly and a saucer of multicoloured condoms.

'These yours?' I asked.

'No, the gay boys.'

'Ah.'

'Have your shower. We have to talk.'

She left me. I showered. I checked the bathroom

cabinet for evidence. There was evidence of dandruff, bad breath and vitamin deficiency, but nothing I could tie in to a murder plot. I slipped into the shower and tried not to think of what Derek and Eric might have been up to in it. I concentrated on rearranging the facts to fit into what I had revealed to Mandy. The water was hot and it was great. It wasn't the sort of shower where you would find a chicken drumstick in the plughole. I was thirty minutes under it and only came out when there was a bang on the door and a shouted enquiry from Mandy after my health.

I towelled off. There was a choice of a nice silk bathrobe or my own street clothes. I chose wisely. Just in case Derek was feeling lonely. I am not particularly homophobic. But gay ex-cops with guns frighten the pants off me. Metaphorically speaking. I combed my hair with my fingers. I was all thumbs. I was nervous. I had to talk truth with Mandy and all I had was half-truths.

I pre-empted. 'Tell me about the car,' I said as she showed me into the lounge.

'No, tell me what you're up to,' she countered.

'Tell me about the car. It may have some bearing on what I'm up to.'

She pondered that for several moments. While she did I investigated her father's drinks cabinet. It was well stocked. She said, 'Make yourself at home.' She followed it up with 'In need of Dutch courage?'

'Just tell me about the car.'

'Like I said, the brakes were cut. If you tried to drive me home like you said you did then the likelihood is you didn't lose control because of your own deficiencies as a man.'

'Ouch.'

Derek appeared in the doorway. He looked sniffily across at me. 'Are you after anything in particular?'

Something a little fruity. A different time, a different place. 'Just a little drinkie,' I said. I produced a bottle of white wine and two glasses. 'Staying?' I asked Derek.

He shook his head. 'I was just going to say, I'm popping down to the shop. Get something nice for tea. Don't be opening those gates for anyone, okay?'

Mandy nodded absently. Derek withdrew. A couple of minutes later I heard the car leave. I poured two glasses of wine and offered one to Mandy.

'I told you. I can't. I'm riding on Saturday.'

'Oh. Well. Waste not want not.'

I sat on the sofa with the two glasses and began to sip. She settled into the armchair opposite and folded her legs beneath her. They were nice legs. She had showered. She was wearing a virgin-white towelling dressing gown. Her hair was damp and combed back. As all this was registering she said suddenly, 'Please tell me what's going on. I'm worried about my dad. He's not normally like this.'

'Like what?'

'With the guns and the security and always looking

over his shoulder. We've only had those gates a few weeks. They're a right pain in the hole.'

I took another sip. I licked my lips. 'I don't really know where to begin.'

'Yes you do.'

'Okay. At the beginning. Like all good stories. I just hope this one has a—'

'Just *tell* me, will you?'

'Well,' I said. 'You must know your father has made a lot of enemies.'

'He has business rivals. I don't know about enemies.'

'Believe me. He has.'

'How do you know?'

'Because I was asked by the Horse Whisperer to find out who'd put a contract out on your father.'

'A contract?'

'A contract, and I'm not talking recording.'

'That explains the car . . .'

'And the three dead Chinamen in my house.'

'The *what*?'

'You heard. I came down here and started asking questions. Lo and behold, three Chinamen break into my house, tie me to a chair and set fire to my feet.'

'Your . . . ?'

I rolled down my socks and showed her the burns.

'Jesus. No wonder you couldn't run. Why on earth didn't you . . . ?'

I shrugged. 'They're not sore. I wanted to run with you.'

She smiled hesitantly. 'I don't understand.'

'It's complicated. The Chinese wanted to know what I knew about your father, his movements. Their English wasn't the best.'

'God.'

'Luckily, one of them found my computer. They gave me a breather on the torture while they checked it out. I managed to free myself, only one of them caught on and we had a bit of a scrap as I tried to make my exit out the window. His gun came loose and we both grabbed it. There was a bit of a struggle and he ended up shot. Before I could get out the other two came for me guns blazing. I just closed my eyes and fired. When I opened them all three were lying dead. As far as I'm aware they still are. Up at the house. There's been nothing in the papers. You can go and check if you want.'

'I . . . God, I don't know what to say.'

'I've been on the run ever since. That's why my clothes were in a bag under the bridge.'

'Do you still have the gun?'

'No. Of course not. I threw it away.'

She unfolded her legs, then refolded them the other way. 'Maybe I will take that glass of wine.'

It was gone, but I got her another.

'Why would anyone want to kill my father?' she said almost dreamily as I handed it to her. I plonked myself down beside her. She didn't object. She moved her legs a few inches to give me more room.

'Mandy. You know as well as I do. He's hardly

going to qualify for the diplomatic corps, is he? He doesn't just step on toes, he cuts them off and chews them. He might wear the nice tweeds and Barbour jackets. But he hasn't changed. He's a circus-tent hustler trying to muscle into the old boys' club.'

'And I'm the hustler's daughter.'

I shrugged. 'Does he owe anyone money?'

'I don't know.'

'Has he reneged on a deal?'

'I don't know.'

'Might we go through his paperwork?'

'He doesn't keep it here.'

'There must be something.'

'Dan – even if there was, I couldn't. It's up to him. I'll have to speak to him. Obviously he hasn't been telling me. I'm his daughter. He's trying to protect me. I've a big race on Saturday, he doesn't want me worried. There's plenty of explanations. He doesn't have to have done something wrong. There are a lot of strange, deranged people out there. I know, I've dated some of them.'

We sat staring at the carpet for some time.

'I'm sorry it's got you into trouble, Dan.'

I shrugged. 'It's my own fault for asking.'

'Still. I shouldn't have pushed you in the river.'

'You'd every right to. If the roles had been reversed I'd have pushed you in, then bashed your head in with a stone.'

'You wouldn't hurt a fly.'

'You're forgetting the Chinamen.'

185

'That was self-defence.'

'Tell that to the Guards.'

'The Chinese aren't into owning or breeding, at least not in Europe. They're into gambling, though. And so is my dad.'

'Is or was? I heard his bookie's operation went bankrupt.'

'Not that I'm aware. Someone else runs it for him, but it's still his and still turns a nice profit.'

'I must have been misinformed.'

'Fuck.' She snapped it out suddenly. 'All I want is a simple life. Look after my horses and win the Grand National.'

'It's not your fault somebody's after your dad.'

'Well why does it feel like it?'

I shrugged.

I got us both another glass of wine. I sat a little closer. I had carried off my lying with aplomb. I had not been particularly deceitful. Just a slight rearranging of the facts. I was wanted for one murder and would shortly be called to account for three others. I was lying to a beautiful woman and stealthily trying to get her drunk; not so drunk that she would vomit down the back of the sofa, just enough to make her fall asleep so that I could root around for a paper trail with which to nail Geordie McClean, and all before Derek returned to conjure something up in the kitchen.

When I looked at her again, she was smiling. 'What?' I asked.

'Nothing.' Her face had reddened slightly, but it could have been the wine.

'No, come on, what're you smiling at?'

'Nothing. I . . .' She trailed off. She tried to hide her smile behind her hand, but it was getting longer. Finally she dropped it away and nodded down. 'You have an erection.'

I followed her gaze. I cleared my throat. 'No. It's just the way the trousers crease.'

'It's an erection.'

'It's the trousers. I'm not *that* big.'

'I know an erection when I see one.'

'That will be down to your long riding career.'

'There's no need for that.'

'You brought it up, so to speak.'

'You're saying it's not an erection?'

'No, I'm saying it *wasn't* an erection. Now I'm not so sure. It's all this talk of erections.'

She giggled. 'You get excited by talk of erections? Derek'll be home soon if you're that way inclined.'

'I haven't been inclined at all for a long time. Why were you looking at my trousers anyway?'

'The carpet was making me dizzy.'

'You can't handle your drink.'

'Perhaps you should put me to bed, then.'

'Is that an invitation?'

There was a clarity in the brilliantly blue eyes she held steady on me that suggested she was not really drunk at all. 'It might be,' she said.

'Well either it is or it isn't.'

'Well it depends on whether the invitation would be accepted or not.'

'Jesus Christ, of course it would be.'

'Just because you want a quick shag.'

'No! Well yes as well. But I really . . .' I was about to start off with the familiar litany, the one that's handed to every boy on the eve of puberty, promptly memorised and then destroyed. I sighed. I just couldn't be bothered with it. It was Patricia's fault. I decided to overturn the habits of a lifetime and tell the truth. 'Mandy,' I said, 'you are lovely, but please don't make me give you all the shit about love and romance and wanting to get to know the real you . . .'

'I don't want that. I just want to know if you find me attractive.'

'Of *course*. Why wouldn't I?'

She shrugged and looked away. 'I just don't feel very, y'know . . .'

I took her hand. 'Let's go to bed. And shut up. You're beautiful.'

She smiled meekly. I stopped her in the bedroom doorway. 'One thing.'

She looked suddenly unsure.

'Will you wear your jockey gear?'

At that point I made my excuses and left.

As if.

It had been a long time since I'd gone to bed with a beautiful woman. With *any* woman. I was out of practice. If she noticed she didn't complain. She was shy but not passive, quiet but not unresponsive. All the same it was important that I lasted more than one minute, but it didn't seem likely. As I moved above her I could feel myself rushing helplessly towards climax.

I looked desperately to the shelves above her bed. I looked at book titles: thrillers, a whole run of Agatha Christies. I tried to picture the elderly Agatha Christie in her underwear, but it did nothing to still the rush towards . . .

Desperately I tried to divert my attention.

A piggy bank.

A framed show-jumping certificate.

A photo of her father handing over a trophy to her.

A photo of a pre-teenage Mandy running on the beach with her mum and dad.

I stopped mid-stroke.

The blood drained from my face, and elsewhere besides. Instantly.

'Dan . . . what's the matter . . . what's wrong . . . what's . . . ?'

Her mother, laughing as she ran, so proud of her daughter, so in love with her husband, so happy with that moment in time.

So Hilda.

17

'You're white, you're shaking . . . am I that ugly?'

'God no . . .'

'Well what then . . . ?'

'I don't know. I . . .'

'I *am* . . .'

'You're not . . . I . . . it's been so long . . . my wife . . . my son . . . I'm sorry . . . it was going so well . . . I was about to . . . It would have been Niagara, but now I need Viagra.'

'I'm so embarrassed, I should never . . .'

'No . . . you should, of course you should . . . It's me . . . not you . . . I swear to God.'

'But . . .'

'But nothing. Come here.'

I hugged her to me. Her mother. Hilda. My brain was fit to burst. My stomach was cramped. My lungs were contracting. I couldn't raise a breath, let alone an erection. I felt something damp against my shoulder, and realised that Mandy was crying.

I hugged her harder and tried to reassure her, but nothing would work. I turned and she rested her head on my chest. As I stroked her arms I saw that there were thin scars around her wrists. Across, like an amateur, not straight up, like a professional. Good thing too.

I said, 'You haven't had a happy life.'

There was a little shrug. 'It's been okay.'

'Your parents divorced when you were young. Acrimoniously.'

She rubbed at her eyes. 'That's a big word to use in bed.'

'I'm sorry.'

'No. You're right.'

'What happened, he got custody?'

'No. They reached a compromise that made each of them happy. Boarding school.'

'That explains the English accent.'

'What English accent?'

'Well now.'

She stroked my chest. I didn't ask about the slices on her wrists. They were self-explanatory. There is a tendency by ugly or average-looking people to presume that beautiful people don't have problems. But they do. Sometimes bigger ones. Just that nobody believes them. I also had problems. I was being lied to on a colossal scale. People were trying to kill me because of lies. I wanted to kill someone because of lies. I said, 'Nice picture.' She followed my gaze up to the beach photo above us.

'Oh, sure,' she said. 'Long time ago. Happy families.'

'Tell me about your mother.'

'Why?'

'I'm interested.'

'I'm naked in bed beside you and you want to know about my mother?'

'Yes.'

'Don't reassure me or anything.'

'I have reassured you.'

'Not enough.'

'You're great, you're beautiful and I fancy the arse off you. I am a sad, inadequate individual who can't perform. Satisfied?'

She sighed. 'Okay. Sorry.'

'Don't worry about it.'

We lay in silence for a while. We heard a car crunch along the driveway, then the back door opening and footsteps in the kitchen.

'Derek won't . . . ?'

'He knows better.' She pushed herself up on one elbow. She sniffed up. 'My mother,' she said, 'lives in Belfast. I don't see much of her. When I got out of boarding school I came to live with Daddy.'

'Why?'

'Because he's marginally less mean and bitter than she is, and I have to live somewhere. Also, I want to ride horses and win the Grand National, and there's a better chance of that than with Mummy. Her horses are nags.'

'What happened that they split up?'

'Daddy always had an eye for the fillies. He liked having sex with women he wasn't married to as well.'

'And Hilda didn't approve.'

'Well, naturally she . . .' She trailed off. Her brow furrowed. 'How do you know her name?'

'I . . . well, I told you. I was doing a book. I've done a little background.'

Her eyes narrowed. The temperature dropped. 'You're still doing the fucking book, aren't you?'

'I . . .'

'All this, all this fucking seduction—'

'It was hardly sed—'

'Just to get fucking information . . . I don't believe you!' She reared up.

'It wasn't like that, I swear to God, I really—'

'You're a fucking bastard—'

'There was very little fucking.' I meant it as gentle, self-deprecating humour. But somehow it missed its mark.

She growled. 'And you think you're so fucking funny. I gave you the benefit of the doubt and you were just laughing at me all the time. You sucked me into bed and made me take my clothes off and all the time you were laughing. You didn't even fancy me. You couldn't even keep your fucking erection. It was all fucking *research*. What're you going to do, describe my tits in great detail? Describe how I move or moan or how I touch a man or how I don't? That

I've cut my wrists before? Oh don't deny it, I saw you looking at them. You're a sad fucking bastard, Dan Starkey, and I'm even sadder for falling for it.' She threw the quilt back and climbed out of bed. I looked at her, me ashen-faced and mumbling *nothings*. She grabbed one of her breasts and thrust it out towards me. 'Take a good look. Do you want a photo? *Here.*' She thrust her groin towards me. 'Interview this,' she spat. She burst into tears. She fled into the ensuite bathroom and slammed the door. I heard the toilet seat go down, and then sobbing.

I sat on the edge of the bed, wondering what to say.

She was wrong.

But not totally.

I said her name several times, without knowing what to say after it.

I said, 'Can I get you a cup of tea?'

'Fuck off!'

'Coffee?'

She hammered the door in frustration. The shock of it made me jump.

'Just get *out*.'

'Mandy . . .'

'Now!'

I sighed, and stayed where I was. 'Look, I'm really—'

'Are you not gone yet?'

'All I did was remember your mum's name. Where's the crime in that?'

'Go away.'

'Please come out.'

'I'm on the toilet.'

'You've been a long time. Are you having trouble working things out?'

There was a pause, and then a very faint giggle.

'C'mon,' I said.

'C'mon yourself,' she snapped, but it seemed less angry.

I sat on the bed for a few minutes, debating whether it would be diplomatic to put my clothes back on. I had the feeling, somehow, that if I did put them on I would never again have the opportunity to take them off in her presence. That a line would have been drawn. A wall built. A Hoover Dam constructed. There were a lot of images that flitted through my mind, and the most dominant one was of Hilda smiling at me, giving me her cutesy encouragement to travel south to investigate the death of Mark Corkery.

I wanted to throttle her.

And sleep with her daughter.

The bathroom door opened a fraction. A panda-eyed Mandy peered sheepishly out. 'Perhaps,' she said softly, 'I misinterpreted.'

'That's okay,' I said.

'I over-reacted.'

'No, you didn't, it's understandable.'

'I hate myself.'

'You shouldn't.'

She smiled hesitantly. 'Do you think,' she ventured,

'that you'd be up to that interview now?'

'With your . . . ?'

'Mmm.'

'I could try.'

She came fully out of the bathroom. She was naked and I was naked and we stood and hugged and kissed and she clung to me like the poor orphaned kid she felt herself to be. We fell back on the bed. As I moved down her she purred, 'Tell me, do you intend to delve deeply?'

'As deep as you will allow.'

'Will the interrogation be painful?'

'Only until I get to the truth.'

'And what is the truth?'

'You tell me.'

She clasped the back of my head and fell silent.

I nudged her awake. Her bedroom was at the back of the house and that, together with the size of the stables, meant that the room didn't get much light, so it felt later than it was. Five, according to my watch. She came dozily back to life as I stroked her back. She said, dreamily, 'What's the smell?'

'My apologies.'

'No, I mean the burning.'

'We burned the place up, sweet pea.'

She sat up. 'No, I really mean the burning.' Her nose crinkled.

I sniffed up. She had a point. 'Dozy Derek's left the dinner on.'

She looked at her watch, and didn't look any happier. 'I better go check.'

'You're not going out dressed like that. Relax. If you're worried, *I'll* go.'

I crawled down the bed and into my pants. Mandy relaxed back into the quilt. I smiled warmly at her. I felt happier and more relaxed than I had in a long time, and that despite the fact that I had lied outrageously to her, wanted to kill her mother, and was suspected of four murders. I'd been in worse situations and was still alive to tell the tale. After all, James was my middle name.

I put on my shirt and my trousers and prepared to pad barefoot up the hall. From the bed Mandy said, 'Put on your socks and shoes.'

'What?'

'Put on your socks and shoes. If you go up there in your bare feet it'll look like we've been having sex.'

'Will it? And if it does, so what? Are you ashamed of me? And meanwhile the house is burning down.'

'Yes. It will look like it. And yes, it does matter. And I might yet be ashamed of you. And I don't think the house is burning down, I just don't want the place stinking of burned potato. Do you have a problem with any or all of that?'

I shook my head. I sat back on the bed and pulled on my socks. Mandy grabbed my shoulders and pulled me back, then kissed me. I sat up and tied my shoes. She kissed me again. She was quite obviously mental, but she was a good kisser.

I went to the door. 'Will I pass inspection now?'

'Wash your hands.'

'What?'

'Wash your hands. You smell of sex.'

'Are you serious?'

'Completely.' I tutted and walked into the ensuite. 'He's not going to *smell* me, y'know.'

'Isn't he? You don't know him.'

I came out. 'Now can I go?'

She nodded. I opened the bedroom door. 'Dan?'

'*What?*'

'Don't be long.'

I rolled my eyes. I closed the door behind me and walked the hall. The smell intensified. It was burning, but not *the house is on fire* burning, burning food. I entered the kitchen. There was smoke coming out of the oven. I wasn't quite sure what to do, not being overly experienced with cookers. Open the door to let the smoke out, or open the door and a huge ball of fire melts me on the spot and takes the rest of the house with it. My inclination, as ever, was to slip out the front door and go home, let someone else worry about it. Except there were dead Chinamen in my home and I'd a nasty feeling that I'd fallen in love, or at least in lust. I'd a nagging fear, or hope, that I wasn't going anywhere without her for quite a while.

I found a pair of oven gloves and carefully opened the door.

There was the merest billow of smoke. I reached

in and removed a casserole dish. Whatever Derek had been cooking had shrunk and blackened and attached itself to the base. I set it in the sink and ran some cold water on it. A stable hand was leading a horse across the yard towards a horsebox as I opened the back door to let the smoke out. He glanced round. 'Derek burned the dinner again,' I said. I gave him a little wave and a reassuring smile. He nodded and went on about his business.

I left the door open, then walked down the hall to the lounge.

Sometimes you can't see the bleeding obvious. I admired the view of the brilliant green Meath countryside. The cool grey of the clouds. A slim Oprah talking silently on the widescreen television in the corner. And Derek lying on the floor. There was blood seeping on to the carpet. Above him a whiter-than-white square on the wall where a painting had been removed to reveal a safe. The door was hanging open. There was nothing inside.

'Mandy!' I yelled.

18

Derek was alive, although slightly bent.

By the time Mandy had buttoned herself into jeans and pulled on a sweatshirt I had him sitting up moaning, which was better than lying down dead. He groaned about the state of the carpet, the blood stains on his shirt and the tragic fate of his glazed turkey à la King. He didn't seem particularly fazed by the untidy gash on the back of his head.

'He's . . . there's blood . . . Maybe . . .' I said helpfully as Mandy came through from the hall and let out an initially shocked yelp before hurrying across to kneel at Derek's side.

'Christ,' she said. Derek started to complain again but she shushed him and patted him and mothered him. 'Call an ambulance,' she snapped at me.

I stood to look for the phone. As I did there came from outside the roar of speeding tyres on gravel. I turned expecting to see Geordie McClean racing up the drive. Mentally I began to prepare myself. I would be blamed. For this, for everything, it was my fate in life. But it wasn't Geordie. A Land Rover, a horse box, the one I'd seen moments before, now travelling at speed away from the house.

I said, 'Mandy.'

She was examining the wound on Derek's skull. 'What?' she said, irritated.

'You better look.'

She was about to growl something fresh, but the look on my face made her jump up. Her joints clicked. Her brow furrowed as she saw the Land Rover and horse box speeding towards the security gates.

'What the . . . ?'

The gates, erected more for privacy than defence against assault, buckled and then burst open as the Land Rover smashed into them. The horse box gave a little jump at the force of the impact.

'Oh holy fuck,' said Mandy.

The Land Rover paused briefly as it came to the road.

And then indicated left and turned.

Indicated.

What sort of a getaway driver *indicates*?

Derek, ignored momentarily, let out another groan, and settled back on to the floor. He looked a little greyer. I called the ambulance. Before I'd finished giving the information, Mandy had dashed out of the lounge, down the hall and into the kitchen. She hadn't asked me to call the police, so I didn't. No point in dragging them in while I was within a thousand miles. I told them Derek had fallen, gave them the address and put the phone down. I pulled a throw off the tan leather settee and tucked it in around him. I told him everything would be okay. He nodded and thanked me and mumbled something about Eric.

I hurried out into the yard. I could hear Mandy's raised voice. Curses.

As I crossed towards the stables Mandy came steaming out trailing anxious-looking stable hands in her wake. She'd a face like thunder.

'Fucking fuck!' she yelled.

'What?' I asked. She hurried past me.

'They've taken Dan the Man,' she said coldly, then thumbed back towards the hapless and helpless-looking stable hands and snapped, 'And those bastards let them.' She shook her head furiously at them. 'Get into the house, look after Derek until the ambulance comes.'

They nodded wordlessly and followed in her wake as she raced into the kitchen. I went after her. She picked the keys to the Ferrari off a hook.

'What're you . . . ?'

'What do you think? I'm going after them.'

'They've a—'

'Of course they've a headstart. But they're driving a fucking horse box.' She jangled the keys. I followed her into a utility room off the kitchen. She lifted another key and opened a cupboard. She took out a shotgun.

'There's an ambulance on the way,' I said.

'Tell them to send another one,' she said, smoothly loading the gun.

'I'll come too,' I said.

She looked at me. And damn it if the vaguest hint of suspicion didn't cross her eyes.

'Mandy, I didn't have anything—'

'Then help me.' She turned back into the kitchen. She lifted down another set of keys. 'The Land Rover,' she said, pressing them into my hand. 'When we come to the junction they're either going left for Dublin or right for Navan. Those are our choices.'

She tore along the hall and pulled open the front door. She hurried down the steps and across the gravel to the Ferrari. She paused for the briefest moment and gave me a look of absolute devastation. 'He's my *life*,' she said.

I nodded. 'Which way?' I asked. We locked eyes.

It was feminine intuition against a lifetime's experience as a hard-bitten reporter and clown.

'I'll take Dublin,' she said.

I nodded once and we climbed into our vehicles.

Mandy was tearing down the drive before I'd found where to insert the key. When I finally made it out through the mangled gates she'd disappeared completely.

I drove down over the bridge where we'd met earlier to the junction, then turned right on to the N3 for Navan. The traffic was heavy, both ways. I crossed against oncoming and received a cacophony of horns for my trouble. I sped. There were all sorts of roads branching off, not to mention lanes and tracks. Whoever had stolen Dan the Man had done the hard bit. Getting lost in horse country wasn't going to be difficult.

But I kept driving.

Something about the desperation and mistrust in her eyes.

Something about proving I could do something right.

Something about having been to bed with her and feeling things I hadn't felt since last time.

I drove, and drove, and before I knew it I was coming into Navan.

It was pointless, pointless, *pointless*.

Hey, did you happen to see the most beautiful horse in the world?

Pointless.

I pulled into a filling station. I bought a Diet Pepsi and a Twix, God juice and God food. There was nothing I could do. There was a coin box outside. I phoned Geordie McClean's house. While I waited for a response I checked my watch. I'd been on the road for forty minutes. A hesitant voice said, 'H-hello?'

'Who's that?'

'B-Barney, who's—'

And then there was some sort of altercation. I heard a muffled 'Fuck off you munchkin,' and B-Barney was quickly removed from the phone. Derek said, 'Who the fuck is this?'

'Dan. Are you okay?'

'Sure. Have you found the horse?'

'No.'

'Fuck. Where are you?'

'Navan. She headed for Dublin.'

'I know. There's been no word.'

'Fuck. Did the ambulance not arrive yet?'

'It did. I told them to piss off. It's only a scratch.'
He sighed. 'Fuck. Fuck. Geordie's going to go through
me.'

'Have you any idea who . . . ?'

'No. Yes. Somebody whacked me from behind. But
it won't be hard to find out. I mean, the gates were
closed, everything's on camera. There'll be a roll-
call for the munchkins and we'll see who's missing.
If youse had waited we could have worked it out
instead of chasing all over the fucking country.'

'We panicked.' I sighed. 'What do I do?'

'Don't tell Geordie, and get the horse back.'

'Thanks a bunch.'

I put the phone down.

It was the smoke that got me.

I'd driven past the turn-off for Ashtown and on
towards Dublin. There was nothing to be gained from
going back to the stables. She was somewhere ahead
of me, she'd a Ferrari, a shotgun and a temper for
company. I just had a Land Rover that smelled of
horse shit and a head that was full of it. I'd just flashed
past the turn-off to a tiny village called Muldudhart
when the traffic ahead of me slowed to negotiate

the clouds of thick black smoke that were wafting across the road. I pulled into the hard shoulder, then reversed at speed back to the turn-off.

Several hundred yards outside of the village I came to the Ferrari, and beyond it the empty, burning horse box. There was no sign of Mandy. The Ferrari was unlocked. The keys were gone. The shotgun lay on the ground. I picked it up. One chamber had been fired. I cursed and threw it down. Then cursed again and picked it up and wiped whatever fingerprints I'd left with the tail of my shirt. Distantly I heard the sound of a fire engine. Inevitably police would follow. I got back in the Land Rover and drove back to the headquarters of Irish American Racing.

As I approached the mangled gates I saw that Eric was standing guard, another shotgun in his big hands. It meant that Geordie was home. I wound down the window. 'How's it going?' I asked.

'What do you think?' he scowled. 'The big man wants to see you.'

I nodded and drove on. It was only a hundred yards up the lane. I used the time to try and think up a suitable response to the inevitable question. *What were you doing when all of this was going on?*

Geordie McClean's face was white with fury. Derek's head was white with a crudely applied bandage. The safe door remained open. Geordie didn't question what I was doing there at all. Derek had filled him in. I filled them in.

'No sign of the horse at all?' Geordie asked.

'Or your daughter,' I added, pointedly.

'Of course.' He sighed. 'I just don't under—' He let loose with a flurry of curses, then put his hand to his brow and rubbed it hard. 'I thought Bosco of all people . . .'

'Who's Bosco?' I asked.

Geordie looked at me. 'None of your business. Dan. Look. I don't know why Mandy agreed to be interviewed behind my back . . . well, probably *because* it was behind my back, but it's over now, things have gotten serious and I have to sort them out. Now, thank you for chasing after Mandy, for the news about the car, I'll get my own people on to it now. I'd appreciate it if you left it to us. And please, keep this under your hat. My daughter's life may depend on it.'

I looked from Geordie to Derek, and then up to Eric now standing in the doorway.

'I want to help,' I said.

Geordie shook his head. 'Dan – you're more of a hindrance than a help.'

'You don't understand. I *saved* Fat Boy McMaster in New York. I can do it again.'

'It was long ago and it was far away,' said Geordie, 'and frankly you've gone badly downhill since. Now please . . .'

'Geordie.'

'Or to put it another way,' said Eric, 'get the fuck out of the house.'

'Geordie. I wasn't interviewing your daughter in there.'

That brought a little colour back to his cheeks. 'Get him out,' he snapped.

Eric caught hold of me by the collar and started to drag me back.

'I don't mean . . . I mean . . . I think I love her . . .'

'Now!'

I was out of the house and tossed on to the tarmac. Eric looked menacingly down at me. And then the menace dropped away and he said, 'Sorry, sometimes I have to do the heavy stuff. It's what I get paid for. Left to my own devices I would probably have given you a thank-you card and a quarter of fudge.' He winked. 'I'd give you a lift, but y'know, better get back inside.'

I pulled myself up into a sitting position. I said, 'Okay.'

'There's a bus goes past the bottom of the road every half-hour, if that's any help. You need money for the fare?'

'No. I'm okay.'

I stood and wiped at the black skidmarks on the knees of my trousers. I nodded at him and turned away. Then back. 'Eric?'

'Mmm?'

'You should get Derek to a hospital. That's a nasty crack.'

'I know. I will. Thanks.'

'And Eric?'

'What?'

'Who's Bosco?'

Eric thought for a moment, then glanced behind him. He stepped forward. 'I think it's really sweet that you can fall in love with someone so quickly. Derek tells me youse were at it while he was being whacked.'

I shrugged.

'She's a lovely girl, except that silly old Hector doesn't appreciate it, and his own daughter too.'

I looked at him.

'So Bosco's the guy stole the horse,' he said. 'Bosco Brown, find him you'll find the horse, and maybe Mandy too.'

'Can you tell me something about him? Does he—'

There was a shout from the house. 'Sorry,' Eric said, 'gotta go.' Then added swiftly, 'He's one of our jockeys. Down Cork way.' He made a little hand movement to suggest drinking. 'That's why we're not getting too hot under the collar. The fucking little people are always giving us grief. Bosco's strictly small-time, he's probably holed up down there in a barn with a bottle of vodka. He'll phone in a ransom demand, except he's not bright enough to realise we can trace it. We'll have them both back in no time, no doubt about it. But if you're going looking yourself, Dan, I hope you find them first, cause when I find him, I'm going to fucking plant him.'

Eric hurried back to the house.

I watched him go for a moment, then walked back down the drive to the mangled gates, and out along the road to the bus stop.

I leant against it.

Eric had been doing so well. My *chum*. Love was sweet. Volunteering information. But just a little too much. *Strictly small-time. Drinking. Cork. If you're going looking* ... Of course I was bloody going, they knew that, and it was all designed to throw me off the trail.

Geordie was frightened silly.

I heard the sirens before I saw the police cars. They weren't stupid. The burning horse box, the abandoned Ferrari and the discharged shotgun, they could all be traced back to Geordie. They didn't need to add me into the equation.

I have long been convinced that sirens serve only to warn criminals and further inflate the egos of policemen. I wasn't complaining. I did what every dashing hero does when pursued by his enemies.

I hid behind a tree.

19

I had two pints to steady my nerves. I sat in the bar at Connolly station. If I craned my head and pressed it against the smoked glass I could just make out the train timetable hanging down from the ceiling outside, but there was really no need. It wasn't like stations in England, where you had to keep an eye on constantly fluctuating times and destinations. Here you'd a choice of three or four, north to Belfast, north-west to Sligo, and maybe a couple more.

Drink can take you both ways. Highs and lows. You're never quite sure which. That's what makes it fascinating. You can be quite positive right up to the fourth pint, then hit the depths with number five, only to resurface beaming once a pretty girl sits down next to you and smiles on number six and *wey-heh!* you've forgotten what you're depressed about and turned into Benny Hill. That's what's different about drugs. Once you're locked into the blues, you've difficulty getting out of them. I've dabbled occasionally.

Just never went along with the party line. They always say, hey, so three or four people die from Ecstasy every year – but thirty thousand die from alcohol. Which makes you think, well maybe they have a point. But then you think, when was the last time someone dropped down dead from a bad pint? Fuck no, to die from alcohol you have to *really* work at it. You have to know what you're doing. I was born too late really, for drugs. When I was growing up dope was the guy who sat at the back of the class and smack was what you did to people's sunburn. Horse was a horse and speed was what took you down the left wing. *E?* We were more into D. And Junior Disprin when we couldn't get the grown-up stuff.

I was waiting for a train, I'd the fifth-pint blues and an overwhelming feeling that someone had spiked me with acid.

I needed to talk to Hilda, but until my ESP developed further I hadn't the means. If they'd been able to hack into my e-mails to her, tracing a phone call wasn't going to be difficult. Besides, it would have been too easy for her to just slam the phone down once I started into *What the fuck do you think you're playing at? People are getting killed all around me because you set me up as the Horse Whisperer without telling me the single most important piece of information I could have, that you were married to Geordie McClean. And by the way I'm screwing your daughter. And by the by, she's missing presumed . . .*

Presumed what?

Kidnapped. Murdered. Raped.

And she was carrying my child.

Just to be melodramatic.

And she was *nuts*.

We'd made love once. She *could* be pregnant. As a woman, it had of course been her responsibility to provide protection, but you couldn't always trust them to do so.

You know you don't fall in love with the first one that comes along.

I'm not, I'm . . .

There was a phone in the corner. I phoned Trish at work. I said, 'Hi-di-hi.'

She put the phone down.

I tried 'Ho-di-ho' a moment later and didn't get much further than the first *ho*.

I took another five minutes' worth of beer and phoned her back. I changed to a nice Ballymena accent. I said, 'Sorry to trouble you, hey, the name's McGimpsey, I've been having terrible trouble with m'tax return. Seems I—'

'What's your tax reference number?'

'My . . . hey, what would that be now?'

The pips started to go. I tutted and put some more money in. She recognised the tutt.

'Dan, what're you playing at?'

I tutted again. 'You've the time of day for some clown from the sticks but you won't even speak to the man who made love to you twice a week for ten years.'

'No, but I'll speak to you.'

'Oh very fucking funny. That's what I need right now. Your fucking sarcastic fucking . . . fuck stuff.' I scowled angrily at my jaundiced reflection in the pint glass I cradled in my free hand. I took another drink and snapped, 'What do you want?'

'Dan. You phoned me.'

'Yes I did. You're right there.'

'Dan, what is it?'

'Nothing. Just checking in. I still care.'

She was quiet for a moment, then: 'So what've you been up to?'

'This and that.'

'What about the new girl?'

'Kidnapped.'

'*Dan.*'

'I need help.'

'I can't, Dan.'

'C'mon.'

'Dan, last time . . .'

'I know what happened last time.'

She sighed. 'What sort of help?'

'Moral support.'

'You can have that.'

'Somewhere to put my head down.'

'No.'

'Money.'

'No.'

'A car.'

'No.'

'It might be easier if you were to tell me what you *are* prepared to offer.' There was silence. I filled it. 'Is there any fucking wonder there isn't any peace up there, never give an inch, no surrender, no fucking compromise. What's done is done, do you hear me? We can't go back in time! I did my best! I didn't mean for him to die! All I'm asking is somewhere to put my head and all you can think about is what some cunt with a beard will think. You've changed, you've fucking changed from the person I loved. You would never, ever, fucking ever have gone out with someone with a beard before, I'll tell you that for nothing. So fuck you, and your progeny.'

I put the phone down, even though there was fifteen seconds left on the clock.

I was wild and crazy and just didn't care. I bought another pint, but there was someone sitting where I'd been sitting. She looked a little embarrassed as I returned from the bar with my drink and she said, 'Sorry, I thought you'd . . .'

'Never worry.' I put my hand on the chair opposite. 'Do you mind?'

She shook her head. She was eighteen if she was a day and had mousy brown hair tied back in a little mousy-tail. Her accent and demeanour were Northern. She was drinking a hot whiskey. There was an open packet of Handy-Andies beside her. I sat down. 'Bit of a cold?' I said.

She nodded and sniffed up. She had a paperback lying face up on the table, perfectly flat.

'I hate that,' I said, nodding at it.

'What? Agatha Christie?'

'No. People who break the spines of books. It's like murder.'

She smiled. 'So do I actually. I just bought it second-hand across the street. It was like that. I was desperate for something to read.' She picked the book up and showed me the title. There was a picture of Agatha on the back. 'I've often wondered,' she said, looking at it, 'why they bother putting the picture of her on.'

'The old-bag picture?'

She nodded. 'The old-bag picture, exactly. When she was actually quite a mover and shaker in her day. Quite glamorous. Pretty even. Why not use that?'

'Maybe they're going for the old-bag market.' I cleared my throat. 'Not, of course, that you're an old bag.'

She put the book down. 'You sounded quite upset on the phone.'

'Oh. I didn't think it was that loud.'

'Drink does that. Turns up the volume.'

I shrugged. 'Sorry.'

'Don't worry. You sounded very passionate. I like that.'

I took a drink. 'So what's your story?'

'Job interview.'

'Did you get it?'

She shrugged. 'Don't care. Fancied a day in Dublin really.' She kicked at bags at her feet. 'Shoes. I've a thing for shoes. Six pairs. You just can't get them like this in Belfast.'

I nodded.

'So what's your story?'

'Oh, the usual. Dead Chinamen in my front room, on the run, that kind of thing.'

She nodded. Then sipped her drink. Then gathered up her Handy-Andies, her Agatha Christie paperback, her precious bags of shoes, and left. She didn't say a word, but looked at me like I was mental.

I sat on the train, drawing pictures on the misted-up window, as we pulled out of Connolly station. Fifteen minutes later, chugging gently towards Drogheda, she slipped into the seat opposite. 'You were serious, weren't you?'

I shrugged. She pushed her bags under the table and set down two cups of coffee. I looked at her. 'I don't drink coffee,' I said.

'It's not for you,' she replied.

I nodded and returned my attention to the misted window. 'Please,' I said, 'I want to be alone.'

'I imagine you already are.'

Something touched my elbow and I looked down to find she'd pushed a newspaper across the table, folded into a little rectangle so I couldn't miss the story she was pointing at on the front cover of the *Evening Herald*. It was about the discovery of three dead Chinamen in a rented house in Ashtown.

'You were telling the truth.'

'No, I just read the same paper. I'm a slabber. Be warned.' I returned my attention to the window.

'The coffee *is* for you.'

'I don't drink coffee.'

She looked at me glumly. Then, 'You didn't ask what job I was going for.'

'I know.'

'RTE. Reporter.'

'Christ.'

'They run a trainee scheme.'

'I don't believe I'm hearing this.'

'Except it's all stacked against you if you haven't got a degree.'

'Please stop.'

'But if I came back with a genuine scoop, I'd be set.'

I sighed. My brow against the cool window. 'Tell someone about a little murder, and all they can think of is me, me, me. I'm not interested in your fucking job. I did not murder anyone. I made it up. It was a joke. Now go away and take your coffee with you.'

'A good reporter doesn't let go of a story just because she's told to go away.'

'Have you ever heard of Veronica Guerin?'

'No, but I've heard of Woodhead and Bernstein.'

I sighed. 'It's Woodward. Wood*ward* and Bernstein. Christ.' I stood up. 'I'm going for a pee,' I said.

I walked down the train. There wasn't a buffet *car*, as such, more of a shop. You bought and went back to your seat. I bought a four-pack of Holsten Pils, then continued on down looking for a spare seat. I hated cub reporters, because I'd been one myself. I wasn't sure whether it was the enthusiasm or the lack of cynicism that annoyed me most. But it did. Jesus Christ, I was on the run, I'd left bodies behind me all over greater Dublin, and she was looking for a leg-up into the profession; what she deserved was a fist-down. I do not of course condone violence against women, unless they're asking for it, and smaller. I stopped off for a pee. It's difficult to stand peeing in a moving train. Really you're meant to sit down. But real men don't, they just get nasty bruises on their foreheads. Or spots on their trousers; using one hand to hold you up and the other curled round your can, you can't pee straight, you *spray* and leave it for the next woman in to clean up the seat you haven't bothered to lift anyway. I drank Holsten Pils and peed at the same time. In one end, out the other. The glorious circle of life, although not quite what the Lion King had been yapping about.

We pulled into Drogheda. I stayed where I was. People got off, people got on. Somebody tried the door. We started off again. I finished the first can then pulled down the window and threw the empty out. My trousers had dried sufficiently for me to face the public again, but I was quite happy where I was, leaning on the windowsill, looking at the countryside humming past. I could have stayed there until Belfast. No interaction required. No one to annoy me. I was just opening the second can when the door was rattled again and a man's voice said, 'Are you going to be long? I'm bustin' out here.'

It was followed almost immediately a second voice. 'Jimmy, there's another further down.'

'I want *this* one.'

He had another go at the door.

There was no reason for me to recognise their voices. To Northerners, Dublin accents all sound the same. I didn't have my thinking cap on. And I was half cut. Besides, I knew what it was like to be dying for a pee.

I unlocked the door. It opened outwards. *Jimmy* had to step back to let me out. He had one hand on the door and was in the middle of saying something to the other guy, so there was a split second when I was looking at him and he wasn't looking at me. It was just long enough for me to recognise Jimmy, Jimmy Farrelly, the chicken man, and clock the other fella, who I knew only as Oil Paintings, his mouth just falling open as he realised who I was. A frozen moment before I yanked the door out of Jimmy's hand, stepped backwards and banged it shut behind me, slipping the lock across and staggering back against the toilet bowl, silently cursing and already shaking and shuddering.

Then the hammering started.

So much for Agatha Christie.

This was *Murder on the Belfast Express.*

20

'Don't be fucking stupid, son,' Oil Paintings said through the door. 'You're in a toilet. We have guns. And lots of bullets. With the noise of the train they won't hear a thing. Come out before we fill you with fucking holes. We only want a chat.'

Well okay then.

'Just give me a moment while I freshen up.'

'Don't be smart,' growled Jimmy the Chicken.

I was in a blind panic, again. I needed Valium and a holiday. All these adventures, and I never learn. If I really wanted to flee the country, what the hell was I doing hanging around in the main fucking train station. Stevie Wonder could have found me.

I had the window down. Fortunately it was an old enough train for the benefits of fresh air not to be outweighed by concerns about potential suicides. Moments before I'd been enjoying the breeze, but now it felt icy cold.

There was another hammer on the door.

'C'mon! I swear to God—'

'Nearly there . . .'

'Shut the fuck up and get out here.'

'Tell us why you're fucking following us, you fuckin' creep.'

'I'm not following you. I'm just going to Belfast.'

'Yeah. Right. We're going to kill you this time, you fucker.'

Well that helped sway things.

There were two choices left, the surrender option obviously being a no-go. Dive out the window of a speeding train – it wasn't going to set any records, but tell that to your skull as it bounces off the ground – or climb up on top, like they do in the movies. It would be a difficult enough little manoeuvre for a fit and sober person, well nigh impossible for . . . Ah hell, if I failed, sure I would only be falling back on the first option. I peered out, and twisting round, up.

The top of a train.

Who're you kidding?

Surrender. Go down on your knees and *beg*.

They're only after money.

Or had been.

Tell us why you're following us. Who were *they* kidding?

You don't like heights. You're half cut. Even if you manage to get on top of the train you'll have you head cleaved off by a passing tunnel.

Maybe you could attach yourself to the hook that the

night mail bag is automatically snatched off as the train races through outlying stations.

Bollocks.

You've been reading too much Dylan Thomas.

There is no night mail. It isn't even the fucking night.

Next stop – Dundalk; how far away?

Fifteen minutes? Far enough. They'd have shot holes in the toilet long before we got to Dundalk.

'Open the fucking door!'

I took another drink.

There was no choice really.

There were two cans left. I put one in each pocket, for ballast, and climbed out of the toilet window. The rush of air hit me immediately, almost sending me flying. I steadied myself then took a firm grip of the inside of the window frame and cautiously felt above me for something to hold on to. There was something metal – I mean, the whole friggin' train was metal – a bar, a frame, enough for me to curl my fingers around. I pulled against it, testing its strength. It seemed okay. But *seemed* was hardly inspirational. What was inspirational was the gunshot that blasted through the door and smacked into the side of the carriage six inches from where I was standing.

I pulled myself up, and out, one foot still on the window ledge, the other scrabbling for a second grip as I dragged myself up the side of the train. I found one. I heaved again. All that work at the gym was paying off.

Whoooaah! and . . .

I was up, I was lying flat on the top of a speeding train, breathing hard, trying not to laugh.

Ridiculous.

Me, on a train, on the run.

Stupid. Freezing. Exhilarating. Petrifying.

What would Bruce Willis do?

He'd get a stunt man.

What would the stunt man do?

He'd check his insurance.

Third party, fire and locomotive.

Ahead was Dundalk. Beyond that the dark hills above Newry. There was no particular significance to making it across the border, besides the fact that God was more likely to be on my side, if he existed, and the fact that I'd not murdered anyone north of it recently. *If I could just stay up here* . . . but I had to *know*. Of course I had to know.

I made sure there was no tunnel in the immediate distance, then inched across to the edge again and peered cautiously back down at the toilet window. Sure enough. Jimmy the Chicken and Oil Paintings were crushed into the window frame, staring back along the line, trying to pick out my crushed or fleeing body.

They kept looking.

And looking.

They wouldn't stick their heads back in; every time I checked they were still gazing back down the line, as if the very fact of their interest might inspire me to pop up from a field and wave a broken arm back at them.

If they'd seen the same movies as I had they'd have known to look up top. But clearly they spent too much time on lesser pursuits like murder. I could just stay where I was for the rest of the journey. Just lie back and enjoy it. After all, I had a ticket. And it didn't say anywhere on it that you couldn't ride on the roof. I smiled. I rolled away from the edge, lay on my back and admired the sky. It wasn't half as cold lying flat like this, and it certainly gave an interesting perspective on the world, like sunbathing on a seventy-miles-an-hour lilo. I raised my hands to clasp them behind my head for a bit of added comfort, and as I did, one of my tins of beer rolled out. I scrambled after it, but too late, it was over the edge.

Deadly from fifteen feet and at seventy miles an hour.

There was a shout from below. I chanced a peek over. I saw Jimmy the Chicken clutching the back of his head, and met Oil Paintings' eyes. We stared at each other long enough for him to raise his gun and shoot at me.

Obviously, I ducked away.

Obviously, I cursed to high fucking hell at my own stupidity as the bullet whistled past.

What to do.

Jump.

Wait for them to climb up. Kick the guns out of their hands then wrestle with them to the death.

Uhuh.

I looked to the front of the train. I could get as far as the driver.

Then what? Hijack it? *Take me to Cuba.*

Fuck!

He would have a radio. He could call the police. They could be waiting to meet the train.

And arrest me. They'd have me back on board and haring down to Dublin before they could type *extradition.*

A hand appeared over the edge, searching for a grip.

It took hold where mine had. I stamped down on it and there was a shout, followed by a shot that came up through the roof and missed my thigh by centimetres. Okay, come on up then. I hurried along the roof, fighting to keep my balance. There was only a couple of feet between carriages, though it felt like a couple of hundred. I nearly lost it, then was across and moving as fast as I could.

I looked back. The hand was up searching for the grip again. I only had seconds. I lay down flat at the end of the carriage and peered over the side. The next toilet along. I was in luck. The window was slightly open. All the carriages were the same; I knew exactly where to place my hands to guide my descent down the side of the train. Another glance along the top: there were two hands up now, Jimmy the Chicken's hair blowing in the wind. In a moment he would see me. I looked forward.

A tunnel. Shit!

Only yards away.

But how wide? Jimmy's head was moving up.

I had to take the chance. I rolled over the side, holding fast on to the grips, but it still swept the air from my lungs. I held on for dear life as the train ploughed into the blackness of the tunnel. The wall was close, but there was just enough room to manoeuvre. My feet desperately sought out the gap in the window, missed, missed, then found it. I cautiously lowered myself, then bent, fraction by fraction so that I could open it further, aware that any overstretched arching of my back could bring it into contact with the wall of the tunnel at full belt and hurl me off to be crushed beneath the train's ferocious wheels.

But I did it.

Still in complete blackness, I dropped from the window ledge down on to the floor of the toilet.

I took a deep breath, then closed the window. As I turned away from it the train emerged suddenly from the tunnel and the toilet was instantly bathed in light.

I smiled at the elderly woman seated before me. Her habit was as black as her face was white. She blinked at me for several moments, then scrambled for the voluminous blue knickers that lay crumpled about her ankles.

I removed the other can of beer from my pocket and pressed it against my cheek. 'Beam me up, Scotty,' I said.

*   *   *

A lesser man would have slugged her, or at the very least poured scorn on her chosen profession, but I made hurried, sightly slurred excuses about the door lock being faulty, then deftly turned it while making a show of examining it. All the while she didn't say a word. Maybe it was shock. Maybe it was a vow. Maybe I didn't care. I opened the door, looked left, then right, then slipped back out into the corridor.

I hurried back along to my original seat. The girl with journalistic ambitions was still there. She looked up with a relieved smile.

'You took your time,' she said.

'Come with me,' I said.

Her brow furrowed. 'What . . . ?'

I walked on. I didn't look back, but I could hear her gathering up her bags. I waited between carriages. She bustled through, holding her shoe bags protectively before her. She was looking at me oddly. I turned and opened the door of the toilet.

'In here,' I said. She peered into the little room, but made no move. 'Quickly,' I said, 'we haven't much time.'

'I don't under—'

Before she had a chance to stop me I wrenched the shoe bags out of her hands and threw them through the door. 'Now . . .'

'Jesus,' she said. She rolled her eyes and stepped into the toilet. I followed after her and closed the door. I pulled the lock and turned to face her. She opened her mouth to protest but I put a finger to my lips and shushed her.

'Please,' I said, 'I need your help.'

'*My* help?' She looked uncertainly from me to the locked door and then back. 'I'm not *doing* anything just to get a story. If you so much as touch your zip I'll break your neck. I'm a brown belt in judo.'

I raised my hands and managed a smile. 'I believe you. If you were making it up you'd have said black belt.' She gave a hesitant smile. 'Look. I'm not trying to . . . Listen, there are two men on this train who're trying to kill me. Please help me.'

'On this . . . You mean the guys who . . . to do what?'

'Last time I saw them, they were on the roof . . .' She looked up. 'Yes, the roof . . . but now . . .' I took a deep breath. 'Anyone comes to this door, they'll find it locked. If they persist, you just shout *occupied*, tell them you might be a while.'

'How long do I have to stall them?'

'Until Belfast.'

'That's one hell of a long shite.'

'Well . . . tell them you're constipated or something.'

'That's none of their damn business.'

'That's the spirit.'

She smiled. 'Move a second,' she said.

I moved a little. She squeezed past and plumped herself down on the toilet. 'May as well get into the spirit of things,' she said, then added, 'Don't worry,

I'm not going to drop my drawers. If you think I'm standing to Belfast you've another think coming. I expect a full and frank interview, no bullshit, no payment, no demand to check my copy, world rights including electronic and a signed statement that you forced me to help you out in case you *are* guilty and the cops try to do me for aiding and abetting a murderer.'

'Okay,' I said. Then added, 'Thank you.'

'Thank *you*.'

'What for?'

'Kick-starting my illustrious career.'

I sat on the floor, my head against the window. The nice steady rhythm of the train against the back of my head served to dull my anxieties a little. I looked at her while she counted her shoe bags to make sure she had them all. It was barely five minutes since the last woman had sat before me on a toilet. This one was a lot younger, and much prettier. Her hair was tawny, her nose button, her complexion fair; there was a little gap between her two front teeth, which would have been handy for spitting through, if the need was ever to arise. I delved into my pocket and produced the remaining can of beer. I opened it and offered the first slurp to . . .

'I don't even know your name.'

'Patricia,' she said.

'Do you mind if I call you something else?'

21

'And that's it. In lurid detail.'

'I love lurid detail.'

'You'll go far. London, anyway. Papers here don't like lurid detail.'

I had told her my recent turbulent history. She peppered it with comments like, *crazy, tragic* and *God Almighty.* She wanted detail. Dates. Times. Descriptions. *Feelings,* for fuck sake. She was thorough. She sat on the toilet and fired off questions in my direction the way Jimmy the Chicken wanted to fire off bullets. I remained on the floor as the Belfast Express sped north. I told mostly the truth, and lies only when there was a danger of the truth casting me in a poor or unheroic light. Come to think of it . . .

It wasn't as if she was ever going to have the opportunity to print it. She wasn't writing anything down, she wasn't taping, it didn't matter if she had an elephant's memory, there was no record, and with no record there was no story. Nobody would print it.

She would have to buy a bag of potatoes and do it herself. But I enjoyed the process, it was therapeutic in a funny way, it enabled me to take a step back and examine the facts objectively, to analyse, to compute, to conclude that yes indeed, once again, I was floating in the river called Creek. But at least I wasn't alone. I had a new and sympathetic ally, prepared to lay down her life, or at least her shoes, to help a wronged man on the run.

We endured a brief hiccup in my story as someone tried the door, once, twice, three times. My companion finally gave an authentically tremulous 'I'll be a while,' as I lowered the window, ready to make a dive for it, but there was no response, and after a while we returned to our urgent whispering. It continued on through Dundalk, then Newry, Portadown and only tailed off as we pulled into Botanic Station. It was one stop short of the end of the line, but that was where Elaine's car was, and I needed it. Elaine was her middle name. Patricia Elaine Taylor. She was endearingly but impossibly cute in a wide-mouthed Julia Roberts heart-of-gold prostitute kind of a way. I could imagine dancing with her, but not making love; cutting a wedding cake, but not removing her underwear. Even in the direst situations I found myself thinking things like that about women. I presumed it was universal, a male thing; of course, I would never find out; as a species we don't talk about things like that. The closest we ever get is mentally filling in the survey in the six-month-old copy of

Cosmopolitan you find yourself reading because the butch girl next to you in the doctor's waiting room has already nabbed the only copy of *Autocar*.

We waited until everyone else who was getting off was off, then stepped out, as close to *one* as we could manage, Elaine with her umbrella already up but angled down, and me close in behind her. The little of me that was still sticking out was hidden by the half-dozen shoe bags. She moved the umbrella a fraction to allow me to scan the rest of the platform and the departing train. I thought I caught a glimpse of Oil Paintings looking our way, but I couldn't be sure. I moved a fraction closer to Elaine, just to be safe.

We walked slowly until the train disappeared from sight, then dashed along the platform and up the steep incline to where the collector took our tickets. Elaine, catching the first Dublin train that morning, had been able to park on Botanic Avenue, almost directly across from the station. I drummed my fingers on the roof of her Rover ('Dad's') as she fumbled in her handbag for the keys, looked apologetically up at me, then smiled as she located them.

She drove with as much speed as the traffic would allow. On a clear road Belfast Central was only five minutes away, but it took us twice that. She tried to pick up the loose threads of my story again as we drove, but I was too agitated. I didn't want to lose Jimmy the Chicken and Oil Paintings. I knew they were the key to it. Although I had no idea what *it* was. Elaine pulled up opposite Central Station, sitting on the brow of a hill overlooking the glass-fronted Waterfront concert hall to the right and the occasionally strife-torn Lower Ormeau Road to the left. There was a pedestrian exit just across the road, but our view of it was blocked by a red brick wall, erected to provide some shelter in the days of bombs and bullets and riots but never removed, although they'd had an entire month to do it.

We watched for several minutes. We recognised two or three passengers from the train scurrying into the fresh wind blowing off the mouth of the Lagan down below, but there was no sign of the terrible twosome.

I slapped the dashboard. 'What am I thinking? They might swagger about at home, but a Dub accent can still get you knifed up here if you wander into the wrong area. They're walking nowhere.'

She started the car again The taxi rank and station car park were at a lower level than the station, again hidden from view to protect the cars from hijacking. We drove up to the right, then turned against the traffic and sped down a slip road which ran past Maysfield Leisure Centre and finished in a dead end beside the car park. The taxi rank was opposite, sitting in the shadow of the station and just a couple of yards from a covered moving stairway which took passengers up to the main station, and the steps which they had to negotiate by themselves to get back down. There was a queue of half a dozen passengers waiting at the rank, with two others already ensconced in the back of a black taxi, which moved off as we came to a halt.

'They're probably long gone,' I said.

'Give it a chance,' Elaine said. 'They might've stopped off for a pint. Hard men do that, don't they?'

'Aye,' I snapped, 'you'd know.'

She looked a little hurt. There was no need for it. She was only trying to help. Nevertheless, I let it sit.

'As a matter of fact, I would know.' She reached across me and opened the glove compartment. As she delved inside she said, 'My dad used to be in the UDA.'

'Sorry,' I said, and smiled at the memory of it. 'So was mine. He attended one of those rallies where you pledged your loyalty to the Queen and you got a balaclava and a stick in return.'

'Oh – right,' she said, nodding, '*that* generation. My granny told me about that. She didn't think the balaclavas were knitted very well. Granda came home from work one day and she'd sewn a pom pom on to it. Nobody took him very seriously after that.'

I smiled. 'You make me feel like I'm about seventy.'

'Aren't you?'

We returned our attention to the taxi rank. Still nothing happening. Without looking at her I said, 'You're far too well spoken for your dad to have been in the UDA.'

'Well he was, for fifteen years.'

'In what capacity?'

She cleared her throat. 'Accountant.'

I snorted.

'It was important. Remember, they only got Al Capone for tax evasion.'

'You're suggesting the UDA are gangsters? That's shocking. Say that to their faces and you'll be up to your oxters in concrete. In the best interests of the Queen, of course.'

She smiled, then turned from the glove compartment brandishing a small disposable camera.

'Inch High Private Eye,' I said. 'You'll get fuck all with that from here,' I added knowledgeably, nodding across to the taxi rank.

'I know,' she said, and snapped me.

She wound it on. I said, 'It really is titchy. Can I see?'

She hesitated, then handed me the camera. I examined it carefully. Then rolled down the window and threw it out.

'What the hell are you doing?'

'Just following the instructions. Says *disposable* on the side. I have a predisposal to disposing of disposable cameras. If you get my drift.'

She had her hand on the door. 'That cost me five ninety-nine.'

'Leave it. I have full picture approval. It's in the small print of our contract. Plus, I'm incredibly vain.' She opened the door. 'I'm serious. Leave it.'

'It's *my* camera. I've other pictures on it. If you're

238

that worried about it, I promise I won't use yours.'

'Well, then I can relax.'

She started to climb out. I put a hand on her arm and pulled her back in.

'Great,' she said flatly. 'What're you going to do, kill me?'

'Ouch.' She sat where she was. 'Look,' I said, 'I really appreciate what you're doing for me. The car'n all. But I'd just prefer not to have my picture taken right now. I don't want you rushing into print before you have the full story.'

'I won't. I promise.'

I raised my eyebrows. She smiled. 'I know. But I really won't.'

She smiled, and always being the sucker, never the suckee, I sighed and relented. 'Okay.'

She got out of the car and bent to retrieve the camera. As she did I caught sight of Jimmy the Chicken and Oil Paintings coming chatting and smiling down the steps. Elaine looked up as I hissed her name, then followed my eyes. She'd never seen either of them before, of course, but she could tell instantly. My bug eyes and white face gave it away.

She stood, clutching the camera, then walked towards the taxi rank.

I hissed again, but if she heard, she ignored me. *What the hell is she . . .?*

Elaine joined the back of the taxi queue, directly behind Jimmy the Chicken and Oil Paintings. They smiled round at her. She smiled back, then examined her camera. Her brow furrowed. She looked through one side, then the other, then held it up to her ear. Jimmy the Chicken and Oil Paintings were watching her, smirking. They said something to her, she laughed, she looked at the camera again, she held it up to them, Jimmy took it off her, looked through the lens, then ran his fingers along the top of it and pointed at something. He handed it to Oil Paintings, who looked where Jimmy had pointed, then looked through the lens at Elaine, who smiled as he took her picture; he then ran the film on and handed it back to Elaine, again pointing at something. She smiled expansively, said something else, both of my enemies then laughed; Jimmy put his arm round Oil Paintings, they both raised their thumbs and put on say-cheese smiles. Elaine took their picture. They all laughed together. Three taxis in succession pulled up. The first two were quickly filled; Oil Paintings opened the door of the third and tried to usher Elaine in; she shook her head and raised her hands. Jimmy the Chicken tried to insist, but she stood her ground, waved them into their taxi, then stood patiently waiting for the next one while they drove off, waving back at her.

The instant they turned up past Maysfield she ran back to the car and dived into the driver's seat.

'At least they weren't vain,' she grinned as she gunned the engine, then took off in pursuit of the black taxi. I shook my head and tutted. 'Listen, mate,' she said, 'I have a photo of them and I know where they're going. What do you have apart from *Most Wanted* tattooed on your forehead?'

'I have . . . you,' I said wearily. 'A lunatic.'

'It takes two to tango.'

'So where *are* we going?'

'Malone Road.'

'Shit.' I had a dread feeling about the Malone Road.

'What?'

'Nothing. Just follow.'

'If we're going to be partners, you better tell me what you mean by *shit*.'

I sighed. 'We're not partners. I don't have to tell you anything.'

She indicated, then pulled in sharply. There was a blast of horns from behind. Elaine ignored it, content merely to glare across at me. 'Do you want to get out of the car now?'

'Be serious.'

'I am bloody serious. I'm putting my neck on the line for you, the least you can do is show a little appreciation.'

'I appreciate what you're doing.'

'More than that.'

'I really appreciate what you're doing.'

'We're losing them.'

'Then drive.'

'Then promise.'

'Then promise what?'

'To tell me what you're doing, what you're thinking.'

'What's the point? Don't you have a home to go to? Won't Daddy be worried about you?'

'He'll be worried about his car.'

I sighed. Fair point. We were both keeping an eye on the black taxi, now at traffic lights halfway up the Ormeau Road, waiting to turn right into Donegall Pass. We knew they were going to Malone Road, and I'd a fair idea which house. But it would be helpful to be sure. The lights changed, the taxi moved forward.

'Okay,' I said. 'Just follow them.'

'Tell me.'

I rolled my eyes. 'If you absolutely bloody insist, the woman who runs the Horse Whisperer lives on the Malone Road. Somehow they've managed to track her down.'

'Okay.'

She indicated, but suddenly inspired, I put a hand on the wheel. 'One thing.'

'What?'

'Will you let me drive?'

'What's wrong with my driving?'

'Nothing, I . . . just like to feel in control.'

'We're going to lose them.'

'Not if I'm driving.'

She blew air out of her cheeks. 'Bloody *men*.'

'Think of the story. Concentrate on that. Front page. By Elaine Taylor.'

'*Patricia* Taylor.'

'Exactly. Let me drive.'

She slapped the wheel in exasperation. 'Okay. *Okay!* You bloody drive. Just don't try anything funny.'

I gave her a pained 'Like what?' as she opened her door and scooted around the back.

I locked my own door, then slipped into the driver's seat, pulling the door she'd left open for me shut. She pulled at the passenger door, once, twice, then knocked on the window. Her face appeared at it, followed by a misty little circle as she said urgently, 'It's locked.'

I reached across and she stood back to let me open it, but instead I rolled down the window a fraction. 'Sucker,' I said.

I closed the window again, locked my own door, then indicated and pulled out. There was something that sounded suspiciously like a kick against the passenger door panel as I moved off, but I didn't stop.

Fifty yards up the road I checked the mirror to make sure she was far enough back, then pulled in. I grabbed hold of the shopping bags full of her precious shoes. I moved across to the passenger door, opened it, then set them carefully down on the pavement. I glanced back. She was running.

The door was closed and I was back out in the traffic again before she got anywhere near. When I checked the mirror again she was standing in the midst of her bags, angrily giving me the finger.

I had stolen her car, but I preferred to think of it as saving her life.

22

I spent an hour and a half watching the house from the safety of Patricia Elaine Taylor's father's car, during which a pleasant early evening had begun to slip into autumnal night. There was a crispness to the air and a half-moon in the sky. There was the possibility of frost. There was a high pressure area building up over the Azores, and Mallen Head was expecting a force nine gale. You can listen to too much weather on the radio. I searched the dial for news but kept managing to miss it; I heard the weather. Again and again. And again.

For the first hour I saw no movement, then halfway through the second the merest glimpse of Oil Paintings as he pulled the curtains in the front lounge. A dull light appeared around the edges of the window. I took a deep breath, nearly choked on one of the barley sugars I had liberated from a bag in the glove compartment, then got out of the car and followed the perimeter wall around to the back of the house.

It was low enough to peer over. Satisfied that nobody was watching, I pulled myself up and over and hurried across the grounds. I skirted the tennis court and swimming pool, then headed for the stables. The door was slightly open and I could see that the interior was lit by a single low-wattage bulb. There was movement within, but it was horse movement. I slipped inside and walked slowly past the half-dozen stalls, making clicking sounds to the horses within, checking to see if by any chance any of them was Dan the Man. Of course, none of them were. Or all of them were. They were brown horses in a bad light. I hadn't a clue. I moved out of the stables, and towards the house.

I entered from the rear, shinning up a pipe and making a dive for a half-open window.

In truth it wasn't the most dangerous leap. There was a sloping and overgrown grass bank behind me to break my fall, if required. But I held on to the ledge and dragged myself in. I lowered myself down on to a carpet and knelt there for several minutes.

As my eyes grew accustomed to the dark, and with the faint assistance of the handily placed moon, I realised that I was standing in what must once have been Mandy's room. There were framed photographs of her on the wall, stretching from when she was not much more than a toddler to her later teenage years. There were four factors common to them all. A riding helmet. A horse. A rosette. And her proud mother. There was make-up on a dressing table and a poster of Frankie Dettori pinned to the door of a wardrobe. There were clothes in the wardrobe, and underwear in the dresser. I was thinking about the nature of sexual fantasy and the bizarre paths along which it can lead you when I was suddenly stopped in my tracks by a low, agonised groan from below. The sort that sends a chill through your bones.

I went to the door and peered out. The hall was in darkness. I padded along it. I came to the room where Hilda had shown me the Horse Whisperer set-up. I tried the door. It was unlocked. I opened it and slipped in, then closed it behind me. I chanced turning on the light. I blinked against the brightness for a moment, then switched it off again. The room was empty. No computers, no faxes, no gossip, no Horse Whisperer.

At the end of the hall I looked over the banister. The stairs and downstairs hall were partially lit by light emanating from the half-open door of the lounge. I could see shadows dancing on the walls. Although not, of course, *dancing*. Or if they were, it was some kind of surreal torture tango. Another hideous groan. I shuddered. I'd had no idea of what I might find in Hilda's mansion. All I knew was that she had used me. Quite possibly she had betrayed me. At the back of my mind there'd been a hint of a suspicion that she might somehow have been in league with Jimmy the Chicken, Oil Paintings and the mysteriously absent Dry Cleaner, that there had been some dispute between her and Geordie over money and she was using me in some bizarre fashion to try and flush it out, but the screams of terror and pain and despair that were coming from that room knocked any such suspicions of collaboration well into touch.

They were killing her.

I sat on the bottom step.

'Tell us, you fucking old hoor.'

A hiss. Like . . . *steam*?

A scream.

'Where's the fucking money, you cunt?'

'Tell us!'

A hiss. Like . . . an *iron*?

A terrible juddery involuntary scream.

Then laughter. A horribly sadistic snigger. 'Look at the fuckin' shape of that!'

'Girlie, we're doing a fucking map of the world on yer tits.'

Hiss. Scream.

'Tell us!'

'Noooooooooooo!'

Hiss. Scream.

Silence.

'Get some water.'

I flattened myself against the stairs, but kept my head raised just enough to see the door open further and Oil Paintings emerge. Beyond him Jimmy the Chicken stood with an iron in his hand. He raised his other hand, then slapped it downwards. I heard flesh meet flesh. 'Come on, you stupid bitch, wake up.' Then he tutted, stepped back and set the iron on a sideboard. He pulled out a cigarette and lit it. He moved out of my line of sight and I saw Hilda for the first time.

I will never forget that vision of torment.

What had she been? A beautiful woman in upper middle age. Proud. Determined. Angry. Vengeful. What was it my mother used to say? Full of *vim*. And that was back in the days when the only vim I knew was the brand name of the scouring powder she used to clean the toilets.

But now.

Naked. Her arms bound behind her. Her legs deliberately spread for the maximum humiliation, then tied to the legs of the chair. But she could cope with that. She was strong. But no one could cope with . . .

Her flesh was melting. Great welts of dripping, corrupted skin hung bloody from her chest. Around those horrific wounds her ribs were clearly visible, pressing outwards as if trying to escape. The arms were blotched and burned. Her legs. They'd been at her for some time. I'd been listening to the weather forecast in the car while they'd been pressing her. Her head was slumped down, her grey hair tangled and dank with sweat. There was a damp patch on the carpet beneath her, urine on her legs.

There were footsteps to my left, and Oil Paintings came back along the hall carrying a pint glass full of water. He re-entered the lounge and pushed the door closed behind him.

There was a splash and a groan and a gloating 'Now where were we?'

I cursed silently.

What's the plan, Dan?

Call the police. I would give myself up for this. Everyone would. But it would be too late. They'd be gone and Hilda would be dead long before they arrived.

What to do, what to fucking do!

I looked desperately about me. Horses . . . *horses*? Hilda was into horses, and half of those into horses are also into the hunting, the shooting and the fishing. It was part of the lifestyle. They went hand in hand. Guns. For hunting. Somewhere in the house. But where? It was massive. There'd be a gun room, somewhere . . . but locked. Keys . . . keys?

There was another yell and a barely audible 'Please . . .'

Frig. There wasn't time.

A weapon. Anything.

The kitchen. A knife. A *carving* knife.

Take a run at them, stab, stab, stab, hope for the best.

I moved cautiously off the stairs, then quickly along the hall and down the corridor leading to the kitchen. The door was three quarters closed but Oil Paintings had left the light on. I hurried through and crossed directly to the drawers underneath the sink. I carefully pulled the first open.

Behind me, a voice said: 'Looking for something?'

My heart stopped. Then started. I turned slowly.

Sitting at the breakfast counter, a forkful of pasta in one hand, a gun in the other, a microwave meal before him, was Dry Cleaner.

I sighed. He smiled. 'Not in enjoying the fun?' I asked.

'Nah. Puts me off my dinner.' He put the pasta in his mouth, then set down the fork. 'Jimmy said he saw you on the train,' he said between chews.

'I didn't see you.'

'Oh no. He sent me on ahead. To do a recce and buy the iron.'

'You *bought* the iron?'

'Oh yeah. Much better value up here. It's the exchange rate.'

'I mean . . . why not just use hers . . . ?'

'Women like this, more money than sense, they send their clothes out to be done. Keeps me in business! Besides. I needed a new one for the shop. Killing two birds with one stone, so to speak. You can put the knife back any time you want.'

I put the knife I'd slipped into my sleeve back into the drawer.

'What now?' I said.

'I should think that's fucking obvious.'

I nodded. I was going to get ironed.

I was tied to a chair. A cheap wooden effort of the type you stand on to change light bulbs, while Hilda was secured to a much superior aluminium number that had once sat around her dining table. She looked at me with a kind of vague recognition. Her eyes were flecked with blood and there was saliva dribbling out of her mouth. I said, 'I'm sorry . . .' across to her, but there was no reaction.

'You will be,' said Oil Paintings.

Dry Cleaner stayed with his pasta. Oil Paintings marched me in. Jimmy the Chicken laughed his head off when he saw me, then decked me. My eye was already swollen and closed by the time they both came to stand in front of me, but that didn't bother me. What did was the iron with the slivers of crisped flesh hanging from it which Jimmy was brandishing.

'So,' Jimmy said, 'about this money?'

'I don't know anything about— Don't, don't, don't . . .' The iron was an inch from my trouser leg. It is a well-documented fact that I can stand anything but bad reviews and pain. 'Just don't. Please. Ask me anything. Better still, let me volunteer everything I know.'

Jimmy laughed. 'You know,' he said, then nodded at Hilda, 'she's a better man than you are.'

'I know.'

'She didn't give us shit for two hours. She's fucking dying and you'd give it all up as soon as the room temperature goes up a degree.'

I shrugged helplessly. 'What can I say?'

'Everything,' Oil Paintings said, stepping forward, 'that includes the word money.'

'I don't know anything about—'

Oil Paintings grabbed my hand. I bunched it into a fist. He squeezed the little finger tight and I opened up. Jimmy brought the iron down on my palm with a delighted laugh and I jerked back in agony . . . *Jesusjesusjesusjesusfuckfuckfuck* . . .

'Now where the fuck is it!' Oil Paintings screamed.

'There is none!' I bellowed.

'Of course there is! Where is it!'

'I swear to God!'

Jimmy stood back up and glared down at me. He spat on to the base of the iron and it hissed. Hilda gave a low groan. 'What do you mean?'

'I . . .' I looked from one to the other. I looked at my hand. The flesh was bubbling. *Fuck!* 'Water . . . please . . .'

Jimmy thought for a moment, then nodded at Oil Paintings. He snarled, then lifted what was left in the pint glass and threw it over my hand. I shuddered again.

'Now,' Jimmy snapped, standing over me again, 'talk or melt.'

As threats go, it was right up there in the top one.

I took a deep breath. There was nothing to lose by telling them what little I knew, and a life, possibly two, to be gained.

'I don't know anything about money— Wait, wait, wait! Let me finish!' Jimmy hesitated. 'Just let me finish. I've been working for *her*, but besides some loose change there's never been any money about the place. I know youse have all fallen out over some scam or something, but whatever money's been ripped off you, it's either gone . . . or it's in a horse.'

'What the fuck are you talking about?'

'You've heard of Dan the Man?'

'Of course we've—'

'There's your money.'

'Talk sense, cunto.'

'Okay. Listen. Listen. He's running in the Grand National, day after tomorrow, right? Owned by Geordie McClean, Irish American Racing, right?'

'Right.'

'He's her ex-husband.'

'We know this, what the fuck has this got to do—'

'The horse is worth millions if it goes to stud, right?' Jimmy and Oil Paintings nodded warily. 'But there's this dispute over who owns it, right? The way I see it, Geordie gave Hilda the horse as a gift, to try and win her back, but maybe volunteered to train him up . . . Meanwhile, okay, meanwhile . . . Hilda's boyfriend managed to lose whatever money he ripped off youse, so Hilda needed cash to pay off his debts. Okay? With me?'

'We're not fucking stupid,' Oil Paintings hissed.

'Okay . . . So she's no money, can't shift a white elephant like this fucking house, so all she has is Dan the Man. Only Geordie's been training him all this time and has realised how good a horse he actually is and won't hand him over.'

'Is this going somewhere?' Oil Paintings growled.

'Shhhh,' Jimmy the Chicken said, 'go on.'

'So big fight. Now if Hilda knows her name's on the paperwork, there's nothing to stop her going to court. But if it's joint names, then it's a bit murkier. She also knows that whatever Dan the Man's worth at stud, it'll double or triple if he wins the National. Plus . . . plus, you ready for this?' They nodded. I prepared to draw one of the women I loved into their sights. 'Hilda's also having a bit of a tug of love with Geordie over their daughter . . .'

'This is getting like fucking *Emmerdale*, Jimmy,' Oil Paintings whined.

'Shhhh,' Jimmy said again.

'She's a jockey as well,' I continued, 'but Geordie's never really going to let her ride in the National like he promised, so Hilda bargains her help for a free ride on Dan the Man in the big race.'

Jimmy's brow furrowed. 'You mean *her* daughter *stole* Dan the Man from Geordie McClean,' Jimmy said, ponderously, 'so that she could ride it in the National. And she's hoping to treble the asking price when it comes to stud.'

'Succinctly summarised,' I said.

Jimmy looked across at Hilda. 'Is that the way it is?' he asked. There was a drip of saliva, but no other response.

'So,' I said, pushing my luck, 'if you wait until the National's over, Hilda'll be flush and you can get your money back. I'm sure she'll give you interest. And expenses.'

Jimmy nodded. 'So where would the daughter be now?'

I shrugged. 'On the way to Aintree, I suppose.'

Jimmy looked at Oil Paintings. 'Liverpool ferry,' said Oil Paintings. 'Direct route.'

'So, uhm,' I said, 'you can let us go now.'

He smiled down at me. 'Now what the fuck would I want to do that for?'

'Because . . . well. I told you how to, ahm, get your money back.'

He came a little closer. He spoke more quietly, but somehow the threat seemed greater. He put his left hand over my burned one, and each time he made a point, he gave it a little squeeze. 'Well, Dan Starkey, Horse Whisperer, whoever the fuck you are, it's like this. Much as I would love to hang around until fuck knows when, that's not really very practical. Y'see, I'm a betting man. I know my horses. I know my jockeys and I know my fucking courses. Now Dan the Man's a good horse, sure he'll maybe fetch half a million at stud, but he's not a great horse, which is what you need to win the National. It's the hardest fucking course in the world. Not only do you need a great horse, but you need a fucking great jockey as well, not some little girl's barely run a race in her life and's only up there because Mummy promised her. See?'

I nodded. He squeezed again. I held in the scream as best I could.

'I'll tell you what'll happen. That girl will think

she's doing okay right up to Becher's Brook, she tries to get him over that fuckin' fence she'll not only break her own neck, but more importantly, she'll break Dan the Man's as well. And then Dan the fucking Man will be worth exactly *nothing*. So where'll our money be then?'

'I . . .'

'It'll be off to the knacker's, won't it?' I nodded. 'Like I say, I'm a betting man, and I'll give you this tip for nothing, don't bet on Dan the Man even starting that race on Saturday. I'll take my half a million now, thanks very much.' He nodded at Oil Paintings. 'C'mon,' he said, 'we've a ferry to catch.'

Oil Paintings grinned at him, and turned for the door. As Jimmy the Chicken went to follow I said, in retrospect stupidly, 'What about us?'

Jimmy paused. 'Good point,' he said. Abruptly he shivered. 'Is it my imagination,' he asked, 'or is it cold in here?'

I looked to Oil Paintings. 'No, right enough,' he said, 'it is a bit nippy.'

'Okay,' said Jimmy, smiling down at me, 'why don't we light a fire?'

23

Maybe it was the intense heat, or the overpowering smell of burning petrol, or maybe the crack of the windows as they exploded; whatever it was, it brought Hilda round. Her head moved slowly up and her red eyes surveyed the inferno with a kind of resigned relief. She had been tortured to within an inch of death, and now it was coming anyway. The house was burning around us, the bad guys were away, it was all going to end. There was nothing left to say.

Except there was, of course.

Her eyes settled on me. As they did, I looked away. I was going to die, and die secure in the knowledge that although I had come to first rescue, then chastise Hilda for betraying me, I had instead failed miserably to save her then managed to betray her daughter to the bad guys. Killed two birds with one stone, even. My only hope was that Hilda was so far gone she wouldn't be aware of it. I looked up at her again. A melted woman with her legs spread. Her eyes were hard and alive and burning into me with as much vigour and vim as the flames that were now licking across the floor toward us.

'You . . . told . . . them . . .'

'I had to, Hilda.'

'You . . . have . . . killed . . . my *daughter* . . .'

'This isn't the time to be scoring points, Hilda, but you might have told me.'

There was a loud crack from above and I ducked down as best as I could as part of the ceiling fell away, crashing to the floor behind me and momentarily dousing the flames that had crept as far as the base of my chair.

I tugged at the ropes, but they were expertly tied. In a movie we would have shuffled our chairs across the floor, got them back to back and then untied each other before making a dramatic charge through the flames as the building crashed around us. Except we would have been younger and better-looking, my companion would not have been hideously scarred and I would not have been on the verge of tears.

The flames were at the base of her chair and were beginning to bite into her legs.

'You . . . have . . . to . . . save . . . her . . .'

'Hilda . . . oh Jesus . . .'

Her legs were on fire. Her whole body was shaking.

'You . . . have . . . to . . .'

'Hilda. Fuck sake!'

'Please!'

'Hilda . . . Hilda . . .'

She was burning alive.

She *screammmmmmmmmmmed* . . .

I screamed.

And then she was burning dead.

Oh fuck! I prayed to every god there has ever been. A second section of the ceiling gave way and crashed down on to Hilda, knocking her backwards and engulfing her completely in the flames.

She was gone.

Swallowed up.

Consumed.

It was closing in on all sides. I looked down. The legs of my chair were burning. I could keep my feet raised, but for how long before they too were alight?

Seconds.

Face it, Starkey, you're toast. Just as you like it, black.

I could feel my arse burning through the seat of the chair.

And then *snap* and *thump* as the cheap legs of the chair gave way and I was suddenly on my arse on the red-hot floor. The sudden collapse had extinguished the flames closest to the chair, but the reprieve only lasted for brief moments. As they bloomed again I was fleetingly in a position to make use of them. The pause in their intensity and my position on the ground allowed me to stretch my wrists back into the fire without burning the rest of me first.

I held them there . . . one, two, three . . . Jesussssss! Then back out. I strained against the smouldering rope, but it wouldn't give. I plunged my wrists back into the flames again, screaming as they burned into my flesh . . . hold it, hold it, hold it! The rope was on fire, it must, it must . . . I pulled hard and it snapped suddenly.

My hands were free. I rubbed my wrists against my jacket for relief from the pain, then turned my attention to the rope holding my feet together. Another crash from above sprayed me with burning shards of wood. Then they were free and I was up.

I looked about me desperately. Which way? *Which way!*

To the door, stupid. No, to the window.

Sheets of flaming death, either way.

Just get fucking out!

I closed my eyes. I put my jacket over my head. I screamed and I ran into the flames.

I was hissing in the swimming pool.

I was smouldering and black, and after a fashion, alive. Hilda's mansion was crashing in the background. There were sirens. I cried tears of relief and anger, but not for long.

I dragged myself reluctantly out of the pool and limped away across the lawns to the perimeter wall. I barely had the strength to pull myself over it. I sat bedraggled on the crisp grass on the other side, breathing hard, alternately cursing and praising God.

I ducked down behind a tree as the first of a series of fire engines sped past.

When it was clear, I tumbled down the bank and hurried along to where I'd left the car. I could see in the distance a police car sitting with flashing lights close to the entrance to Hilda's mansion, and a cop trying to hold back the small crowd of onlookers who'd come to enjoy the spectacle.

I'd left the keys hanging from the branch of a tree overhanging the footpath beside the car, but it took several minutes to discover *which* branch.

I got them, opened the car door and slipped in behind the wheel. As I put them into the ignition a hand landed on my shoulder and I jumped, banging my head off the roof.

'Nice fire,' a familiar voice said.

I turned to look at Mouse in the back seat. 'Jesus wept,' I said.

'Nice to see you too, Danny boy.' He leant forward out of the darkness. His familiar oval face and perky smile.

I should have kissed him, but: 'What the fuck are you doing here?' had to suffice.

'As your luck would have it, a wee doll stormed into the office trying to sell me an exclusive about a journalist on the run and all sorts of murder and mayhem in the horsey world. I put two and two together and got you.'

'So where is she now?'

'Typing.'

I sat back and sighed. I was hurting. 'Are you going to run . . . ?'

'No, of course not. How much of it is true?'

'Off the record and allowing for standard female journalistic exaggeration?' He nodded. 'Oh, about a hundred per cent.' I started the engine. It was agony to turn it with my burnt hand.

Mouse couldn't help but notice the agonised expression. 'Do you want me to drive?' he asked.

'Yes,' I said, never the brave soldier. He squeezed forward between the seats as soon as I'd moved across to the other side. As he reached beneath the seat to move it to a better position he glanced across at the fire. 'I hope she's insured,' he said.

'She's dead.'

'Oh. God.'

'I know.' I glanced at the clock on the dash. Nine thirty. 'What time's the last sailing of the Liverpool ferry?'

'What am I, Captain Birdseye?'

'*Mouse.*'

'Ten, I think. What's—'

'Then get this fucking wagon moving. The big place where the boats are.'

'The docks.'

'That'll do.'

He got into gear and pulled out. Another fire engine was arriving. 'Do you want to tell me what went on in there?' Mouse asked.

'No. Just watch the road.'

'Swell. How is it you tell a wee girl not long out of school all the facts, but you don't think of confiding in me?' I looked at him. 'On second thoughts, don't answer that. It's glaringly obvious.'

I smiled through the pain barrier. 'If you would just lose the 'tache.'

He shook his head, and drove. The docks were less than ten minutes away. As he drove I said, 'You didn't think of coming in and rescuing me or anything?'

'I'm a watcher, not a doer, Dan, you know that.'

'So what did you see?'

'Three guys leaving in a car. Then four guys following the three guys.'

'Tell me about the four guys.'

'They were Oriental.'

'Certain?'

'They were pulling rickshaws.'

'Fair enough.'

He wasn't the sort to jump lights. If he was really pushed he might rev the engine a bit. I drummed my fingers on the dash and cursed at him. He gave me a lot of guff about doing his best and and how it wouldn't help anyone if we were both flattened by a lorry or stopped by the cops. He didn't *understand*, but there was nothing I could do.

He said: 'I'm here for you, aren't I? How many of your other friends are here? Come to think of it . . .'

'Just step on it.'

'I'll step on you.'

He did increase the speed a little. He went through

two lights in a row on amber and stopped indicating when he was overtaking pensioners. In his own mind he was probably Mad Max.

He said, once, with real feeling, 'Are you okay?'

I nodded. 'I'm never having another barbecue again.'

For no sane reason he said, 'I saw Trish the other night.'

'Oh.'

'She was having an argument with some guy with a beard. He slapped her and got thrown out of the pub for his trouble.'

'I hope you went after him and killed him.'

'No, Dan, I'm a—'

'Watcher, not a doer. So what else did you see?'

'Them hugging each other, later. It warms the cockles of your heart.'

'I'm going to warm his cockles over the fucking—'

The ferry. Up ahead. Brilliantly lit. And pulling out.

'Fuck!' said Mouse, slapping the wheel.

'Fuck!' I said, slapping the dash.

We screeched to a halt.

Actually, we indicated and pulled over, braking gently a hundred yards short of the entrance to the ferry terminal. And he didn't say *fuck*, he said *flip*. I had a best friend who said *flip* and wouldn't break the speed limit even if it was a case of life or death. Even when it was more than that. It was life *and* death. I got out of the car and kicked one of the tyres. A security guard checking vehicles in the short-stay car park opposite looked over. I ignored him.

Mouse got out and stood beside me. 'Sorry,' he said, kicking another tyre, although relatively gently, and glaring critically at the car, 'more power in a fart.'

I nodded. What was the point?

We sat on the bonnet. The docks had been transformed in recent years. They were bright and modern and there were restaurants and bars and live entertainment nearby, where previously they'd been dark and dilapidated and there'd been live ammunition. And I kind of liked them the old way. There was something romantic about the abandoned warehouses, the bricked-up terraces and the dank streets, particularly when you'd lost your virginity around here, thanks to three bottles of cider and a pasty supper. Particularly when her name was Patricia.

She let men slap her, then hugged them.

Me, she slapped back.

I loved her still, but now there was someone else. For both of us.

The ferry was already fading from sight. It was modern, all enclosed. It had a McDonald's and a four-star restaurant and a kids' club and there was *no smoking*. I'd only ever been on the old one where smoking was compulsory and hot and cold running vomit was virtually guaranteed.

'Remember the old ferries?' Mouse asked. 'Hot and cold running boke. They were disgusting.'

I smiled. 'Great minds think alike.'

'Fools seldom differ.' He sighed. 'So who's on the ferry?'

'Hilda's daughter. Three hoods, four Chinamen and a horse called Dan. It's not serious. I just don't want her killed.'

'Patricia hears, she will be.'

I shrugged. 'Patricia can go fuck—'

And then stood stunned as my eyes fell on a Land Rover and horse box emerging from the short-stay car park. It paused for just a moment at a junction at the end of the slip road to allow another car to pass by, then turned right towards the exit from the ferry terminal; but a moment was all I needed to get a clear glimpse of Mandy at the wheel.

24

'I can't, Dan. I told the wife I was only popping out for a few pints after work. We have guests for dinner. If I phone her from Scotland she'll murder me. Especially after last time.'

'What happened last time?'

'You and me. Cannes. I was in bed, for Christ sake. I told her I'd forgotten to lock up and went downstairs and out the door and drove to the airport in my pyjamas.'

'There's an airport in your pyjamas?'

'Stop it. I was in France a week. Mind you, I think it was Tuesday before she noticed.'

We looked at the ferry. Different ferry. Different port. Larne. Twenty miles up the coast, two hours across choppy waters to Stranraer. The long way round. Mandy had just driven the horse box up and on to the ship. I was at the desk paying for my ticket with Mouse's money. I promised to pay him back. I was lying. He said it didn't matter. He was lying. Our friendship has existed on that basis for many years. He handed me the ticket and said, 'Dan, you should learn to say no.'

'I say no all the time.'

'Aye. *No, don't shoot me. No, I didn't do it.* I mean, in the first place. You should do your job and go home at night and put your feet up.'

'I've nothing to put my feet up *on*, Mouse.'

'That'll change. You two will get back together again.'

'Aye, they said that about Burton and Taylor.'

'They *did* get back together.'

'Aye, for about an hour. Then he died and she joined the cast of *The Flintstones*.'

'But what an hour it was.' He sighed. He gave me some more money. I thanked him. He said, 'Don't waste it. Buy something nutritional.' I nodded. We shook hands like adults and then I turned for the ferry.

'Dan,' he called after me. I turned. 'Yabba-dabba,' he said.

'Yabba-dabba.'

It was cold and dark outside. I went up the plank. It wasn't a plank, of course. It was like boarding an aircraft. I did a quick tour. I bought a McDonald's strawberry milkshake and then went to the news-agent and asked for a packet of Opal Fruits. The girl looked at me and I groaned and said, 'Starburst.' She nodded and lifted them off the shelf. 'They used to be called Opal Fruits,' I said. 'They changed the name because the Americans call their Opal Fruits "Starburst".'

'Oh,' she said.

'And do you know why they call them Starburst?'

'No.'

'Because the astronauts took them into space. Existed on them. They're packed with fruit juice. There's a dozen square meals in this packet, and all for just thirty-two pence.'

'Thirty-five.'

I handed her the money. 'You're okay. You're young. You don't remember. The glory days of Marathons and Pacers and Toblerones.'

'We still have Toblerones.'

'Yes, but they're the size of fuck all. Used to be you'd break your teeth on them. Like Wagon Wheels.'

'You couldn't break your teeth on a Wagon Wheel. They're soft.'

Behind me a man in a blue tracksuit said, 'No, I know what he means, Wagon Wheels used to be huge.'

I looked from him to the shop assistant and sighed. 'Maybe they still are. Maybe we just got bigger.'

We all nodded sagely for several moments, then she gave me the change from fifty pence and I went looking for Mandy and the horse with my name. If she was concerned about Dan the Man she'd stick close, so unless they'd started letting horses meander the decks, the obvious place to start was down below. I went down to the car deck and started looking.

It didn't take long. There were three Land Rovers, three horse boxes, but only one had Bosco Brown drinking vodka up front. The window was an inch open and there was a trail of cigarette ash along the top of it. He was singing along to 'All Kinds of Everything' by Dana. I remembered her winnning the Eurovision Song Contest with it when I was a kid. She also had a hit with 'Something's Cookin' in the Kitchen'. She had a lot to answer for, but now that she was a member of the European Parliament she probably wouldn't have to, and get well paid for it. I peered through the window. Bosco had his eyes closed. I satisfied myself that there was no gun in his hands, then banged hard on the glass. He jumped, his eyes wide and darting around until they settled on me and he uttered a tremulous 'Don't hurt me.'

'Relax,' I said. He didn't. I realised he'd barely had a glimpse of me before, back at Geordie McClean's when he was stealing Dan the Man, so probably he didn't know who I was, and was thinking the worst. 'I'm just looking for Mandy,' I said, as jauntily as I could. 'She up top?'

If it was his life or her life, he chose her life and nodded. I left him to soak. I took another tour of the upper deck. It was crowded with football fans going to a European qualifier in Glasgow. Their scarves were red, white and blue and they sang about being up to their necks in Fenian blood. It was all good clean family fun. I spotted Mandy sitting alone with two drinks at a table in a corner of one of the bars, trying to ignore the chants of the football supporters packed around the beer pumps behind her.

I slipped into the chair opposite. 'Hello, stranger,' I said.

She didn't seem surprised to see me. 'Hello, Dan,' she said after a while.

'You don't seem surprised.'

She held up a mobile phone. 'Bosco called. I got you a drink.' She nodded at one of the glasses in front of her.

I lifted it and took a drink. Then I rubbed a thumb across my lower lip. 'So let me get this straight. You took off in pursuit of your kidnapped horse, or horsenapped horse for that matter, and tracked it to the Glasgow Rangers True Blue Fuck the Pope Supporters Club. So what do they plan to do, stick King Billy on Dan the Man on Saturday?'

'No, Dan.'

'Damn. Okay. Let me have another go. You took me to bed either as an alibi or to make sure I was offside while Inch High whacked Derek. All that shit about *oh I'm so unattractive* and *oh I'm so ugly* was just a delaying tactic to get Dan the Man out of there.'

'You catch on slow.'

'It didn't mean anything to you?'

'What did you expect?'

She looked away. A shadow of something crossed

her face. I shrugged. I took another drink. 'Fair enough,' I said as I put the glass down. 'And by the way, your mum's dead.'

There was a sudden explosion of 'The Sash' from the bar.

We walked around the boat until we found an empty corner of a lounge, behind a bank of one-armed bandits, and only then did she collapse against me. I hugged her to me and she cried and cried and cried. When, eventually, I told her what had happened, I spared her the details. I left in Oil Paintings, Jimmy the Chicken and Dry Cleaner and left out their free ironing service; I left in the fire and left out the horrific manner of her death. She asked faltering questions and I told only the truth, except when I was lying.

Gradually, gradually, she came round. She said, 'I'm sorry for being horrible to you. I was just trying to remain . . . *focused*.'

'The race?'

She nodded vaguely. 'It all seems so irrelevant now.'

'Or even more important.'

She smiled weakly. 'We were just having fun, fucking Dad around. No. That's not fair. It wasn't fun. We were serious. He messed us around and we were taking revenge. It was a little bit dangerous, but it was also the most exciting thing I've ever done. An adventure. But now . . .' She wiped at her eyes. She stared at the floor. I raised her head and kissed her on the lips.

'I'm sorry,' I said. After a little I asked softly, 'So who does own the horse with my name?'

She reached into her jacket pocket and produced a dozen sheets of folded A4. 'Read for yourself.'

I read. I nodded and *hmmmed*.

She could see I was lost. She took them off me and folded them back into her pocket. 'I do.'

I nodded. Like I'd figured, more or less.

'Seventeenth birthday present. From my dad. Another attempt to buy me.' She gave a little laugh. 'Worked, too. Love that horse.'

'So why all the . . . ?'

'Shit? Because I was a minor, so he's named in the paperwork as the owner, but only until I'm twenty-one, when it transfers.'

'You're . . . ?'

'I'm twenty. Did you think I was older?'

I shrugged. She grinned. 'So he can do whatever the hell he wants with it until I'm twenty-one as long as it's in my best interests, and who would argue against selling a horse for millions as opposed to keeping him in your back garden and riding him once in a while purely for the pleasure of it?'

'Jimmy Stewart probably would.'

'Jimmy . . . ?'

'Nothing. Old man's joke.'

She looked at me sympathetically, then continued. 'He kept dangling the prospect of riding him in the

National to keep me in line, but I knew he wouldn't let me. It's all about maximising profit, isn't it? He'll let a proper jockey ride him and then sell him the moment he crosses the line in first – and he will cross in first. He'll cream off millions and maybe he'll share some of that with me, but that's *not the point*. I want to win the race.'

'The problem is,' I said, 'you want to have your cake and eat it. You want to keep Dan the Man all to yourself, and win the National.'

'And why not? He's *mine*.'

'Fair point. And your dad badly needs the money.'

'Yes, I know he does, things haven't been going well.'

'And by now he'll know you and your mum were behind this; he's not stupid.'

'Yes, I know.'

'And vicariously he will probably blame you for your mum's death.'

'I didn't . . .'

'Well if youse hadn't started all this shit she might still be alive.'

'I know, but . . . stop telling me off. I'm *sorry*.' The tears began to flow again. I felt like a heel. In fact, a stiletto. I offered her a Starburst. She accepted, and began to unwrap.

'They used to be called Opal Fruits,' I said. 'I'm sure Eric and Derek love them.'

She nodded vaguely. 'I don't understand why those . . . *monsters* . . . would do that to Mummy. I mean, what's Dan the Man to them?' She looked up at me. 'They're the ones cut the brakes on my car? Why Daddy's had all the security?'

'Far as I can work out, they feel they're owed a lot of money and don't mind how they get it.'

'Owed money by . . . ?'

'Well, Mark Corkery to start with, and by association your mum. And by association with her, your dad. Like I say, they don't mind where they get it. They just follow the money chain until they get what they want.'

'Christ. So what will they do next?'

'Well they're after you. Or more directly, the brown horse.'

She looked startled. 'What?'

'I thought when you doubled back from the Liverpool ferry you must have suspected you were being followed.'

'It was a precaution. I thought Daddy would have people watching for me. I mean, the worst he'll do when he catches me is stop my allowance. But these guys. After *me*? Jesus. How did they even find out I was—'

'Your mother let it slip. They slapped her about a bit. I'm sorry. Anyway. It doesn't matter now. They're halfway to Liverpool.'

She gave a little sigh of relief, then rested her head against me for a while. There were all sorts of dark, dangerous thoughts going through her mind. I could feel them banging against the inside of her skull. I stroked her hair and she managed a wan smile and squeezed my hand. 'That's nice,' she said, gently. 'You're nice,' she added.

'And you're not as hard as you let on.'

She nodded against me. 'What're we going to do?'

'I don't know. Win the Grand National?'

'Okay. We'll do that.'

Twenty minutes before docking we went down to the car deck. Bosco had roused himself. The ash was gone from the window. There was no hint of alcohol in either the vehicle or his demeanour. He nodded at me somewhat sheepishly, then said, 'All right?' to Mandy.

She nodded and went to check on Dan the Man. She raised a half-shutter on the side of the horse box and he poked his head out. She patted his nose and gave him a kiss. I rubbed his nose as well. Mandy and Bosco exchanged glances. Dan the Man licked my hand and I gave a little shiver. Then he tried to take a bite out of my jacket and I pulled sharply away. Mandy laughed, then pushed his head gently back inside and re-secured the shutter.

All around us people were beginning to drift back to their vehicles. I didn't take any notice of doors slamming behind me, but I did take notice of the cool metallic object that was suddenly placed firmly against the back of my head and the expressions of horror I could see on the faces of Mandy and Bosco before me.

I turned slowly.

'Ah so,' I said.

'Ass hole,' said the Chinaman in perfect English, then cracked the gun across my brow.

25

I nightmare.

Sometime I would like to see an X-ray of my skull, just to admire the damage. I've taken more heavy blows than Frank Bruno and am constantly surprised that I don't talk as little sense. Perhaps I will. When I go to sleep, I do not dream, I nightmare. Double it when I go under through violence. I dredge up horrors from the past and relive them with anger and fury and fear. There are many horrors down there. A black friend plunging off an apartment block. A starving wife. A dead baby. The crack, crack, crack of guns on skulls, the thump, thump, thump of a heart racing to breakdown. *Dan, you should learn to say no. Dan, you should learn to say no. Dan you should—*

'Dan?'

Somewhere, far away.

The baby boy who would never grow up.

The wife who would never look at me the same way again.

The horse with my name.

Exhaust fumes. Engines revving.

I opened my eyes. 'What?'

Mandy, looking relieved, Bosco, smoking, taking a swig from a bottle of Vladivar. 'Are you okay?' she asked.

Another stupid bloody question. But I nodded anyway and sat up. My head throbbed. I was on the floor of the car deck. There was no Land Rover, no box, and no horse. I rubbed at my brow, winced.

Mandy smiled.

'What the fuck are you smiling about?'

She smiled some more. 'Just glad to have you back.'

'Aye.'

I stood up. A little shakily. Dizzy. There were only a few cars left. Mandy took my arm and helped me back up towards the passenger deck. We joined the queue to get off.

'You look remarkably relaxed considering millions of dollars' worth of horse just walked,' I said.

Mandy nodded. 'But the important thing is, you're okay.'

'Don't talk crap, what's going on? Have the cops caught them?'

Bosco, walking behind, snorted. Like a horse.

'No.'

She was grinning.

'Will you stop that fucking grinning and tell me what's going on!' Ahead of me a father glared round. I glared back. His eyes flitted up to the blood on my brow and then away. He picked up his pace and ushered his three kids a little further forward. We joined the end of the queue to get off. 'Please,' I added.

'Hold up your hand.'

'What?'

'Hold up your hand.' I tutted and held it up. 'The other one.'

I dropped, I raised. 'What are you . . . ?'

'What do you see?'

'Four fingers and a thumb. I'm not concussed. Now what . . . ?'

'What do you *see*?'

'For Christ sake . . .'

'Well if you don't want to know . . .'

'I *hate* cryptic.' I rolled my eyes. 'Okay, four fingers and a thumb. A tragically short life line. And although I don't smoke, what looks like nicotine fingers.' I examined them a little more closely. I looked at Mandy. 'What is this? I got knocked out and youse got me addicted to smokes in, like, five minutes?'

Behind me, Bosco snorted.

'It's dye,' Mandy said. 'Brown dye.'

'There's a reason you dyed my fingers brown?'

Mandy burst out laughing. 'No! You fool! Not you – the horse. That wasn't Dan the Man. It was a lookalike. We just had to touch him up a bit. When you rubbed his nose earlier it came off on your fingers – you didn't see Bosco and me nearly cracking up when you did it, did you?'

'I . . .' And then I laughed again. 'You cunning little bitch. The classic double bluff.'

She shrugged. 'I try.'

'So they've stolen what, a donkey?'

'No, the merely average, as opposed to the great. Hopefully they won't find out for days. Poor Maximum Bob, he's going to end up on a menu somewhere.'

'As will you, when they find out.'

She shrugged. 'You didn't tell me there were Chinamen on our trail as well.'

'Well that's just the way the fortune cookie crumbles. I didn't want to weigh you down. I thought Jimmy the Chicken and his crew were enough to be worrying about.' I shook my head. 'Mandy McClean, you are one smooth operator. And verily, your father's daughter.'

'Please,' she said, 'I use my mother's name.'

'Okay. Hilda,' I said. She grinned, but it faded quickly. The memory of her mother was still etched on her face. She was lucky she couldn't see what my memory of her mother was. 'This begs the question,' I said, 'as to the true location of the horse known as Dan.'

'Well now,' said Mandy.

We stepped back down on to the dock. The cool sea air tasted cool and sea-like. There was chanting coming from Rangers supporters already opening cans of beer as they waited to board the fleet of buses lined up along the dock. Mandy's hair blew around her face. There was a half-moon in the sky. Bosco walked ahead of us. I caught her arm and pulled her back. 'Stop messing around,' I snapped.

She pulled her arm free. 'If you ever lay another finger on me again, except when we're in bed, I'll break your spine.'

I held my hands up in surrender. 'Just *tell* me.'

'It's like real life Dan, the poor catch the ferry, the merely average get squashed into a cargo plane, the high-flyers, well, they fly in style. I have a mate works for a contract company that flies horses between here and England, the rest of Europe, every day. Dan's travelling under a false name with nine other horses. He'll be in stables by now, not far from Aintree. There. I trust ninety-five per cent of you, Dan, but the other five is just stopping me telling you which stables. Okay?'

'Okay.'

'Good. Now we have to catch a train. Bosco has *our* tickets. If you want to join us, you'd better hurry.'

'You *will* wait.'

'Will I?'

She walked off. I waited for her to turn and smile or wink or offer encouragement, but she kept walking. I checked my pockets for the money Mouse had given me. Not that it mattered. If I couldn't afford a ticket I'd just climb on to the roof.

Somewhere around the border between Scotland and England, Bosco got involved in a card game with a couple of squaddies several seats back. They were all drunk. There'd be a couple of minutes of cursing, then hysterical laughter. He came back once to check that Mandy was all right, and then a second time to borrow a tenner off her. We didn't see him again for the rest of the night.

Seeing as she was so flush, I borrowed a tenner off her as well and bought a bottle of whiskey and half a dozen cans of Diet Coke at the bar. Whiskey and Diet Coke isn't one for the connoisseurs, but who gives a flying frig about connoisseurs? It gets you drunk and you don't put on any weight. They'd run out of ice, but there was a trolley with an ice compartment selling ice pops for kids, and I bought some of those. We stuck them upright into our drinks and laughed at our crappy-looking cocktails. And then after a while she got maudlin about her mother and I gave her a sympathetic ear, which was like a normal ear, but with more wax to filter out the emotions. She loved her mother, and she loved her father, but they'd fucked her up. They do that. She loved Dan the Man more than anything in the whole wide world, and coming hot off my own rough-tongue experience I asked her if she'd any interest in bestiality and she threw a sharpened ice pop at me. We laughed then, for a while, and then we looked at each other, and out of the window, and listened to Bosco giving them the Irish blarney and them saying they loved the Irish, now that they weren't shooting them any more.

Mandy was talking, and she was beautiful and sad

and interesting, but I was drifting. I was thinking about Trish and where to go next, and my life and how to get it back on track. If I wasn't dead by the end of the week I was going to have to make radical changes. Mouse was right. I had to start saying no. He would get me work. There was no doubt about that. Something that wouldn't put me in the line of fire. I could review films. Or the theatre. Or restaurants. I would attend fashion shows and coffee mornings and promote charitable causes. People were dying in Africa and had no choice about it. I was dying because I always made the wrong choice. In future, I would go with the opposite of whatever my instincts told me. They said left, I'd go right, unless it was into oncoming traffic. Yes, things were going to change. There had been too much death and too many bullets and although it seemed like there had been a reasonable amount of sex, most of it had been tied into those very same periods of death and destruction and seemed now more like callous acts of self-destruction rather than the expressions of love they were supposed to be. Or were they supposed to be that at all? The sexual instinct . . .

Bugger.

Another five minutes and I'd be on to the meaning of life and why are we here and then I'd be gone for days. I shook myself, I blinked across at Mandy. She was still talking about her mother. A childhood memory. I smiled at her. She was so different from

Trish. Like chalk and cheese. What I wanted to do was phone Trish and tell her all about this remarkable new girl I'd met, because although we were barely speaking, Trish was still my best friend and would be able to advise me what to do, how to play it. I wondered if she was thinking of me. Or the man with the beard. I would lamp him when I got home. Or haunt him, if I didn't.

Mandy fell silent for a moment, and I dived in. 'Back at your mum's house, before the fire, I noticed all the Horse Whisperer equipment was gone.'

'Yeah.'

'So what's the story, morning glory?'

'She sold it. Lock, stock and two smoking barrels.'

'The equipment or the . . .'

'The equipment *and* the . . .' She sighed. 'It was getting too much for her. Dad was closing in, God knows who else too.'

'Still,' I said, 'I thought it was her baby.'

Mandy shook her head. 'More Corkery's, with Mum providing the technical know-how. She only really kept it going after he died out of badness, to get at Dad, but once we dreamed up this whizz with Dan the Man, there didn't seem much point in going through all the other hassle. So she got an offer she couldn't refuse.'

'God. How much? Does *everything* revolve around money?'

'Of course it does. She got the grand sum of one pound, plus a promise to take over any outstanding legal problems and keep sticking a knife into the industry's seedy little underbelly.'

'I see. So who . . . ?'

'I can't tell you that. The whole point of the Horse Whisperer is it's anonymous.'

I sighed. 'It's you, isn't it?'

'Could be.' She blew air down her nose and added playfully, 'Or it could be Bosco. Could be the conductor on this train. You'll never know.'

'What about your dad?' I asked.

'He's not going to buy it, he hates that kind of thing.'

'Buy it through an intermediary, then kill it.'

'No, don't worry about it. It's safe. The Horse Whisperer lives.'

'I'll drink to that.' We replenished ice pops, then clinked glasses. I gave her my wise old man look. 'You know, if your dad's worked out that you've stolen Dan the Man, he'll just sit and wait for you at Aintree. Take him back, just like that. One could regard this big double-bluffy circuitous effort as a colossal waste of time.'

'No. He thinks he's connected, but he's got nothing on my mum. All those years in the business, plus the Horse Whisperer? It's all fixed. He won't be able to lay a finger on us till Dan the Man's in the parade ring at the earliest, and even then I'll have lawyers standing by, plus the world's press if he tries anything dramatic. Actually racing's just going to be the icing on the cake.'

'You're not going to scare Jimmy the Chicken off with lawyers. What's to stop him or his mates making a grab for the horse?'

'Because they won't get within a mile of Aintree. Since the IRA forced the cancellation of the race in ninety-seven security's been wound up tight as a drum. They try to get weapons through, they'll be jumped all over.'

I took another drink and stabbed myself in the eye with an icepop.

'That's why they call this train the red-eye,' Mandy laughed.

'No,' I corrected, wiping at it, 'they call it the *sleeper*. The red-eye's the first train in the morning.'

'Don't get all high and mighty with me, Mister Know-All. Just because you stuck an ice pick in your eye.'

'An ice *pop*. Just you watch yourself, girlie. Last time you got drunk you vomited all over my furniture.'

'No, last time I got drunk I slept with you and stole a horse.'

'Well the time before that.'

We sat quietly for a couple of miles. Then came cries of anguish from Bosco's direction. I smiled at Mandy, she smiled back.

'You've planned this well, haven't you?' I said.

She shrugged. 'I didn't plan for my mum to die.'

'I know. But you've done well.'

'Maybe. You were right, what you said back on the

ferry, about winning it for her. I mean, if I wanted to win the National before, now I *really* want to win it. They say will power's half the secret.'

'That and a horse that can get over monster fences.'

'Well I don't think there's much doubt about that. Dan's the best ride I ever had.'

'Can I have that in writing?'

She ignored me. 'What can stop me?'

I shrugged. There were too many answers to that question for it to compute in my damaged brain.

26

I didn't like it. I'm suspicious and pessimistic at the best of times. The journey out to the Livermore stables, twenty-five miles from Aintree, owned by one of Hilda's oldest and dearest friends (though I wasn't convinced that the dearest didn't refer to how much she charged to feed big brown beasts straw), had assumed something of the spirit of a triumphant procession. Bad guys vanquished, superhorse awaiting glory over a couple of modest fences, millions in the bank, victory over her hated father, whose heart would melt at her audaciousness and they'd be reunited. Whereas I've always leaned more towards the unexpected death and horse as Fray Bentos scenario.

Mandy wasn't exactly all smiles, her mother's death didn't allow that, but there was a quiet confidence that grew the closer we got to the stables, a slightly superior air about her that made me nervous. Maybe it was adrenalin. Maybe it was fear.

Maybe it was just me being sensitive. I'm the sensitive type.

Mandy ordered the taxi from the station with a barked command that made me jump. We had breakfasted on bacon sarnies. None of us had any luggage to speak of, though I carried a lot inside. Or was that baggage? The Chinese had made off with what little Mandy and Bosco had brought with them. Bosco himself had the hangover to end all hangovers, although he was two hundred pounds to the good from his poker game. The soldiers had drifted in and out of drunken comas, allowing Bosco to cheat outrageously. Nevertheless, you can't buy good health and the taxi stopped twice to allow him to throw up on the side of the road. Mandy tutted. I held my nose.

She kept looking at her watch. We had to get to the stables, pick up the horse, negotiate the traffic back to Aintree, then allow Mandy and Dan the Man time to get themselves *as one* for the biggest race of their lives. I imagined there was more to it than *giddy-up*. I had visions of Dan the Man warming up in his dressing room, pawing the air, thinking, *Come on, son, you can do it, you're the best, you're the greatest*, then they'd fight over the mirror.

'Excited?' I asked.

'Damp with it,' said Mandy.

'Glad I asked.'

The driver was looking at her in the mirror.

'What's the plan after the race?' I asked.

'In what sense?'

'You and me.'

'Don't know. I'll be busy with the press. You'll be wanting to write your book.'

'Oh yeah. The book.'

I looked out of the window. She put her hand on my arm. 'What do you think,' she asked, 'happy ending or sad ending?'

'For you, me or the horse?'

'All three.'

'Well, bearing in mind that I usually get the short straw, I'd say happy, sad, lots of sex, respectively.'

She smiled. 'I'd settle for happy, happy, happy.'

I nodded. 'So would I.'

'This the place?' the driver asked. We looked ahead to the open metallic gates and the big sign which said *Livermore Stables*. The correct answer to his question was *Of course it's the fucking place, can't you read, dimwit?* but we settled for, 'Yup, this looks like us.'

There was a lane leading up to several stable blocks about half a mile away, but the driver made no effort to enter. He looked back at us without any hint of apology and said, 'Don't want to get horse shit all over the car. Puts people off.'

So we paid him and got out and tipped him fifty pence on a £25 fare and he snarled something we couldn't make out and then roared off. We started walking up the lane. The driver had a point. There was horse shit everywhere.

As we got closer, then closer still, Mandy's cool confidence finally dissolved and she dashed towards the stables. Bosco glanced at me, then hurried after her. I brought up the rear. There were three stable blocks set in a triangle around a cobbled yard. There was no sign of activity. There were horsey sounds, sure, but nothing in the way of human beings.

I don't like it, it's too quiet.

You'd be suspicious in heaven.

I don't like this, it's too good.

And zap, you're in hell.

So, wasn't I right to be suspicious?

Mandy emerged from the first block, then dashed across to the second. Bosco followed, shrugged across at me, then hurried after her again. She emerged from the second, and hurtled into the third. And then, finally, there was an excited shout. Bosco wandered out of the second, looked at me again and said, 'Guess she found him.'

'Yippee,' I said.

I sauntered over. The stables were suitably stable-like. There were half a dozen horses still *in situ*, but the rest of the stalls stood empty. Gone racing, I guessed. Mandy was kissing Dan the Man on the nose. He was licking her throat. It felt like I was intruding. Bosco busied himself getting a halter and reins and other leathery things horses and strange men like to wear. When Mandy eventually broke away she beamed across at me. 'Isn't he beautiful?' Before I could respond, she continued with 'Aren't you just beautiful?' She kissed him again. 'I am going to be *so* proud of you . . .'

She unhitched the door and led him out, still patting him. I gave him one myself. For Ulster. Mandy nodded at Bosco. 'Go and see if you can find Trudy up at the house, we're going to have to get moving.'

Bosco handed her the leather gear, then headed for the yard again.

I said, 'I'm happy for you.'

'Thank you.' She looped the leather over the horse's head. He snorted appreciatively.

'That's some tongue on him, that is,' I said. 'He could look you in the eye and lick your belly button at the same time. If I could do that I'd be made.'

'Stop it.'

Bosco was back in the doorway in world record time. Literally. Or perhaps he never truly left. Perhaps the unhappy man with the two unhappy flunkies had something to do with it. We stopped, we looked, we knew the game was up.

'Daddy,' said Mandy.

'Darling,' said Geordie McClean.

Derek and Eric stepped out of his shadow. Each of them carried a shotgun, hung lazily over their shoulders. I knew they wouldn't shoot Mandy, I wasn't so sure about myself.

'Howdy,' I said, 'long time no—'

'Shut the fuck up, Starkey,' Geordie growled.

'Okay.'

'How did you know?' Mandy asked, her voice still defiant, yet a shade tremulous.

'Well I pulled in every favour I was owed. And

when I exhausted both of those, I consulted your friend and mine. The Horse Whisperer.'

'*What!*'

'Yes my dear, shot by your own side. Funny really, I'm at last beginning to see the value of it. When all else failed, I spotted a juicy little snippet about a horse in hiding at these very stables. Didn't take much to work it out.'

Mandy pulled Dan the Man a little closer. 'You can't stop me, Daddy. He's mine.'

'I can stop you, and he's mine until your birth-day.'

'You *gave* him to me.'

'Yes, and you can have him stuffed and mounted when I'm finished with him, but for the immediate future I need him back.'

'That's not fair, and it's not right, and I won't let you take him.'

'Fair and right? Enter the real world, darling. I'm afraid you can't stop me.'

Her back straightened, her mouth tightened. 'What're you going to do, shoot me?'

'I don't think that will be necessary.' He nodded at Derek and Eric. They advanced. Dan the Man whinnied, threw his head up. Mandy looked despairingly back to her father.

'Daddy, please, don't . . . if not for me, for Mummy, she wanted me to have him, she wanted me to run in the National, please . . .' Derek hesitated.

'Your *mummy* is dead because she got involved

in things she knew nothing about. Because *you* demanded to ride in the National. I tried to protect you from it, but you wouldn't listen and here you are up to your neck in it. Well it stops here, okay? Derek?'

Derek put a hand on her arm. She tried to pull away, but he held firm. Eric pushed himself between Mandy and the horse and took hold of the halter. Mandy made one last appeal.

'Daddy, *please* . . .'

Geordie lit a cigar. He said nothing. As Eric led Dan the Man towards the stable door, Bosco stepped suddenly into his path. 'Let him go,' he hissed, raising a diminutive fist, 'or I'll crack you on the head even better than I did your fruity friend.'

Eric laughed. 'That's quite a mouthful, Bosco. And so is this.' He punched him between the lips and Bosco was spitting teeth before he hit the ground. Eric smiled across at Derek, who smiled back. Geordie smiled proudly at both of them. Even Dan the Man bared his teeth. The only ones not smiling were Mandy and me. And she was glaring. At me, of course.

'Are you just going to stand there?' she wailed.

I nodded.

'What sort of a man are you?' she shrieked.

'I'm Leo,' I said. 'The cowardly lion. Geordie, about this book . . .'

'Not now, Starkey, we've a race to win.' He nodded at Derek and his weeping daughter. 'Put her in the car.' Derek began to push Mandy towards the door. She dragged her feet, but the fight had gone out of her. Geordie threw his cigar to the ground and stepped on it. He couldn't have had more than two puffs of it. He was still smiling. He looked back to me. 'You're welcome to come along for the ride.'

I looked at him, slightly incredulously. 'You've changed your tune,' I said.

'Better the devil you know, eh?'

I shook my head. 'You're quite pleased with her really, aren't you? Daddy's girl nearly got away with it.'

He nodded as he walked off. 'Yup,' he said, as much to himself as anyone, 'she's certainly full of spunk.'

'I know,' I called after him, 'mostly mine.'

I was hoping for a reaction, but there was nothing. Derek and Eric smirked when they realised he hadn't heard. Geordie and Mandy started arguing again beside the car, but I'd had enough of it. I turned and wandered back into the stable. I was thinking that journalism was too dangerous for me. Even writing biographies and novels had proved detrimental to my health. I needed an ordinary, dull job. Something to do with big complicated forms or digging holes for no obvious reason. I could paint long walls white, and then repaint them the next day black. I could count pebbles on the beach or hunt for fossils. I could shampoo dogs or replace tiles on old roofs. I could sell hot dogs by the seaside or collect hymn books in church.

I needed excitement like I needed a hole in the head.

I needed the love of a good woman, and by good I mean one who goes to church on Sundays and wears a bonnet and makes cakes. We wouldn't bother with sex; it only complicates things. I would become a monk. I would live on an island, although not Wrathlin. I would fish. I would study ancient myths and legends or become an astrologer.

I would phone Patricia and ask her advice.

I needed a mobile phone. That would solve a lot of my problems. I could talk to her any time, any place, anywhere. And she to me. If she'd only known where I was half the time, I'm sure she would have called. She's had her own dark moments of late, and no matter what the state of our love life, she knows there's only one person in the world who understands her. And it ain't some fucker with a beard.

Another thing: I didn't want to smell horses ever in my life again.

I wandered back towards the stable doors. I'd thought they were all gone, I'd heard an engine and not bothered to turn, but as I was about to step back out into the sunshine I realised that what I'd heard wasn't their departure, but another vehicle arriving. And now that I was closer, the sound of raised voices.

I moved deftly into the shadows.

Derek and Eric had their shotguns raised and pointed at a Land Rover and horse box parked in the middle of the triangle. Bending over the bonnet, pointing guns, were Jimmy the Chicken, Oil Paintings and Dry Cleaner.

Jesus. Any moment now Brian Rix would enter stage left with his trousers around his knees.

Didn't anyone *ever* give up?

I knew instantly what had happened.

They'd been reading the Horse Whisperer as well.

'I won't tell you again,' Jimmy the Chicken was shouting, 'put those fucking guns down!'

Derek and Eric held firm.

'Now!' yelled Oil Paintings.

'Why don't *you* put *yours* down?' Derek shouted back.

I pressed myself into the stable door frame. Jimmy and Co. hadn't spotted me yet. If I backed up quiet as a mouse with slippers I could exit through the door at the other end of the stables. Then run away and really get that less dangerous job.

'Put your fucking guns down or the fucking horse gets it!'

They had their guns trained on Dan the Man.

'Be sensible!' shouted Derek. 'It's the fucking horse you want.'

'Don't tell us what we want, you cunt!' Jimmy shouted back.

Geordie said, 'Come on now, take it easy, there's no need for all this, let's just settle down, we'll work something out.'

'Daddy! They're the ones killed Mummy!' Geordie's eyes narrowed as they turned to his daughter. 'They are! Ask Dan!' She pointed towards my shadows. Guns shifted. 'Please don't let them take my horse!'

'Get the fuck outta there!' Dry Cleaner yelled. 'And don't try anything stupid.'

As if.

I stepped shyly into the limelight, hands raised. 'I saw nothing,' I said. 'I didn't have my contacts in.'

I don't know about horse brains, but it looked like Dan the Man was starting to feel the tension. He was raising up on two legs and whinnying. Mandy jumped to grab hold of the leather. After two attempts she got it and began to talk gently to him, holding him firmly down at the same time. She also managed to look thunderously from her dad to me to Jimmy the Chicken.

'We want the fucking horse, so let him go!'

'Can't do that,' Derek growled, his eyes flitting from Jimmy, to Oil, to Dry.

Jimmy moved slowly out from behind the Land Rover. 'We're going to come over there and take him. Just stay where you are and no one'll get hurt!'

'You come any closer I'll blow your fucking arms off, and that *will* hurt.'

'Then let him go!'

'No!'

'That horse is ours!'

'Ours!'

'He's mine!' Mandy yelled.

'Shut up, Mandy!' shouted Geordie.

'No! He's mine!'

'He's ours!' yelled Jimmy the Chicken, coming closer, gun raised, held tight, sweat on his brow. Oil Paintings and Dry Cleaner followed, slowly, cautiously. Derek and Eric moved between the advancing trio and the horse, guns held just as high, eyes narrowed, fingers already squeezing lightly on triggers, just waiting for the final application of pressure.

Soon the only thing between the Jimmy camp and the Geordie camp was little old me, hands aloft and heart in my shoes.

There was almost complete silence. I looked from one set of gun barrels to the other. I swallowed. 'I guess this is what they call a Mexican stand-off,' I said in a vain attempt to keep things light.

'No,' replied a voice from the roof of the barn, '*this* is what you call a Mexican stand-off.'

Five Chinamen, five guns. Holy manoley.

27

Shouting, yelling, five guns up top, three on one side, two on the other, five and three and two makes . . . ten. Say six bullets apiece – although six as a figure is a hangover from Western six-guns and movies where the bad guy has used up all his bullets but only the good guy knows it – so, say, for inflation and modern technology, ten bullets apiece . . . .minus Derek and Eric's shotguns of course, two apiece, presuming they're double-barrelled, makes a grand total of . . .

Shut up!

Stop that head whirring!

One moment, one moment amidst the yelling and swearing, one moment on one hair trigger and we would all be dead, including the horse with my name. It needed someone to stop it, someone with the will power, the tact, the diplomacy and the bravery to stand up and be counted.

Cometh the moment, cometh the man.

Bosco stepped out of the stable, hands raised, and

for a moment all guns pointed to him. 'This isn't going to helth anyone,' he said.

'What?' said Geordie.

'What?' said Dry Cleaner.

'What?' said the English-sounding Chinese.

'This isn't going to helth anyone,' Bosco repeated.

'Helth?' said Geordie.

'*Help*,' said Mandy. 'If your brutes hadn't knocked his teeth out he'd be able to say it properly. *Help*,' she repeated.

'Exactly,' said Bosco. 'Listen, folks, we're all going to end up dead, what's the pointh in that?'

'Pointh?' said Oil Paintings.

From above came a low roll of laughter from the lead Chinese. Jimmy the Chicken grinned, and lowered his gun a fraction. 'Okay,' he said, 'fair point. Maybe we all need to cool off, no point in throwing the bathwater out.'

Derek and Eric, one gun on the Chicken crew and one on the Chinese, remained steady as rocks. Geordie McClean moved up behind them and gently put his hands on their shoulders. They relaxed, just a little. Everyone looked to the Chinese. Their team leader lowered his gun, the others kept theirs in place.

'Okay,' said the Chinese. 'We will talk. With safeguards. One representative from each side to meet in the middle of the square.'

'It's a triangle,' I whispered.

'Okay?' said the Chinese.

Eyes met eyes. The impasse seemed to stretch interminably.

Then Geordie made the first move, walking confidently across the cobbles, everyone watching. Even the horse. There was a moment of panic when he reached into his pocket as Jimmy the Chicken went to join him, but Geordie slowed down enough to show that he was only getting a cigar out. He offered one to Jimmy, who refused. Then came the Chinese. I half expected him to do a double somersault from the roof and land barefoot on the cobbles, his chest bare, his lethal hands raised, ready to inflict mayhem, but as it was he merely disappeared for a minute while he made his way down and reappeared through the stable doors, carefully brushing bits of straw off his immaculate Armani suit. *Enter the Clothes Horse.*

Mandy, leading Dan the Man, came and stood by my side. She slipped her hand into mine and squeezed. I gave her an encouraging squeeze back. We watched. We couldn't hear what they were saying across the way, it was all conducted in urgent whispers, but the finger-pointing gave us an indication that things had not started well.

'Jockeying for position,' I said.

Then they split and returned to their respective sides. Bar Geordie, of course, who stayed where he was, puffing quietly on his cigar, keeping his own counsel. Once he nodded across at Mandy, but when she ignored him he did not look in her direction again. After five minutes Jimmy walked back across to Geordie. A minute later the Chinese joined them and they began another session.

'How can he even talk to those scumbags?' Mandy whispered.

'Who're we talking about here?' I murmured back.

'Stop it. You know what I mean.'

'As Michael Corleone would say, it's just business.'

'Who's Michael Corleone?'

'The Godfather.'

'*Whose* godfather?'

'The film.' She looked blankly at me. 'You've never seen *The Godfather*? The film? Al Pacino. Marlon Brando.'

She shook her head. 'Why, is it any good?'

'It's one of the greatest films ever made. Surpassed only by *Godfather II*. The winning sequence was rather dashed by *Godfather III*. I can't believe you haven't seen any of them.'

'I've better things to do with my time.'

'Like what?' She patted Dan the Man. 'Oh please,' I said. 'Sitting on a brown horse jumping over fences. Get a life.'

'As opposed to sitting in a dark room watching pretend things.'

'Shhh. Here they come. Nevetheless, I enjoyed our chat. We should go out on a date. To the pictures. Or a ride, whatever takes your fancy.'

'Why are they walking in our direction?'

'Your direction.'

'I don't like this.'

'Neither do I. Though slightly better than if it was my direction.'

'Mandy.' Geordie stopped in front of his daughter, flanked by Jimmy the Chicken and the Chinese. I stepped to one side, just to give them space. 'Mandy,' Geordie said again.

'Whatever it is, the answer is no.'

'Mandy, don't say that. Hear us out.'

'Or we'll kill you,' said Jimmy the Chicken.

'Stop that!' Geordie barked. There was another moment where guns were raised all around, then it slowly passed. Mandy looked from her father to the other two, then returned her disappointed gaze to Geordie.

'What?' she said.

'Mandy, we have a problem. Nobody wants to get hurt here.' He clasped his hands together. 'We're from Belfast, so we know violence doesn't get anyone anywhere, these days it's all about compromise and taking the bomb and the bullet out of the equation.'

'Stop the bullshit, Daddy, and tell me what youse want.'

'My girl, indeed.' He sighed. 'Okay. Mandy. In order for us all to come out of this healthy, and indeed wealthy, we've decided to take a gamble. Rightly or wrongly, these gentlemen are owed money by your mother, and they believe, by association, by me as well. I simply don't have the money to pay them. As you must have suspected, businesswise things have not been going well. The stables, with the exception of Dan the Man, have been a disaster. Plenty of little winners, but not enough to keep my head above water. Everything I have is mortgaged to the hilt. I can barely meet the bloody payments as it is.'

'Get on with it!' the Chinese hissed.

'Okay. Okay. Mandy, love, Dan the Man is the only thing that can save me, and us. There are two alternatives – this ends in a bloodbath or we draw up an agreement, here and now, splitting ownership of Dan the Man three ways. You and me—'

'That's two—' Mandy began.

'That's one,' said Jimmy the Chicken. 'You and her's one.'

'I know. I know,' said Geordie. 'Just stay with me on this honey, trust me.'

'Huh.'

'Please. Listen. Jimmy, here, is two, and the Chinese delegation is three. We split Dan the Man three ways. I know it's not what you want, but at least we all live to fight another day, and we make some money when we come to sell him.'

'I don't understand,' Mandy said.

'What's not to understand?' Jimmy the Chicken snapped.

'You said it was a gamble. You said you'd decided to take a gamble. Where's the gamble? You're just selling me out. Big gamble.'

Geordie glanced at Jimmy and the Chinese, then cleared his throat. 'Well that's where you come in.

Your dream's going to come true. Just like I promised.'

Mandy looked suspiciously around the three of them. 'Meaning . . . ?'

'Meaning you're gonna ride the big fella in the National,' said Jimmy the Chicken. 'He'll be worth ten times as much if he wins.'

'And if he doesn't win,' said the Chinese, 'we're going to kill your father.'

It was a rogues' gallery all right, and could never be anything other than a temporary alliance. But in the strange way that bizarre ideas sometimes capture the public imagination, so their ridiculous gamble came to be regarded as something else entirely, as a sound business investment that would pay great dividends. Once Mandy accepted that she had no choice but to ride in the Grand National, the air of hostility that had surrounded the negotiations lifted; guns weren't exactly put away, but they were certainly lowered. Almost immediately the players began to place bets amongst themselves as to the winning time, the second-placed horse, third, fourth, first to fall, first riderless horse to finish, first to be put down, first to injure a drunken spectator, all spending the money none of them yet possessed, nor indeed was likely to. It was fascinating, or would have been if I didn't know that all three parties had at one time or another tried to kill me; it was probably the only thing they all had in common.

Mandy hurried Dan the Man into a horse box. Geordie, Jimmy and the Chinese agreed that Bosco would go with her to provide support. They weren't worried about her trying any funny stuff. After all, they had her dad. And for all the big deal she made about hating him, I knew she wouldn't let him be killed.

I said, 'Maybe I should go too.'

'Maybe you should shut the fuck up and sit there,' Geordie replied.

'Do you want me to go with her, boss?' Derek said.

Geordie shook his head. 'No. Stay here. We'd be outgunned for sure if things turn nasty.' He turned to look at Jimmy the Chicken, chatting with the Chinese over to the left. He gave a slight shake of his head. 'The things you do,' he said to himself as much as anyone.

Bosco opened the Land Rover door and climbed in. Mandy finished securing the horse box and then hurried round to the passenger door. She stopped, looked at me, then said, 'See you later alligator.'

'In a while crocodile.'

As she went to close the door, Geordie took hold of it.

'Mandy,' he said. 'Wait.'

'I haven't time. I've still to get to the fucking races. I have to give him a run-out. He'll be in no shape to run if he doesn't.'

'Just . . . I'm sorry. Your mum and I . . . we've been

playing games all our lives. We loved each other, we just couldn't . . . well, you know.'

'No, I don't.'

'Well then believe me. I know I promised Dan the Man to you. But some things are more important. Win the race, we'll work it out. And if you don't want to win it for me, then win it for her.'

'I always was.'

'Okay. Good luck.'

She turned away. She stared straight ahead as Bosco drove her out of the stable yard towards the biggest race of her life.

And mine.

28

Geordie McClean entered the house like he owned it. Just pushed open the snibbed front door and walked into the hall. We followed in behind. The Chinese crew went into the lounge on the left and switched on a television while Jimmy the Chicken, Oil Paintings and Dry Cleaner retired to the kitchen to look for drink, pausing only to rip the telephone from the wall.

Typically, each of them carried a mobile phone, but it was agreed that these would be off limits for the duration of the race, just in case anyone tried to pull a fast one. However, they all had businesses of one shade or another to oversee, so I was nominated, seconded and elected as Mobile Phone Carrier with the strict instruction to answer all incoming calls, taking only a message, and the warning that I'd be put to death if I attempted to make an outgoing call. I was to remain in plain sight. I had eleven mobile phones switched on and secreted in various cavities about my body. Even if I survived this particular adventure, I would probably die from a brain tumour.

The house was ramshackle and smelled of horses. The owner of the stables had several runners in the support races at Aintree and had taken most of her staff with her. Those who remained were tied up in the cellar. Four stable lads and a stable girl. Nicely counterbalanced by the unstable gangsters already getting excited about the racing on the TV upstairs. I sat at a table in the dining room opposite Geordie McClean. A sliding glass door gave us a view of the lounge beyond with its widescreen television. I leaned across and lifted a banana from a bowl in the centre of the table. I peeled it and took a bite, though only after some hesitation. I had to be careful. After scoffing the rest of the Starbursts on the train, I didn't want to overdose on goodness. Geordie took an apple. He rubbed it on his coat, then took a bite.

'Talking of fruit,' I said quietly, 'the only two with nothing to gain from all of this are Derek and Eric.'

Geordie, unprepared to speak with his mouth full, crunched at his own pace, then said, 'I know.'

We watched through the sliding doors as first Derek, then Eric, entered the lounge carrying little wicker baskets filled with crisps and other nibbles, although they still took care to hang on to their shotguns. Jimmy the Chicken, Oil Paintings and Dry Cleaner were already gleefully working their way through the crate of Charger and bottles of VAT 19 they'd discovered in the kitchen.

'So, uhm, why would they put their lives on the line for you?'

'Loyalty. I gather it's not a concept you're overly familiar with.'

'That's rich coming from someone who's selling his daughter out.'

'I'm not selling her out. I'm selling her *horse*.'

'Well, you know what they say about horses.'

'No. Please tell me.'

I blinked at him. 'Horses for courses.'

It was completely and utterly meaningless in this context. I knew it, he knew it, Derek in the doorway knew it, but ignored it. He said, 'Cheese puff, boss?'

Geordie nodded and Derek slid the wicker basket across the table to him.

'Starkey here,' said Geordie, 'was just doubting your loyalty.'

'On the contrary,' I said, 'I was just admiring it, given the circumstances.'

'What circumstances?' asked Derek.

'That you've nothing to gain from saving your boss from this den of vipers.'

Derek's brow furrowed. 'Don't you mean den of *iniquity*?'

'Yes.'

'And isn't it *nest* of vipers?'

'Yes. We're getting away from the point.'

'The point, my friend, is that when Eric and I got thrown out of the force, Mr McClean gave us a roof over our heads, no questions asked. He pays us extremely well, we enjoy our work, we travel, we meet important people, we have fun, we have a clothing allowance, we like the man and understand the business he's in. It's not a question of what we have to gain, it's a question of what we have to lose if something happens to him? Understand?'

'Understand.'

'Now, cheese puff?'

I took a cheese puff. Eric rapped on the glass divider. 'Race starting in five minutes.'

I stood and slid the door open. I looked back at Geordie. 'Coming?'

He shook his head. I stood in the doorway. The Chinese were squashed on to a beige leather sofa on the left, three on the cushions and one on each arm rest. Their guns were down, but handy. Jimmy and Oil Paintings, to the right of the television, had an armchair each while Dry Cleaner leaned against the windowsill. Derek stood in the doorway, shotgun clasped under his arm. Eric busied himself arranging the nibbles on a glass coffee table.

'There's our boy,' said Dry Cleaner, pointing at the screen.

There was a flurry of excited jabber from both sides of the room as we caught our first glimpse of Dan the Man, nostrils flared, head erect. A caption underneath gave his number, his weight, the handicap, the odds, the colours, the owner (G. McClean) and finally the name of the jockey, although that seemed almost an afterthought. The camera only dwelt on

318

her for a moment, and that from the back. She was wearing green and white silks. Her cap was pulled down low. The camera swiftly moved on to the next horse. There were over forty horses in the parade ring and they all had to be covered.

Jimmy snapped out, 'Turn the friggin' sound up, someone,' over the chatter and there followed several minutes of confusion while they tried to decide which of several instruments sitting on top of the television controlled the volume: there was one for the DVD player, one for a video, one for a cable transcriber, one for a PlayStation and one for a music centre. 'It's like fucking mission control in here,' Oil Paintings whinged. By the time they'd settled on the right control and the volume was finally up to required levels, the horses had left the parade ring and commenced their initial gallop along the course. I tried to pick Mandy's colours out of the crowd, and failed.

There were two joint favourites, Emperor of the South and Talisman, and the rivalry between them seemed to have been built up to the point where they were continually being picked out by the cameras at the expense of the other horses. Still, I'm sure the horses weren't worried. They were all about to face the race of their lives and the very real prospect of death over what the commentator described as the toughest course in the world. The Chair, Becher's Brook. Fences which have entered the English language as synonyms for big fences horses die jumping over. Dan the Man was described as an outsider. *'But then aren't they all really, in this race.'* The live pictures were replaced for several minutes by computer-generated shots of the course from the point of view of a horse going over the jumps, and they were realistic enough to make me feel a little queasy; that or Derek had slipped something into the cheese puffs.

The cameras went live again, and this time I caught the briefest glimpse of Dan the Man galloping towards the start, with Mandy sitting forward in the saddle, her bottom lifted several inches off it, a bottom that seemed larger than I remembered, and I suffered another little twinge, this time of guilt at the memory of the whiskey and bacon and Starbursts I'd forced upon her over the past few days. The camera never lies, but it does distort and exaggerate. But in her profession, a couple of ounces could make all the difference between victory and defeat – and on this day, life and death.

I knelt by the coffee table and snapped up some Twiglets. Eric smiled at me and said, 'I always eat when I'm nervous.'

'I'm not nervous,' I said, 'I'm petrified.'

'Take a wee drink,' he said, pointing. The bottles and cans were ranged around the feet of Jimmy the Chicken and his comrades. I gave a little snort of surprise. All this upset around me, and the first time I'd thought about taking a drink. Maybe it wasn't that big an addiction. If I could just stick to murder and mayhem I'd be able to leave the sauce alone. *But just a little one for now, seeing as how we're all nearly friends.*

I moved across the carpet on my knees, and lifted one of the bottles of VAT 19. I raised it to my lips and took a slug. Jimmy the Chicken tapped his gun against the glass, and I lowered it. His smile was not warm, and his eyes were colder still.

'Don't think I've forgotten you,' he hissed. 'When this is sorted out, you're a dead baby.'

I blinked at him. His choice of words was, I thought later, purely coincidental. But something snapped the moment he said them. Without thinking I dropped the bottle and grabbed him by the throat. I pulled him off his chair and the two of us tumbled around the floor for a few moments like primary school wrestlers until we were pulled apart. I was pinned down, breathing hard, a dribble of alcohol on my chin and one third of a Twiglet sticking out of my mouth.

Jimmy, held back by Dry Cleaner and Oil Paintings, glared at me, then shrugged his way out of his friends' restraints. 'You're a fucking lunatic, Starkey,' he said as he lifted his gun and pointed it at me. I don't really think he was going to shoot me, but the threat of it was enough to encourage the leading Chinese to raise his own gun and aim it at Jimmy. 'No,' the Chinese said simply.

Oil Paintings and Dry Cleaner eased their own guns around towards the Chinese.

Eric's shotgun was out of reach beneath the coffee table.

Derek's was already off his shoulder and shifting

from party to party. There was a crunch from the dining room as Geordie bit into his apple.

'What do you mean, *no*?' Jimmy the Chicken snapped. 'He tried to fucking kill me.'

'I mean,' the Chinese said, 'that he is ours. He killed my three brothers in Ireland. When the time comes, *we* will kill him.'

Jimmy the Chicken almost smiled, but he kept it in. He glanced at me immediately, and I raised an eyebrow. He had a way out, and he wasn't going to waste it. He snapped his eyes back to the Chinese. 'Okay,' he said, 'I understand. You have him. But if you take my advice, you'll finish him sooner than later.'

The Chinese gave a little bow. 'Thank you. But we keep him until later. Then we take our time, okay?'

'Okay,' said Jimmy, and everyone relaxed. Even me. It wasn't the time for a slanging match. That would only lead to more mayhem. I'd lost my temper and risked everything, now I had to claw it back; if it meant taking the blame for the deaths of the Chinese, then fair enough. It was buying me time. I retreated slowly to the coffee table. As I did there was a roar from the television and all eyes turned to the start of the greatest race on earth.

All bar mine. I took a handful of Twiglets. Eric, eyes never leaving the screen, said, 'If you're thinking about going for the shotgun, forget it, I'd have your head off quicker than Quavers.'

I nodded. The shotgun *was* tantalisingly close. But I hadn't even thought about it. I had had one of my rare moments of clarity, and realised that there was a plan swinging into action, a plan that would bring all this to a tidy conclusion. I couldn't quite work out what it was, or who exactly was involved, but there had been a clue up there on the screen that had been plain to me, and must also have been plain to . . .

I glanced around, through the sliding doors to where Geordie sat. He was biting into his third apple. The two previous cores sat browning together in front of him. His eyes were fixed on the screen. He was calm. He was focused. But had he noticed? I looked at Eric. Was he in on it too? And Derek?

No one was giving anything away.

It's Emperor of the South, from Malinga Boy, with Terracotta, Lemon Popsicle, Queen for a Day, Snoopy's Progress, Talisman, Prep School and Dan the Man as they come to Becher's for the first time . . .

They were edging forward in their seats. Cans of beer were at half-mast.

There had already been half a dozen fallers, but this was their first big challenge. There was an audible intake of breath as the leading pack jumped.

And Prep School is a faller! He's taken joint favourite Talisman down with him! There's still a long way to go, but it's Emperor of the South from Malinga Boy, Terracotta, Lemon Popsicle, then Dan the Man, Snoopy's Progress . . .

'Come on, Dan the Man!' yelled Dry Cleaner.

'Ride that fucker!' shouted Oil Paintings.

The Chinese were on their feet, screaming.

Then Jimmy the Chicken and Oil Paintings and Dry Cleaner were on theirs. Both sides were together in the middle of the floor. Derek, then Eric and finally Geordie McClean, his view from the dining room now blocked, crowded into the lounge as well.

Every fence was claiming victims. Horses were crashing into the sodden ground, crushing their riders. The roar from the crowd began to intensify. The director gave us a shot back up the course to show the riderless horses standing stunned or lying still on the ground, like the aftermath of some ancient battle. And ancient it was.

It was man and beast versus each other and nature.

Only the strongest, only the best would survive. It wasn't just getting over the fences, it was picking their way through the vanquished, placed like mines to destroy their chances of glory.

There, then, the money didn't matter. There was no owner.

There was only the race.

Only the victory.

And Dan the Man was moving up the field.

Emperor of the South, Malinga Boy, then two lengths back it's Dan the Man, Terracotta, Lemon Popsicle's a faller . . .

'Come on you, beauty!' screamed Oil Paintings.

'Come on, Mandy!' yelled Derek.

Geordie's fists were bunched and beating into his legs with every stride the horse took. His brow was furrowed and sweating, his eyes narrowed and intense. 'Go! Go! Go!' he yelled, and I knew that he didn't know. That none of them did.

I knew. But didn't know what to do. How to deal with it, because I didn't know what *it* was.

Jesus.

They were on their second and final circuit of the course. They were coming up to the Chair for the second time. The commentator was reaching a high pitch of excitement which was only matched by the yelping of the Chinese.

Emperor of the South is over safely! Malinga Boy clips the ... Malinga Boy is down ... he falls in the path of ... no, Dan the Man's okay and gaining on Emperor of the South, a tremendous ride by ... Snoopy's Progress is another faller at Becher's ...

'Come on!'

'Come on!'

'Catch him!'

'Catch that fucking horse!'

'Come on, you bastard!'

'Fall!'

'Fall!'

'Fall!'

And as if by magic.

... and it's Emperor of the South, from Dan the Man as they approach the third from home, it's ... Emperor of the South's a faller, a faller, three from home and Emperor goes down, it's Dan the Man and Mandy McClean on course to be the first female jockey to win the National ...

'Yes!'

'Yes!'

'Go!'

'Go!'

Just two fences to go . . . way back, way back it's Sultan's Charm, Echo Beach, Primo Levi, then Milton Keynes, Barbarossa . . . I think that's it . . . Aintree has taken its victims again this year but for the moment it's Dan the Man with an unassailable lead as he approaches the second from home . . . and he's . . .

Silence.

Over!

Geordie was jumping up and down, still thumping his legs.

The Chinese were shaking with nervous excitement. Jimmy was screaming, the veins standing out from his throat.

I moved, quietly, backwards. Nobody was watching. This was the time to get out. It might be my only chance. I stood in the doorway. Down the hall and out. They wouldn't know until I was halfway down the lane.

Maybe they wouldn't care. They'd be millionaires all, at least in their own minds.

But I stayed where I was.

Always a sucker.

Dan the Man.

Dan the Man just has to get over the last fence to win the Grand National! What a race! What a ride! The National always throws up a hero! This year, for the first time, it's a heroine! Here she comes, no one else in sight, just the final fence . . .

She jumps . . .

Almost slow motion.

And she's . . .

So slow. All the gangsters, like one big gangster, mouth open, drooling, sweating, eyeballs on stalks, so tangled up in greed that they couldn't see the wood for the trees.

And still I couldn't move from the door. Escape, live. Stay, die.

But still.

And she's over!

Over the final fence in the Grand National! Dan the Man's into the home straight and galloping towards the history books!

They were jumping, hugging each other, screaming at the tops of their voices, brothers together.

Fifty yards, and Dan the Man slows almost to a canter, all the hard work is done!

Dancing in the front room, throwing their heads back and whooping in delight. Geordie in amongst them, with the most to lose of all of them, impervious.

But wait a minute!

I don't . . . I don't understand this! She's pulling him up! Dan the Man is stopping! He's twenty yards short of the finish! What's . . . I don't believe this! The crowd is going mad! She's pulled him up! He doesn't appear to be injured . . .

It spread around the room like a virus. They stared stunned as Dan the Man sat quite calmly, yards from the line . . . and then stunned turned to anger, and the anger to fury . . .

'What the fuck . . . !'

'Come on!'

'What the fuck's the matter!'

'Please!'

'Do it . . . he's going to catch . . . !'

But it was too late. Sultan's Charm galloped past the stationary beast to victory in the Grand National.

All bets were off.

Now! Go! Run!

I turned. I was about to put my hand on the handle when the door was blown off its hinges, flattening me. I blinked up through the dust and splinters of wood and there was a split second while I lay stunned, looking at the police outside, and they at me, and then they charged into the house, trampling all over me. All around there was the sound of glass breaking, of urgent shouts and screams. One of them stopped for long enough to bash me with a truncheon, then slipped cuffs over my wrists.

I lay, face down, and listened to the sounds of fighting. But no gunfire.

After several minutes of staring at the floor, stunned, dizzy, I was dragged to my feet and propelled out through the door and into the arms of a waiting policeman. I blinked in the bright afternoon light. There were half a dozen police cars with flashing lights. There were transit vans with blacked-out windows. There was Mandy, arms folded across her chest, looking pensive.

I was being dragged towards the closest transit when Mandy spotted me and tried to get them to let me go, but they weren't having it.

'Not until we get this sorted out,' the one holding me snapped. 'Everyone goes down to the fucking station.'

Mandy stepped back. Her father was being dragged out by two cops, struggling furiously. Jimmy the Chicken, on the other hand, though cuffed and sporting an already closing left eye, almost sauntered out. The Chinese came out relatively meekly. Derek and Eric came out last, just managing to touch fingers as they were separated and led to different transits.

Mandy looked up at me as I sat in the back of the van.

'Did you know?' she asked.

I nodded.

'How?'

'Bosco's arse isn't as nice as yours, that's how.' I sighed. I was alive. Mandy was alive. 'They'll never let you ride in another National,' I said.

'Doesn't matter. As far as everyone's concerned Dan the Man won. He proved he was the best. It was men who fucked it up, not him. I just didn't want to give that shower of shite the satisfaction.' She looked across the yard and her eyes fell on her father, his feet planted firmly against the base of the rear door of the transit opposite, resisting their best efforts to push him in, his mouth working furiously, but his pleas of innocence falling on deaf ears. Then his knees were chopped from below with a truncheon. They buckled immediately and he was bundled inside, still shouting.

Oil Paintings and Dry Cleaner were pushed into the transit beside me, each of them cuffed and bleeding from nose and mouth. As Jimmy the Chicken was brought up he made a lunge for Mandy. She jumped back and he was whacked over the head and thrust past me on to the floor of the transit.

Mandy rolled her eyes. 'Don't worry,' she said, 'it'll all be sorted out. You haven't done anything wrong.'

I sighed. 'No it won't. I'm wanted for murder all over the shop. Even if it's thrown out of court, they'll keep me in prison for months on remand. Jesus Christ, what a mess.' I sighed again. She tried to look hopeful. I sighed for a third time and said, 'Will you wait for me?'

She looked away. Several of the police cars were already moving off.

'Will you?'

She shrugged. 'I don't know, Dan. I'm going to be busy. I have a book to write.'

They closed the doors before I could reply.

Or spit.

29

'So you bought the Horse Whisperer for how much?'

'A pound.'

'Mouse. Why would you do a thing like that? What do you know about horses?'

'Nothing. But I know about *news*, and that's what it's all about. Now that Geordie's gone bust, all those libel actions and court orders have disappeared. All I need to do is tone down some of the more bizarre allegations, attract some advertising, and I'm on to a winner. The web's the new way, Dan. I'm sick and tired of print.'

'I don't believe I'm hearing this. After what happened to me.'

'Dan, don't be sore. The Horse Whisperer will be the making of me, don't begrudge me that. I'll be a dot-com millionaire.'

'While I was running around getting my arse shot off, you were buying it from that old bitch. I can't believe *she* did that to me either. If she hadn't been burned to death, I'd fucking set fire to her.'

'Settle, petal.'

I sighed. I took another drink of Diet Pepsi. 'You actually led Jimmy the Chicken and those Chinese bastards to us, you know that, don't you?'

Mouse shrugged helplessly. 'It was running on autopilot. I owned it, but I hadn't started editing. Everything went in, right or wrong.' He smiled. 'Still, all's well that ends well.'

'That's right, Mouse. Mandy is at number three in the fucking bestsellers with her book. And where am I?'

Mouse looked at the table, he dabbed the tips of his fingers in several drops of Diet Pepsi. 'You've never had much luck on the book front, Dan, have you?'

'I've never had much luck on *any* front, Mouse.'

It was six months down the line. Mandy had written her book in the time it had taken me to compose the first paragraph of the Great Irish Novel. I was still casting around for the second.

We were sitting at an outside table of a café in Botanic Avenue. There was a Chinese restaurant opposite us. I kept a watchful eye on it, just in case. It was the kind of nice sunny day that Belfast sees about once a year. Men wore T-shirts and women short skirts. I had on my black jeans and jacket and shades and my very dark mood hung over me like a cloak.

Mouse sat back and sighed. 'Things were motoring along quite nicely until that first upset with Trish. It's all been downhill from there.'

'That was seven years ago.'

'Well you know what they say about bad luck.'

'What?'

'Ahm. Not sure. But things will change.'

'Can you promise me that?'

'No. But they have to. They can't get any worse, can they?'

Mouse stood, buttoning himself into his coat. He had to get back to the office. His new office. His was a twenty-four-hour-a-day horse news operation, and he'd already offered me a job. When I'd finished laughing, I'd said no. He put out his hand and we shook awkwardly.

'Do you ever hear from her?' he asked.

'She's off on some fucking book tour. She sends the occasional postcard, but no royalty cheques.'

'No, I mean Patricia.'

I shook my head. 'As one door closes, another slams shut in my face. Life's a barrel of fucking laughs.'

Mouse turned to go. Then he stopped, turned. 'Dan – one thing.'

'Yeah. I love you too.'

'No, I mean yeah, but one other thing. Who did kill Mark Corkery?'

I smiled at Mouse. 'No one. I think the car just fell on him.'

Headline hopes you have enjoyed THE HORSE WITH MY NAME, and invites you to sample Colin Bateman's latest novel CHAPTER AND VERSE, out now from Headline.

1

Julie's voice is nicotine.

'She doesn't see me comin'. I have her by the hair, pull the head straight back, then slit her throat.'

The woman who put the *dead* in *dead*pan.

'I use a knife – the knife she bought me on our first anniversary. She doesn't even make a noise, the blood just burbles out.'

'Burbles?'

Ivan glances up from his fingernails. Michelle, right at the back.

'Burbles, yeah – okay?' says Julie, her voice caught between embarrassment and threat.

'Let her finish, Michelle,' Ivan says. 'It's not easy.'

Julie nods curtly at him, then returns her attention to the page. Her fingers follow the words. 'The blood just *burbles* out . . .' She tosses a defiant look back at Michelle. Michelle tosses it back. '. . . And then she collapses in my arms. She's dead. I kiss her once—'

There's a chorus of *ooooooohs!* from the rest of the

class. Julie waits for them to settle again before continuing. 'I kiss her once on the lips, then I bury her in her own garden, just where we used to sit in the summer.' She nods to herself for a moment, then adds a quiet, 'The end.'

They applaud politely. They enjoyed it, but they're nervous about being asked next.

'Ah, yes, very, um, descriptive, Julie.' Ivan gets off his desk and taps his chalk on the blackboard. 'Of course, the title of our essay assignment was actually *What I Will Do On My First Day Home From Prison*. I, ah, wouldn't show that to the Parole Board.'

They laugh. He likes to make them laugh. Julie gives him a limp-wristed bog-off wave. 'Oh Mr Connor,' she says, 'what would you know about writing fiction?'

Ivan smiles. 'Okay, who's next?' Eyes are averted. 'Come on, we're all friends here. Eileen?' A shake of the head. 'Betty?' Not even a shake, just a stare at the floor. A small, elfin-featured girl slowly raises her hand. 'Donna? Right, off you go.'

Donna licks her lips, pushes hair from her brow. 'The—'

'Stand up so we can see you, Donna.'

She gets up. Her voice is soft. 'The light of the ark surrounds me, the dark of the night astounds me . . .'

'Is that a poem, Donna?' Ivan asks.

'Yes, Mr Connor.'

'It *was* an essay I specifically . . .' He trails off.

He glances at his watch and sighs. 'Okay, let's hear it.'

'Will I start again?'

'Come on, girl!' Michelle shouts. 'Spit it out!'

'All right, Michelle. Yes, Donna, from the top.'

She nods slightly. 'The—'

'Shit!'

Donna looks up sharply to see Mr Connor with his foot on a chair, and the broken end of a shoe lace held up as evidence of a legitimate excuse. 'Sorry, Donna. Please . . .'

Donna swallows, takes a deep breath. 'The—'

At that moment the bell rings and class is over. They're up out of their chairs just as if they were back at school, then they remember they're volunteers for this class, and they aren't going anywhere. They slow down. Ivan scoops up his own books and joins the exodus. He doesn't notice Donna, still standing with her poem in her hand.

Ivan is forty years old, he wears an old raincoat, his hair is long and straggled. He has been teaching this class in the women's prison twice a week for the past eight weeks. It pays reasonably well, enough to tide him over until the new contract is sorted out. He looks at his watch. He's caught in heavy traffic, not moving. Ben Elton would get a novel and a million quid out of it. Ivan's Metro is decrepit. He's listening to Dvorak on a tape. His most recent novel, *Chapter & Verse*, sits open on the passenger seat. The passages he will shortly read at Waterstones are highlighted in yellow. Beside the book there's a half-eaten packet of Starburst, although he will call them Opal Fruits until he goes to his grave.

He lifts the book and reads aloud, his voice strong, confident: 'But it was not only by playing backgammon with the Baronet, that the little governess rendered herself agreeable to her employer. She found many different ways of being useful to him. She read over, with indefatigable patience, all those law papers . . .'

He stops because he's aware of being watched. He looks out and then up at the cab of a lorry, facing in the other direction, and the bearded driver laughing at him. Ivan closes his book, sets it back on the passenger seat, then grips his steering wheel with both hands. A moment later music booms out from the truck. Someone with at least a fingernail on the pulse of popular music would recognise it as rap, but to Ivan it is noise. And noise annoys.

Ivan scratches suddenly at his head. He thinks he may have picked up nits in the prison.

Ivan hurries across the busy road, freezing rain slicing into his face. Halfway across he steps out of the shoe with the broken lace, and before he can go back for it a car drags it along the road for a hundred yards and he has to hop after it. Look at the great author! Stepping off his lofty pedestal to pursue an Oxford brogue along the tarmac! He picks it up and hugs it against his chest.

Campbell is watching him from the Waterstones doorway. His agent gets 10 per cent of everything he earns. Ivan's coat is ancient, but at least he has one. Campbell is damp and cold. Ivan hurries up, full of apologies.

He isn't nervous until he sets a damp foot in the bookshop, but the moment he crosses the threshold, the weight of literature and competition is suddenly upon him. Thousands and thousands and thousands of books. Half of them appear to be about a young boy called Harry Potter. Ivan admires anyone who can make that much money, yet hates Her with a vengeance. He wonders if She will ever write *Harry Potter and the Provisional IRA*, or *Harry Potter and the Palestinian Question*. He loves corrupting popular titles and idles away many hours of his writing life at this very pursuit. His favourites are *Love in the Time of a Really Bad Flu*, *The Day of the Jack Russell* and *A Quarter to Three in the Garden of Good and Evil*.

As he moves through the shop Ivan becomes aware that the aisles are actually very crowded. This is a good sign. Campbell pushes ahead of him, then comes to a halt at the edge of a seated area; a hundred seats and they are *all filled*. Butterflies flap in his stomach. This is better than he could ever have hoped. At previous readings he has been lucky to scrape up a dozen hardy souls. He glows. Word of mouth. He has never quite been popular enough to be considered a cult, but perhaps this is the beginning of something. He is ready to be acclaimed. He observes the microphone, the small lectern, the table with the bottle of Evian water, the glass, the chair, the pen for signing books afterwards.

The manager of the shop steps up to the microphone and taps it once. 'Ladies and gentlemen, sorry to keep you waiting, but our author has at last emerged from the nightmare that is our traffic.' They laugh. 'Our guest tonight is quite simply a writer who needs no introduction. Universally acclaimed, a master of the English language . . .' Ivan swallows nervously, takes a first step forward . . . 'put your hands together for Francesca Brady!'

Ivan freezes. Applause erupts around him. Posters curl down suddenly from the ceiling. A mile-wide smile, expansive hair, red-red lipstick, the cover of a book, but the spitting image of the author now emerging from the audience not six feet away from him. His heart is racing. His first impulse is to dive on her, force her to the ground, and then batter her to death with a copy of *Insanity Fair*, her latest 'novel'. Ivan always makes that little quotation-marks sign with his fingers when anyone mentions *Insanity Fair*, or even Francesca Brady. She writes fat romantic books for fat romantic people. She dresses them up with smart one-liners so that she can appear hip, but she's really – *ugh!* – Mills and Boon for the e-generation, and every time he thinks of her he suffers a vowel problem. Francesca Brady takes the stage with a modest wave, pretends to look surprised at the posters.

Ivan jumps as he's tapped on the shoulder. There's a boy of about twelve, wearing acne and a Waterstones identity badge around his neck like a US Marine with a dogtag – and why not? Bookselling is war, and the enemy never stops coming.

'Mr Connor? We've been looking everywhere for you. You're in the basement. Follow me.'

BEN, it says on the dogtag. BEN turns and leads Ivan back through the crowds of people still arriving to hear Francesca Brady. She's milking the applause – 'Thank you, thank you, I keep looking behind me thinking a real author must be standing there – and they're all bloody laughing as Ivan, Campbell and BEN hurry down the stairs into the basement.

BEN charges ahead. Ivan glances back at Campbell, who shrugs helplessly. Signs for *Astrology*, *Military History*, *School Texts*, *Gay & Lesbian*, *Erotica* flash past like inter-city Stations of the Cross. Finally they emerge into a small circular area in which there are set about thirty chairs. Ivan quickly calculates that 77 per cent of the chairs are filled. Something salvaged, at least. There is already a small, balding, middle-aged man standing at the microphone, the literary equivalent of a warm-up guy, a no-hoper, a glorified typist who's stumbled into a book deal because he's slept with someone famous or been held hostage in an obscure country for several years. No problem.

There is a lectern. A table with a bottle of Evian water. A chair. A pen. The man is saying: 'For me, philately is not so much a passion as a way of—'

Ivan becomes aware of BEN waving urgently at him from three aisles across, under a sign that says *True Crime*. Campbell gives him a gentle push and Ivan skirts the outer ring of chairs; BEN turns and hurries away. Ivan passes through *Science Fiction*, *Science Fantasy*, *Terry Pratchett* and then finally arrives at a tiny rectangular area set out with a dozen chairs. Seven of them are filled. There is a lectern. A microphone. A table, chair, bottle of Evian water and a pen for signing copies of his books, which sit in several tremulously high columns on another table.

Ben taps the microphone. He squints at the folded piece of paper he has removed from the back pocket of his black jeans. He glances up at the giant air-conditioning system which whirrs and blows above him, then speaks into the microphone.

'Ladies and gentlemen, sorry to keep you waiting, but our author has at last emerged from the nightmare that is our traffic.' He pauses for laughter, but it is not forthcoming. 'Our guest tonight is quite simply a writer who needs no introduction. Universally acclaimed, a master of the English language, put your hands together for Ian Connor!'

Campbell hisses, 'Ivan!'

'Ivan Connor!' BEN shoots back quickly, but he has already stepped away from the microphone. His voice is not drowned out by the applause, which is on the dead side of restrained, but by the air conditioning, which booms and coughs like an approaching storm.

Ivan steps forward. He sets the hardback edition of

Chapter & Verse down on the table and pours himself a glass of Evian. His heart is racing again. There is no reason for him to be nervous, but he is. He always is. He lifts the glass and sets it down somewhat precariously on the narrow base of the lectern.

'Th-thank you all very much for coming,' Ivan says into the microphone. 'I, ah, am gonna . . . *going to* . . . read from my new novel.' He holds it up for them to admire, but the book slips out of the dust jacket and crashes down onto the glass of water, which immediately cracks. Ivan makes a desperate attempt to retrieve the situation, although it looks to the audience as if he is indulging in some kind of bizarre performance art, juggling broken glass, damp novel and handfuls of water. Meanwhile, the dust jacket floats gently away on the breeze from the air conditioner.

Ivan smiles foolishly while BEN removes the broken glass and soaks up what he can of the water with a Kleenex. Ivan tries to peel apart the damp pages of *Chapter & Verse* in order to find the section he intends to read. Campbell hides himself in *Graphic Novels*.

When they are ready to start again, Ivan decides to ignore the water incident. 'The, um, new novel . . . which is set in England in the eighteenth century, an era which I'm sure you're all . . .' He blinks at them. 'Anyway, this is from Chapter Three.' He clears his throat. 'He took Rebecca to task once or twice about the propriety of playing backgammon—'

'Speak up!'

He glances up at a gnarled, elderly man sitting at the back.

'Y-yes, of course: He took Rebecca to task once or twice—'

'Louder!'

'HE TOOK REBECCA TO TASK ONCE OR—'

'Philately!'

Another man, in the second row, is on his feet, waving a finger at him.

'I'm sorry?'

'Stamps, man! We're here for the stamps!'

BEN bounds up to the microphone. 'B2,' he says. 'The stamps lecture is in B2. Third down on the right.'

As the man shuffles along the row of seats Ivan is aghast to see five other members of his audience, including the deaf man, get to their feet and shuffle after him, leaving only an old lady in the front row.

Campbell retreats into *Occult*.

Ivan waits until some strength returns to his legs, then smiles weakly down at the old lady. 'Mother,' he says, 'I can read to you when I get home.'

'You can read to me now, Ivan. I didn't come all this way not to be read to.'

He shakes his head. He laughs. He does love her. 'Well,' he says, reaching up to move the microphone, 'at least I won't be needing this.'

Except the spilled water has soaked into the wires, and the moment he touches it there's a crack and flash and the author of *Chapter & Verse* is hurled into the air.